Gracie's Revolution

A Johnson Station Novel

By Marj Charlier

SUNACUMEN
PRESS

Palm Springs, CA

ISBN-10: 09860952-4-9
ISBN-13: 978-0-9860952-4-5

Dedication:

To my aunt, Wilma Smith, the Gilman, Iowa, librarian for the past twenty years (above), and Tom Lutgen, a reader's best friend and a librarian at the Rancho Mirage, California, Public Library.

Without libraries and librarians, we could have no revolutions.

Gracie had to put her book bag down on the sidewalk to unlock the door to the Johnson Station Library, and she still fought with the key for a good minute before the latch clicked open.

It was her own fault.

The first time she opened this library door, she found the lock tricky. But then, full of optimism and confidence, she had declined an offer from the hardware store owner to replace it. She'd get it figured out, she'd overcome it, and she'd be stronger for it.

Now twenty-five years later, she shook her head at the thought. Oh, what youthful pride!

Unfortunately, it was too late to accept that offer for a new lock; the hardware store had closed ten years earlier.

As she slipped inside the heavy oak door, a large envelope fell from the mail slot, nearly tripping her. She slammed the door shut against the brisk fall wind and swore. Bending over stiffly, she retrieved the thick manila packet.

She grimaced. The return address was that of Gregory Thungaard, the new chairman of the library board and a thorn in her side.

He'd been on a tear lately, pushing a pro-censorship agenda, and she figured that's what the package was all about. It was the last thing she wanted to look at.

Gracie walked through the door to her small glassed-in office and threw her book bag, purse, and the fat envelope onto her desk. Following her usual routine, despite the unwelcome package, she strode quickly through the stacks and into the bathrooms to make sure everything was okay: no new leaks in the plumbing, no messes left behind by late-night library patrons that went unnoticed and unattended last evening by her assistant librarian, Karen.

Gracie had already had coffee that morning at the regular Wednesday morning klatch in the café two blocks down Main Street, but she decided to start a pot anyway to chase off the chill while the old furnace labored to warm up the building. Gracie ran her fingers over the sparkling counters of the little kitchenette off her office while the coffee pot sputtered and dripped the first cup into the carafe.

Waiting for the coffee to brew, she studied herself in the full-length mirror on the wall of the kitchenette—a mirror installed back when she wore nylons to work and checked for runs a couple of times a day. Even though her legs were now bare, it was still part of her daily routine, taking measure of her appearance, flaws first: her slightly heavy thighs, her wide-set eyes, her thin lips. Then she allowed herself to appreciate her shoulder-length gray hair, which she wore longer than most women her age to show off how thick it had remained. Now nearly sixty, she was content with how she wore her age.

Fresh cup of coffee in hand, she sat at her desk and flipped on her computer. While the system booted up, she turned to the big envelope from Gregory. Its contents weren't going to get any less irritating if they sat around all morning. It was better to get it over with.

Gracie slit one long side of the envelope open and replaced the letter opener alongside its matching scissors in the expensive cherry box where it belonged. She'd received the boxed set from the previous chairman, a kind old codger who led the board for some forty years, never interfering with her operation of the library or her decisions. The gift had marked her twentieth anniversary as librarian.

Why did he have to retire and make room for that jerk Gregory?

Oh yeah. He died. Well, how inconsiderate of him!

The contents of the envelope slid out onto her desk, and

she recognized Gregory's stationery and handwriting on top of the pile. What did a retired farmer need gold-embossed stationery for? she had wondered the first time she saw it. That was before she learned of his political ambitions. He was running for a county supervisor's seat. Even though that vote was still a year away, rumor had it that he already saw as a first step to the state senate and then the governor's mansion.

The package, as she suspected, contained documentation supporting his push to cull the library of books he didn't like. She leafed through the pages, grimacing at the headlines on the articles he'd copied for her.

The only thing Gracie had ever done for the town in the thirty years she had lived there was keep this library open and free of political interference. If Gregory destroyed it by culling books and putting a chokehold on her programs, the town would suffer, and Gracie would feel she let Johnson Station down.

She couldn't let that happen.

As if on cue from a benevolent god, the big front door swooshed open, and Caroline stomped into the library. Gracie looked up at the welcome interruption and waved her into her office.

Caroline was a regular, a voracious consumer of books about rearing children and managing family life, although she had no children of her own. No husband either, for that matter. She was big-boned and clumsy, with strong facial features, and now in her late thirties, she had little chance of attracting a man in time to outpace her biological clock.

Gracie felt for her, but she could imagine how many men had entered Caroline's life only to beat a hasty retreat once she launched into a discussion of her favorite topic: childcare. In lieu of the children she longed for, Caroline cosseted injured dogs and cats and an occasional ferret or gerbil at a veterinary clinic in the county seat, a town twenty miles east. She was good at it, from what Gracie had been told.

"Hey, Caroline!" Gracie called out. "I have just ordered two books I think you'll love."

"Oh, really?" Caroline stumbled over the transom into Gracie's little office and plopped down on the chair opposite the desk. She didn't look as excited about the news as Gracie had expected.

"*Rearing the Hyperactive Child without Ritalin* and *The Germfree Miscalculation.*" Gracie read the titles off a handwritten list. "The second one is about how keeping your house too clean can actually make your child sicklier in the long run."

"So I've heard. They sound interesting," Caroline said, but her body language said something entirely different. She thrust her legs out in front of her and frowned. Mercurial Caroline was in one of her more somber moods.

"Something else on your mind?" Gracie asked. She lowered her voice to signal her intent to keep Caroline's confidence, although it was unnecessary for any other reason than its palliative effect. There was no one else in the library.

Caroline fidgeted with her fingernails and mumbled: "I don't know how to ask you this without you thinking I'm a horrible person."

"Why would I think that?"

"Well, there's this book I've been hearing about. I read about it in *People* and I saw a piece on it last night on *Entertainment Tonight.* Everyone seems to be reading it. You know, I'd just order it from Amazon, but my prude of a sister's on my account, and I don't want her to see it."

"Ah," Gracie said, sitting back and fighting a smile. "*The Intern's Travels?*"

"Yes. How did you know?"

"Two other women have asked me if I'm going to get it this week." Gracie's policy was to put a book on her shopping list once three people asked for it. *The Intern's Travels* was the salacious tale of a young woman who wanted to become an international high-end escort, but first, she had to go through an apprenticeship with a teacher of sorts, who not only taught her much new about sex, but also how to travel like a jet-setter.

Gracie didn't have to ask the library board's permission to buy any book, but when it was a controversial title, she usually sought their advice. Now that Caroline was her third regular patron to ask for it, she would bring it up at the next board meeting. And with Gregory harping lately on community morality and standards, it was likely to be a difficult discussion.

"That isn't the kind of thing you usually read," Gracie said, then immediately felt horrible for it. It wasn't her place to monitor someone's reading list. Was she the town's morality police?

"Forget I said that," she quickly added. "Totally inappropriate. You can read anything you want, and it's not up to me to decide what it is."

"But do you think it's a bad thing to want to read it?" Caroline had obviously heard Gracie's first judgmental comment and missed her retraction.

"No, I don't. It's not my place to chaperone our readers."

"It's getting a lot of publicity, but I don't know if it's any good," Caroline said.

Gracie hadn't read it yet and couldn't comment on that. "So, what else is going on around here?" she asked, changing the subject. Keeping Caroline around a little longer would postpone having to read Gregory's material.

"Hmm. I don't know. If it weren't for the horrid football team, nobody would have anything to talk about." Caroline had two nephews on the high school team, and she was right: the boys had the distinction of being on the worst squad in the conference, and it wasn't exactly a powerhouse of a conference.

"Well, at least they're getting some exercise," Gracie said. "Better than sitting in front of the TV every afternoon."

"And they found another meth lab outside of

Thomasville." Getting to share bad news oddly seemed to be cheering Carolyn up.

"My mother must be turning over in her grave." Gracie shook her head sadly. Her mother had been a nurse in the 1960s, and the county health department hired her to travel around to high schools and give lectures about the dangers of drugs. All students hated those assemblies, but Gracie hated them the most. The older boys in the back of the gym made fun of her mother while she was talking, and Gracie vacillated between wanting to defend her and wanting to disown her.

"Oh, and did you hear about the INS raid?"

"Yeah, I did." Gracie thought it was sad: workers dragged out of the poultry-processing plant on the edge of town and sent away on buses, regardless of whether they had families expecting them home for supper or not. It wasn't as if they were vagrants, squatting on corporate property. They were working, and from what she understood, it was grueling, hard work.

"How do you suppose their wives and children are going to support themselves now?" Gracie meant it rhetorically, but Caroline apparently thought she wanted an answer.

"I don't know!" she said. "And did you hear that Gregory Thungaard is running for county supervisor?" Caroline was off to her next bit of news.

"Yes, I knew that. He's my library chairman, you know."

At times, it was a struggle, but Gracie would never let anyone but her closest friends know what she thought of Gregory. Her role was to keep as many books in circulation as possible, and that meant welcoming everyone who stepped through her door. Keeping her personal opinions to herself had been the key to hanging onto her job over the past twenty-five years. But it was getting harder each year—especially since Gregory came on board.

"Oh, you are lucky!" Caroline exclaimed. "He's so smart. Heck, if I had his money, I could buy books instead of borrowing them!"

"I think he's not the big breadwinner in his family," Gracie said, coming close to expressing an opinion. She bit her tongue.

"So, are you going to order it?"

"Order what?"

"*The Intern's Travels.*"

"Oh, right. I'm considering it," Gracie said. "It's probably one of those things I had better check out with our board first."

"Why? Do they get to decide what we read?"

"Not necessarily, but I want to make sure I'm not offending anyone. Especially your idol, Mr. Thungaard."

"You worry way too much about offending people, Gracie." Caroline laughed. "You need to let down your hair sometimes, too."

After Caroline left, Gracie turned back to the tasks she had set out for herself, neatly delineated on her "To Do" notepad. She wanted to get everything done before Karen arrived at five to take over the evening shift. Karen covered Monday through Thursday evenings and Saturdays. The library was closed Friday and Saturday nights and all day on Sundays.

But as much as she tried to focus, Gracie kept thinking about that INS raid. The Hispanic workers who came into the county over the past decade to scald, pluck, eviscerate, and dismember the miserable chickens that arrived day and night on the beds of semi-trucks had constituted the only diversity in Johnson Station's population since the last socialist was run out of town in the early 1970s. There certainly were some in town who would see the return to an all-white populace a step toward making Johnson Station great again, as if that was all it would take, but Gracie wasn't one of them. The town was already withering into a dusty wide spot in the road like so many other small towns in Iowa.

The closure of the poultry plant put a hundred or so residents of the county, including those Hispanic immigrants, out of work, and Gracie imagined those who weren't deported would move away in search of another food processing job that hadn't yet been filled by a computer or a robot.

Perhaps they and their minimum-wage paychecks wouldn't be missed much. But Gracie would miss their chattering children in the library. She had purchased a few dozen bilingual children's books to help them teach their parents a little bit of the English they had picked up so naturally in school.

For a time, the Hispanic child care center in town had brought the kids over for a reading session once a week. But with the deportation, the daycare had closed and its largely immigrant staff had gone to work at the two other centers, both owned by long-time residents, descendants of the original Norwegian families. The weekly visits stopped, and now those books would sit for months—maybe years—on the shelves, untouched, unopened, and unloved.

Gracie saw it as one more damper on the town's vibrancy. In the years since she had taken her job, Johnson Station had been a roller-coaster of progress and decline, but lately the trends had been one-sidedly deleterious. Just when she thought there were no more businesses to close, a couple more would announce a going-out-of-business sale and mail postcards referring their clients to a surviving enterprise in Newton, Pella, Marshalltown, or Des Moines.

The library, under Gracie's direction, had bucked the trend, blossoming from one room in the back of the town hall to this pleasant one-story storefront on Main Street, donated by the family of its deceased owner. The book collection had grown from donations of used books from local residents thanks to an annual budget approved by the town council.

Over time, Gracie had started and discontinued programs that reflected the changing demographics of the town—a big children's program in the late 1980s, a boisterous college preparatory study group during the maturing of the Echo Boom, and then book clubs for aging Baby Boomers.

Now, even the book clubs had petered out and Gracie feared that Gregory would meet little opposition to culling the library shelves to his liking. If he decided to fire her and replace her with a more like-minded librarian, would anyone care? What was to keep the town council from eventually deciding the library was too expensive, unnecessary, and oversized for the shrinking populace?

Perhaps it wouldn't be much of a loss to the world if the entire town dried up and blew away. Ten blocks by ten blocks, it spread out evenly from the center of downtown. In the middle, two blocks of storefronts faced each other from either side of the street, most of them now empty, and the rest occupied by insurance agencies and law offices. Now people went to Des Moines for clothing, hardware, home furnishings, and most of their groceries.

The farmers who owned the land outside of town declined to sell, preserving farmland and preventing suburban sprawl, but leaving no room for new construction. So, despite its proximity to jobs in Des Moines, every year the town got older, poorer, and less populated.

The town's council was constitutionally opposed to apartment buildings, so nothing was likely to change. Whenever anyone brought up economic decline, the council and the mayor pointed to the Chamber of Commerce. But so far, all it had done was put some baskets of petunias on the downtown street corners—beautification, they called it.

࿚

It was near the end of the day when Gracie's cellphone rang. She dug it out from under a pile of paper.

"Katie's getting married," Gracie's daughter, Janice, announced. As usual, Janice had skipped all manner of salutation and jumped right in. "I'm going to come home and host a shower for her. Can I use the house?"

"Of course, you can," Gracie said. Whatever brought her daughter home to Johnson Station was fine with her. She and Janice weren't friends like many mothers and daughters were, but she loved her only child, and the youthful energy of Janice's gaggle of girlfriends brightened up the house. It, like the library, could be too quiet some days. "When are you coming? How long can you stay?"

"Just the weekend, a week from this coming Saturday. Will that work?"

"Of course, honey. And how is work going? And everything else?"

"Just fine, Mom. I've got to get back to work, but I'll see you in two weeks."

Janice's terse tone wasn't unusual. Gracie got very little information about her daughter, whether on the phone or in person. When she did come home—once every three or four months—she spent most of her time with her friends and very little time with her mother.

Gracie had raised her that way. She wanted Janice to be independent, a little adventurous, a little wild—everything Gracie had given up being when she got married and settled in Johnson Station with Jens. The last thing she wanted was for her daughter to end up back here, married and pregnant. She wanted her to do something special with her life.

That was Gracie's dream, and Janice had fulfilled it. She'd gone to college, attended Drake Law School, and ended up in Chicago working at a large corporate law firm that specialized in real estate. Janice's legal expertise was helping developers get subsidized housing projects approved, which made Gracie proud. Her daughter wasn't just making a lot of money and living an exciting urban life, she was also doing something for the less fortunate.

After Janice hung up, Gracie called Richard, the man townsfolk called her "boyfriend," lacking a better term.

"Janice is coming home in two weeks, so I guess we'll have to postpone that trip north," she said. "I'm sorry, but you know how little I get to see her."

Richard sighed. "I know how little you wanted to go."

He was right, she didn't want to go. Richard had talked her into going to Minneapolis to watch a baseball game. She wasn't a big fan of baseball, for sure, but even more, she didn't want everyone in Johnson Station to know she was going away with Richard. As town librarian, she felt that would be sending the wrong message. But that wasn't why she was begging off now.

"That's not fair," she protested. "I agreed to go. But I want to see Janice."

"Um, yes, it is fair. Janice just happens to be a handy excuse."

Gracie let that pass without comment—not because she didn't want to talk about it, but because someone she'd never seen before walked into the library, looking lost and lonely.

~2~

Forty years before, Gracie had made jokes about her mother's regular morning coffee klatch with her "old-biddy" friends. Now, here she was, at Blixt's—Johnson Station's only café—waiting to exchange gossip over watery coffee with her best friends in their own version of that cliché of small-town routines. Blixt's Formica tables, linoleum floor, and water-spotted windows were indistinguishable from those in the café her mother had frequented back in Thomasville, located two counties to the west, when Gracie was a teenager.

Gracie had no reason to visit Thomasville anymore; her parents had died forty years before, both from lung cancer in their early forties. However, she could still see it in her mind's eye as clearly as she could see Johnson Station through Blixt's front windows.

That was the thing about so many small towns, she thought, sipping nearly tasteless brew and waiting for her friends to arrive. No matter how different the cheap ersatz storefronts were that merchants tacked up to "modernize" their aging downtown structures, the towns had ended up looking pretty much the same in aggregate: wide, featureless main streets with pots of petunias on the corners, compliments of their cookie-cutter chambers of commerce.

Johnson Station was bigger than Thomasville, but only by about a dozen square blocks. Gracie frequently wondered how she ended up staying, why she gave in to the inertia that kept her in this sleepy, enervating place for thirty years. When Jens died five years earlier, she thought she might find a way to move back to Chicago—back where they had met, fallen in love, and gotten married, and where Janice now lived.

Instead, after she had buried Jens, she stayed put in Johnson Station, continuing to run the town's tiny library. Maybe she knew deep down that she no longer had the energy needed to navigate a busy city. Or maybe she had ended up happy enough where she was, happy enough at the library, and happy enough with her tidy life that she didn't need to turn it upside down for the sake of a lifestyle that she had probably idealized over the past three decades.

"Where are you girls?" she muttered aloud, glancing at her watch. It was only 8:01. They weren't late by most standards. She looked up just as Marcia rounded the corner on the sidewalk outside and stepped up through the café door.

"Hey, sweetie!" Marcia cooed, leaning over the table for the two-cheek kiss that had become the group's customary greeting. She threw her huge purse into the seat across from Gracie and slid in. "Jackie's not coming this morning. She had to take her granddaughter to Des Moines for a doctor's appointment."

There were those who probably saw Gracie, Marcia, and Jackie as three peas in a pod—all approaching sixty, and all having spent nearly their entire adult lives in this one place. But each carried her six decades differently. Gracie stumbled forward from the waist as if she were carrying a pack of Nineteenth Century tomes on her back. Jackie strode slowly and erect with teacher-like authority. And Marcia glided down the street at the pace of a person twenty pounds lighter and ten years younger than she was.

"How about—" Gracie started to ask Marcia, but then she saw Belinda's large form darken the café doorway. "Ah, here she is."

Gracie moved over to the other side of the booth, next to Marcia. Belinda liked to face the door so she could see who was coming and going, and since there were only three of them, Gracie ceded her big friend the entire bench.

Gracie had known Belinda, Jackie, and Marcia since their

children had entered kindergarten together, the same year Gracie became the town's librarian. That didn't mean they'd been close friends for all twenty-five of those years. At one point Gracie and Jackie weren't speaking to each other because Gracie's SUV had hit and killed Jackie's dog, a shaggy cocker spaniel with a wandering spirit. Another time Marcia came into the library and found one of her daughters necking with her boyfriend in the back of the stacks. She blamed Gracie.

For the past ten years, however, they had been a regular three- or foursome at the same booth in the front of the café on Mondays, Wednesdays, and Fridays. Irascible Belinda had never been particularly popular with the other three, but Marcia and Jackie had become Gracie's best friends. If any one of them was going to miss the eight o'clock coffee, she let someone know. And throughout the weeks, they watched out for each other, pitching in when someone was ill, or needed a ride to the auto shop or help moving a piece of furniture.

Gracie thought there were plenty of compromises that one had to make to live in a small town. But her friendships constituted a big chunk of the compensation for the empty storefronts, the lack of privacy, and the paucity of choices in everything from groceries to nightlife. The amount of water that had flowed under the bridge since they first met meant there were things she'd never have to hide from these three friends and mistakes she'd never have to explain.

"What's new?" Belinda huffed, plopping down on the empty seat across from Marcia and Gracie. When carrying her two hundred fifty pounds around, Belinda was perpetually out of breath. But once settled, she was like a rock: immovable and cool, the very picture of self-satisfaction, a bland smile concealing her disappointment over her weight, her children, her husband, her meager retirement checks. Gracie tolerated her—barely. She could be sarcastic and funny, but she was usually obsessively focused on her problems.

"There is absolutely nothing new in this town, and there hasn't been for at least ten years. Maybe longer," Marcia said. She waved down Betty, the café's aging waitress, who shuffled over with two more cups of coffee.

"Just three of you today?" Betty set the cups down in the middle of the table on little paper coasters along with two spoons and a handful of tiny half-and-half containers. She turned away without waiting for an answer.

Belinda took a gulp of coffee and spat out most of it on a napkin. "Ouch! Hot! You know I've been thinking that what this town really needs is a big-time scandal."

"You mean our children aren't scandalous enough for you?" Marcia asked, her mouth forming a puffy smirk. "I don't know if Johnson Station could handle much more than what they already contribute."

Marcia and Belinda rambled for a bit around that regular topic of café gossip: the love affairs that bounced around the town's twenty-and thirty-somethings like a pinball. Between Marcia's three daughters, Jackie's two sons, and Belinda's two sons and one daughter, there'd been at least eight different permutations of sleeping arrangements over the past couple of years. And those were just the ones Gracie knew about. Occasionally, a couple would get married, reducing the pool of eligible partners for the others, but the exclusivity only lasted a few months—a couple of years at the most—and they would get divorced and back in circulation.

And now Marcia herself seemed on the verge of having an affair with a banking client, although for her sake, Gracie hoped only the two of them knew about it. Thinking about it, she frowned.

"You're sure quiet," Marcia turned to Gracie. "Did you get up on the wrong side of the bed today? Troubles at the library or something?"

"No. Nothing other than the usual nit-picking by the board," Gracie said. But what was nagging at her? She had been looking forward to coffee that morning, and now her mood had shifted.

"Hey, speaking of your board, did you know that Gregory wants to be the governor?" Belinda asked.

"Yes!" Gracie was tiring of the subject, but apparently, no one else was. "I have heard that rumor, but as far as I know, it's just a rumor." She waved her hand dismissively. "He's got a long road ahead before he's close to that, anyway."

"I can't imagine someone from Johnson Station ever gaining enough political clout to get elected to state office," Marcia said, in a way making the same point. "Usually it's just guys from Des Moines or Cedar Rapids."

"Or Davenport. Or Waterloo," added Belinda.

Belinda and Marcia continued to list the bigger towns in the state as if they needed to compile the definitive list, but Gracie's attention was drawn to the back of the café where none other than Gregory himself was holding court with a handful of the town's businessmen—contractors, store owners, the bank manager, and a bunch of retirees. The men usually entered through the back door, the one that accessed the parking lot off the alley, and gathered at a large community table at the rear of the café for their morning klatch. Before she switched seats with Belinda, Gracie hadn't seen that Gregory was there.

His body language was fascinating. He was a big man with a balding head and a square jaw. He sat with his chair pushed back from the table far enough that he could rest his elbows on his knees.

Gracie couldn't hear them, but Gregory's contributions to the conversation were lengthy, delivered as complete paragraphs. As he talked, he moved his eyes from one man's face to the next, nodding and making eye contact with each in turn. Each time he finished with one of his little speeches, he looked down at the floor in front of his feet, feigning humility.

It was quite a political performance. And the men at the

table were eating it up.

Gregory looked up and saw her watching him. He flashed a sardonic smile and turned back to listen to someone at his table.

"What are you staring at?" Marcia nudged her with an elbow. "Didn't you hear Belinda? She wants to know if we're doing our regular Friday-night thing this week."

At least once a month, the four friends convened at Gracie's house for Friday Afternoon Club—named after the same end-of-the-week celebrations Gracie remembered from college. If it was nice out, they sipped cool Pinot Grigio on her back deck overlooking her neglected garden. If it was rainy or cold, they sat inside around her large kitchen table with Syrah or Cabernet.

"Oh, is it this week?" Gracie fought to return her focus to her own table. If it was this week, she needed to warn Richard. Of course, everyone knew she and Richard were friends; they sat together in church occasionally, and they had run into other people from town at restaurants in Des Moines from time to time. But she didn't want people to think he was living with her.

"Yes, it's this week, and even if it weren't, I'm in the mood for some good wine. This has been the week from hell," Marcia said. She was still working full-time as a loan officer at the bank, and this was the time of year when farmers came in droves to close out accounts for the year and set up financing for the following spring's seed and fertilizer. Gracie knew that Marcia's budding love interest, Carl, was one of them.

"Hey, Belinda," Gracie pointed toward the men's table in the back. "There's the mayor. Maybe you can tell him about that scandal you're wishing for."

Belinda turned around as far as she could, given the limited amount of space between her chest and the edge of the table. Straining to see around her, Gracie watched several of the men raise their hands in greeting as Mayor John Walton approached the table. Gregory wasn't one of them.

Gracie noticed something the others might have missed: a condescending smirk on Gregory's face. He sat back with his arms folded across his chest and watched John as if amused by the deference the businessmen were paying to him as mayor. Apparently, Gregory's political star had already risen high enough that he didn't need to court the friendship of so lowly an eminence as the mayor of Johnson Station.

Or perhaps he had already bought him off and now expected the courtship to extend the other direction.

Either way, Gracie could see how it might spell trouble for her going forward. The mayor appointed the library board members, and if Gregory had control of the mayor, the board would soon be packed with his like-minded sycophants. Her battle for the open and diverse library she had built over the past twenty-five years could easily be lost.

"This should be interesting," she mumbled. "Or worse. Or much worse."

⁓

Caroline wasn't the only borrower at the library whose reading habits and lifestyle were misfits.

Liz was probably anorexic, a condition that Gracie once wished she could catch for a month or two—just long enough to lose that extra ten or twenty pounds she carried around. Watching Liz's pained face pass by her office window once a week for the past fifteen years, though, Gracie had changed her mind. Clearly, *being* slightly overweight was less of a burden than harboring a debilitating terror of *becoming* slightly overweight.

Instead of eating, Liz read cookbooks voraciously. She loved books that didn't promise to save your life: no gluten-free, sugar-free, soy-free, lactose-free, low-fat, vegetarian, vegan nonsense for her. She wanted to see photos of full-figured, densely marbled, richly sauced, heavily buttered, or overstuffed chunks of meat. She would read about salads, too, as long as they offered something to salivate over, like a rich balsamic dressing or creamy dabs of ripe cheese.

The good thing about lending cookbooks to Liz was that they always came back unmolested. Un-splattered, un-dog-eared, and un-warped. She treated them like they were twelfth-century Bibles, rare and beautiful, to be handled like treasures and heirlooms. Certainly, she never cooked from them, or she wouldn't still weigh less than a hundred pounds.

"Hey! It just came in yesterday!" Gracie called out to her as Liz opened the heavy front door just far enough to squeeze her slim frame through. It was Friday, just about closing time, and Gracie was looking forward to the end of her week and the FAC with her friends.

Liz's perpetually sad face—was she sad or just hungry? Gracie wondered—brightened, and for a moment, she looked like she could, on a good day, be kind of pretty. Pretty in a Gwyneth Paltrow-like, pink-eyed, bony-jawed way.

Liz paused in front of Gracie's window between her office and library, stood sideways, and smoothed down the pleats on the front of her khaki trousers. She frequently looked at her reflection that way, making sure that she was slim enough, oblivious to anyone watching.

If she wasn't thin enough, then who was? Gracie shook her head and looked away. Finally satisfied with her appearance, Liz peeked around the doorjamb. Gracie waved her in.

"*Prune?*" Liz asked.

"Yes, *Prune.*"

Gracie picked up the thick cookbook on her desk and waved it at Liz. "I don't know if you can lift it, though. I think it weighs more than you do."

Chef Gabrielle Hamilton had named her new cookbook after her New York restaurant, Prune, and it had been out for months, but Gracie had only recently managed to find room in the budget for it. At nearly thirty-two dollars, it was one of the priciest items she'd purchased that year.

"Did you look through it?" Liz asked. She was excited.

"Yes. I'll have to say, I was underwhelmed. But then, I'm not a foodie. I guess I prefer a cookbook with pretty pictures. This is a little dense for me."

"Ha, then you probably like the food porn on Facebook!" Liz slipped into the guest chair in Gracie's office and pulled the big cookbook onto her lap.

"If I did Facebook."

Gracie watched as Liz devoured a handful of pages, randomly turning to different sections of the cookbook before slapping it closed.

"This is great!" she said. "Thanks so much for getting it."

"If it takes you more than a couple of weeks to get it back, no worries. No one else has asked for it yet. I'll call you if I need it back sooner."

Liz nodded and settled back in the chair, balancing the cookbook on her bony knees. "So what else is going on?"

Since her twin girls had secured their driver's licenses six months before and no longer needed her to cart them around to soccer and their social activities, Liz had seemed a bit lost. She had given up her job as a physical therapist in Des Moines to be home with them after they were born, and now, her nest was emptying. She seemed at times at a loss for what to do with her day, other than read cookbooks she never used. Going back to work, given how out-of-date her PT skills probably were, was out of the question.

Her visits to the library tended to be on the long side— an excuse to stay out of the house a little longer, to communicate with someone other than two snarky teenagers. She professed to having a wonderful marriage and being madly in love with her husband, but even when he wasn't travelling for work, he put in long hours at his job in Des Moines.

If she had it to do all over again, Liz had told Gracie many times, she'd travel and write about food. Anthony Bourdain was her hero, and she followed his blog and his TV shows like he was a messiah. If she had it to do all over again . . . she would say, sighing and looking off into the distance.

"I don't know of anything that's going on." Gracie was sorry she didn't have something interesting to entertain the bored housewife with. "What are the girls up to?"

"Soccer. Oh, and this speech class or speech coaching thing—I don't really know what it is—that Gregory Thungaard is sponsoring. Do you know anything about that? They seem to be really excited about it. Gail is doing some dramatic reading for this contest they're going to in Des Moines, and Gina is doing something called extemporaneous speaking."

"Yes, I did hear about it." Gracie knew that Gregory was tutoring some of the high school students, although the contest in Des Moines was news. His work with students was one of the few things that softened her dislike of the man: he was contributing to the kids' educations by providing something the school district was too poor to fund.

"I think it's great that he's doing this." Liz, echoed Gracie's thought. "He's being very generous with his time. Given how busy he is with his politics and his farming stuff, I'm surprised he can find time for it all."

It was the second time in a week that Gracie had to hear her nemesis praised for his great qualities. She slumped back in her chair.

"Well, I think he's pretty much done with farming." Gracie tried not to sound negative. "He's rented out the last of his land. I think he's just focusing on his run for county supervisor."

"Oh." Liz paused to absorb what appeared to be news to her. "But, still. I mean, where else are these kids going to get help with public speaking, that sort of thing?"

"Right. It is a good thing. I just hope he isn't trying to indoctrinate them with his political ideas." Immediately she regretted saying it. She knew Liz only as a cookbook reader, not by her political leanings. What if she, too, was conservative with strong religious convictions?

"Oh, for sure!" Liz said. "He's a whack-nut when it comes to politics. But I think he's just helping them get comfortable with an audience. At least I hope that's all he's doing."

"Me too." Gracie was relieved. "I hate to see our kids brainwashed before they get a chance to think on their own."

"Well, I'll let you know if I see signs of little Rush Limbaughs in my girls' chatter."

~3~

Gracie looked up from the reading on her desk. The stranger—the one who had come into the library exactly one week before, looking lost and lonely—was back.

"Sara," the woman had reciprocated when Gracie introduced herself on that first visit. Sara didn't seem shy as much as wary, and she shook her head convincingly when Gracie offered to help her "find something."

"Thanks, but I'm just looking," she said, as if she were browsing Macy's housewares department. "I'll let you know if I need anything."

"Are you new in town?" Gracie asked. She didn't need to; she knew the answer. In the more than two decades she'd run the library, she'd seen twelve-year-olds grow up to be mothers and fathers, middle-aged people die of old age, and new people move in and out of town. There weren't many faces she didn't recognize.

"Well, kind of." Sara looked puzzled. "Or maybe not. I'm not sure."

Her face registered distrust and then something like embarrassment, and Gracie decided to leave her alone. She nodded politely, and retreated to her office. She glanced up once in a while to see the woman browsing a few different aisles, including those that held literature, biology, social sciences, and contemporary fiction. Sara, she decided, must truly be "just looking."

Sara left with no books. She held onto the door jamb of Gracie's office as she stuck her head in to say "thanks" and give a little wave. Gracie noticed the broad, white indentation on the ring finger of her left hand. Whatever she once wore there had been on her finger for a long time, and had been removed fairly recently.

Maybe that had something to do with her "just looking." Divorce, Gracie knew, could raise a lot of questions.

Now, a week later, Sara was back. This time she had a piece of paper in her hand.

"Hi, Sara!" Gracie jumped up from her desk again and met the woman as she was heading into the stacks. She leaned over to peer at the paper in Sara's hand.

"Is that a list of books?"

Sara quickly folded the paper.

Gracie nodded an apology. "Can I help you find anything?"

"Nah." Sara scrunched up her nose. "I don't want to be a bother. I think I can find these on my own. I'll let you know if I need your help."

As she did the week before, Gracie looked up occasionally from her windowed office to note Sara's meandering. The woman appeared to be in her late forties, maybe even a little older. She still wore her hair in a youthful style—long sweeping bangs and thick curling-ironed waves of highlighted tresses that hung just past her shoulders. Pretty and petite, she was dressed in a conservative skirt and low heels—standard office attire, her blouse wrinkled in a way that looked like she had been wearing a seat belt for some time—perhaps driving in from a job in Des Moines.

Sara stopped in the stacks a few times, each time pulling out a volume and skimming through some pages while standing up. Her path though the books was just as meandering as it had been the last time.

Again, Sara stopped by her office on the way out, again without a single book in her hand.

"Thanks again," she said. "Nice place here."

Gracie took that as an opening, and motioned for the woman to come in and sit down on her guest chair.

"Oh, I shouldn't bother you." Sara looked unsure.

"No bother." Gracie nodded, waving out at the empty street outside. "There's nothing else for me to listen to but the mice in the attic and the whine of the old furnace."

"How poetic!" Sara laughed. She sat down on the edge of the guest chair, as if not ready to commit to a conversation.

"So what brings you to town?"

"How do you know I'm not from here?"

"I know just about everyone in town," Gracie said. "Especially someone your age. I've been librarian for twenty-five years, and if you'd been here before, I'd know you."

"Yikes." Sara frowned. "Maybe everyone doesn't want to be known." Still, she settled back in the chair a bit further.

"True." Gracie diverted her eyes. Sara would tell her however little or much she was willing to divulge if Gracie stayed patient. "You don't have to tell me anything, and you're still welcome in our library anytime."

Sara laughed in quick little huffs. "Okay, I'm fine with that. Actually, I have a friend who lives here."

"That's great."

"She's on your board."

Gracie looked up. "Caitlin or Lorena?"

"Caitlin."

"Oh, great! Yes, she's one of the board members. I would love to get to know her better. And I'm very pleased to have a friend of hers in town. Of course, you'd be welcome in any case."

Sara smiled and looked down at her hands in her lap. "Well, thanks. But I'd better get going." She stood up and tilted forward in a subtle bow. "I'm going to Caitlin's for dinner."

"Say hi to her for me. And, remember, if you ever need any help finding something, I'm here for you."

Sara threw her the same little wave as before and slipped through the heavy front door. The woman's stealthy visit was something Gracie had seen often in teenagers and young adults. She was seeking an answer there among the wisdom stored in those shelves of books for a question that was weighing on her—a question that she didn't even want to admit to having.

That's what Gracie loved about her job—helping people sort through mankind's vast treasure trove of culture and knowledge stored on paper between cardboard covers. Even in a time of digital storage and electronic communication, some people needed and wanted a guide, and many worried about how much privacy they could expect if they searched online.

She stood up to stretch and get the blood flowing in her legs. She briskly circumnavigated the stacks, turned down the heat, and returned to her desk. She had to get to work!

First on her list was planning the next board meeting, now just three weeks away. She always sent out the agenda at least a couple of weeks in advance to give everyone time to make sure it was on their calendars and to think about the topics to be discussed.

Clearly, one of the items they would discuss at the meeting—and Gregory would pontificate tediously about— was the package he'd sent. She'd put off dealing with it for a week, but she needed to be ready for his arguments. She glanced through the half-dozen articles he had copied, stapled together, and stuffed in the envelope.

For one article, the editors had compiled a list of books that "good" Christian schools had taken off their library shelves for what Gracie imagined was promoting sex, drugs, rock music, alcohol, vampires, tattoos, piercings, break dancing, short skirts, Communism, certain presidents, interracial marriage, or dogs and cats living together— anything kids might actually want to read about.

There was also a copy of a Christian magazine's list of books that young people *should* read. The list was much shorter and contained mostly sanitary romances and "safe" histories—no mention of minorities or the disenfranchised— and young-adult series the editors said contained "uplifting" messages "for today's youth."

The front door banged open loudly against the front wall, startling Gracie. As if opening his package had summoned the man himself, there Gregory stood in her office door.

Of all the interruptions she enjoyed—usually, that was just about any that broke up the silence and monotony of her office—Gregory's occasional visits weren't among them.

"Gregory!" Gracie stood up to invite him into her office, but unlike Sara, he needed no invitation. He strode in officiously, sat in her guest chair, and with straight arms, put his hands on his knees. His pose had the effect of pushing his shoulders up around his ears.

It wasn't a good look. His thin grey hair was combed straight back off his forehead, revealing a tan line left by whatever seed-corn or baseball cap he'd been wearing in the sun lately. His pants pulled up tight against his knees, not yet adjusted to the recent thickening of his thighs, and his shirt buttons stretched open over some newly acquired central padding. Gracie couldn't keep from smiling at the impression that, sitting down, he'd just transformed himself into a kind of plump gremlin with big shoulders for wings.

"Oh!" Gregory nodded at the materials on her desk, his face attempting some semblance of a smile. "I see you got my package. I hope you find it self-explanatory."

Gracie sat down, looked down at her hands, and bit her tongue. Why wouldn't she find it self-explanatory? Perhaps Gregory thought she might need someone to explain it to her. As if his demeaner weren't condescending enough, couldn't he refrain from suggesting she couldn't read his propaganda?

Gracie only nodded. Contributing to any conversation with Gregory was only likely to extend it, not change his mind about anything, and prolonging this visit was the last thing she wanted to do.

"I hope you'll read carefully the sections about young adults," Gregory continued. "I liked that part about 'uplifting' literature for 'today's youth.'"

Gracie stifled a gag reflex and took a deep breath.

"Don't you think that's insightful?" He pleaded her to join his repartee.

"You mean 'uplifting' for yesterday's youth," she said, unable to resist his invitation to disagree. "Yesterday, like one hundred fifty years ago."

"But good literature is that which has stood the test of time!"

"Really?" She reached into the pile and pulled out the list of "classics" recommended for young adults and handed it to him. "Which of these do you remember ever reading? Have they stood the test of time for you? Can you tell me if you would have read any of them if they hadn't been assigned in school?"

Gregory took the list and reached into the breast pocket of his sports jacket for his reading glasses. With one hand, he wrapped them on his head, over one ear and then the other, and tipped his nose up to adjust his eyes.

"I loved all of these," he asserted. "I remember Moby Dick. And David Copperfield." He took a minute to look down the list before handing the paper back to Gracie. Apparently, nothing else on it had left an impression.

"What made them good literature—other than their age, that is?" Gracie asked, accepting the paper and sticking it back in the middle of the pile. "Can you give me an idea, perhaps, of the 'uplifting' value of David Copperfield?"

Gregory pulled his glasses off and studiously wiped them clean with a cloth he retrieved from their case as if buying time while he tried to remember what Dickens wrote about.

"Well, Gracie, I'm not here to discuss any particular novel on that list." He stuffed his glasses case back in his pocket and forced another smile. "You know, it's been years since I was in high school."

"Yes, I do know. And perhaps that's why you don't know what students want to read these days. Particularly what they want to read that a teacher hasn't assigned to them."

At that, Gregory sat up and flashed an irritated scowl. "I'm not interested in what they want to read. I am interested in what they should read!"

"Well, I, for one, do remember the lessons from David Copperfield, and I keep several copies on hand for those students who are assigned to read it in their English class. But outside of their classroom assignments, I don't think it should be up to you or me to decide what they should read."

"And I think it should. I and every other leader in this town. I think you are skirting your moral responsibility to these kids and to the community by allowing any book on those shelves out there, regardless of its contents. It's time we brought back some discipline to our public institutions, including this one."

With that he stood up. Gracie could feel his hot eyes on the top of her head, but she refused to look up to meet them. She gathered the papers on her desk, and stuffed them messily into the big envelope. Finally, when she had crammed all the pieces back in, she looked up.

"Anything else, Gregory?" she asked, feigning sweetness.

"Yes." He stood mute for a moment, and Gracie wondered if there really were anything else he had to say, or if he just didn't want to leave without scoring a win, however inconsequential. "I expect you will read this material fully and be prepared to discuss it at the next board meeting. You can rest assured, I will be ready for your response."

If sounding like she was agreeing with his vapid clichés was the quickest way to end the conversation, she was willing to do it. "Yes," she said cheerfully, masking her irritation. "I'm sure you will rest assured and will be ready." It wasn't what he'd asked, but he didn't seem to notice.

"Terrific!" he exclaimed. "I look forward to our fruitful discussion, then."

He turned and smoothed down the front of his shirt. He looked out her office door at the stacks in the main room of the library.

"We have an institution here that can lead young minds down the right path," he said, waving his arm to take in the stacks of books outside Gracie's door. "Let's not squander that opportunity."

With that grand revelation, he walked out into the library, turned stiffly toward the front door, and disappeared from Gracie's sight. She closed her eyes and heaved a deep sigh.

As she heard the door close with a heavy thud, she shook the pages back out of Gregory's envelope onto her desk. She flipped through the stapled sheets she hadn't yet read. The fattest one was an article from a rural magazine out of Kansas about a small-town library that had thrown out most modern literature in favor of old classics.

Sure, some classics, but probably not *To Kill a Mockingbird*, *Animal Farm*, or *Catcher in the Rye*. She would read the article to prepare for the meeting, but she'd rather listen to fingernails scrape down the length of a chalkboard.

Finally, she returned to his note.

"Dear Johnson Station Library Board Members," it was addressed.

> *I sensed a reluctance among you all to discuss the matter of providing quality reading materials to our community while ensuring that our children do not stumble upon publications that introduce negative images of America, foul language, sexually explicit descriptions, and violent episodes. To assist in a more thorough review of this subject, I've attached some thoughtful articles on communities like ours ...*

"And blah, blah, blah." Gracie glanced over the rest of the long, pedantic note.

"I look forward to a more fruitful discussion next month," he concluded. That again. He signed the note with a flourish—like John Hancock's signature on the Declaration of Independence. Very arrogant and totally in character.

If only he'd continued farming until a ripe old age like most farmers did. Instead, he'd sold a big chunk of his farmland for a princely sum to the poultry-processing plant a decade before and then rented the rest to those who wanted to make more efficient use of their huge tractors and combines. He kept only a couple of acres where the house stood. His wife had inherited the farm, but he carried himself like he'd earned the cash he now wielded like a weapon. With it, he intended to save the county—and eventually the entire state—from its road to perdition, and of course, buy himself a high-flying political career.

Gracie respected the town's religious residents and their minister, Terry. But Gregory had acquired his religious fervor only recently, suspiciously just before deciding to go into politics. But worse for her was his indifference to the role of a library in a small town. Early on, she had tried to warm his heart with stories of kids who didn't have books at home, families who couldn't afford psychiatrists, entrepreneurs who taught themselves accounting, or the precocious kid whose curiosity was unbounded.

He saw the library as only two things: A cost to taxpayers (bad), and a way to enforce a kind of moral straightjacket on the residents (good).

What kind of a person insists on being called Gregory instead of Greg, anyway?

Gracie pulled Gregory's propaganda back together, and got ready to turn the library over to Karen for the evening. As she walked through her final checks, she tried to remember what sections Sara had visited. Then she decided not to. She hoped Sara would eventually trust her to help find what she was looking for, but she certainly wasn't going to spy on her, even if that was something Gregory would want her to do.

For a minute, Gracie stood quietly and thought about her responsibilities to her community—community writ large, that is—grateful to Sara for reminding her of them, whoever she was and for whatever reason she was here.

That evening, Gracie watched Janice drive her pretty little Subaru up to the sidewalk that led to the back door and sit behind the steering wheel for a few minutes, apparently finishing a conversation on her cell phone. Her daughter rarely reminded her of herself; she didn't hear her own voice in her daughter's, or see any of her mannerisms reflected in Janice's body language. However, oddly, without talking with her about it, Janice had picked exactly the same car Gracie would, had she been interested in replacing her aging Buick.

Janice finally finished her phone call and got out of the car. She reached into the back seat and pulled out some clothes on hangers, slammed the door shut with her hip, and retrieved a small overnight bag out of the trunk. She fidgeted with the load, not noticing that Gracie was holding the door for her until she was just a few feet away.

"Mom! You scared me!" Janice jumped back as she looked up. "Don't be hopping up like that."

Why Janice assumed she'd be sitting down and needed to "hop up" to open the door, Gracie couldn't imagine. But she knew it was just the first of the dozens of little slights her daughter was going to throw at her this weekend, and if she started to let them get under her skin already, it wasn't going to be much fun having her daughter home.

"I'm just trying to help." Gracie immediately regretted her words. That "help" was exactly what Janice didn't want—at least this minute. Ever since she was two years old, she had shrugged off Gracie's attempts to help her get dressed, help her get up on a chair, or keep her from falling down the stairs one minute, and then feigned helplessness the next, when she wanted Gracie to wait on her.

Janice leaned over slightly as she walked through the door to accept her mother's cheek kiss. She walked through the kitchen and headed straight down the hallway toward the stairs.

"I'll be right back." She called over her shoulder. "I'm just going to put this stuff away, and I'll be back down."

A half hour later, she reappeared in an outfit clearly chosen for a night out in Des Moines: strappy, high-heeled sandals; tight jeans that reached halfway down her calves; and a long, sheer silk tunic over a short camisole that stopped somewhere above her belly button. Her short dark hair stuck out in all directions in short, stiff spikes, and she had made up her face in a flawless way Gracie had never mastered. Nobody dressed up like that for an evening in Johnson Station.

"It looks like you're heading out already?" Gracie didn't mean it as a question, but it came out that way, like she was wishing it weren't true.

"Yeah, I'm meeting Katie in Des Moines to go over our plans for tomorrow." Janice rummaged through her purse. "Where did I put my keys?"

"I was hoping we could at least chat for a few minutes before you took off." Gracie tried to sound cheerful instead of resentful.

Janice looked up, her keys hooked around one finger, and sighed.

"Sure," she said, rolling her eyes and plopping down on the nearest kitchen chair. "What do you want to talk about?"

Why did she have to act like she was still in high school?

Gracie had thought, back when she dealt with Janice's petulance and impatience daily, that by the time she was thirty or so, they'd develop some kind of an adult relationship. Maybe they'd never be friends, but she had hoped that Janice would start treating her with some respect.

"Well, I'm not asking about anything in particular." Gracie sat down across the kitchen table. "Just what's been going on in your life, you know. That sort of thing. How is work? What's going on in Chicago?"

"Nothing." Janice glanced at her watch. "Nothing is going on. Work is work. I can't think of one interesting thing to say about it."

"Well, then tell me about your plans for the shower this weekend. When is it and what can I do to help?"

"Oh yeah. We're having it tomorrow at two. You don't have to do anything. I'm going to pick up a bunch of stuff in Des Moines in the morning, and the girls are all bringing some wine and champagne and stuff. Maybe you could set out some wineglasses. That would be nice."

"You have food?"

"Yeah, that's what I'm picking up in Des Moines."

"What did you get Katie?"

"A few things for her trousseau." Janice looked at her watch again and stood up. "Look, I've got to run, but you should feel free to join us tomorrow and see what I got her. How's that?"

Gracie let her daughter run out of the door to her car without turning to watch. She'd seen her daughter pull away from her so many times over three decades that she knew exactly what it looked like.

~4~

"Where's Janice?" Richard climbed the wood steps to the deck where Gracie was nursing a very large glass of Pinot Noir. "And where's the bottle that came from?"

"Kitchen counter." Gracie was staring straight ahead as if in a trance.

"Okay, don't mind if I do." Richard let himself in the back door to the kitchen. Gracie heard him open two or three cabinet doors. He'd been in her kitchen regularly for nearly three years now; why did it take him so long to learn where she kept things? At least he didn't expect her to jump up and get a wineglass for him, as Janice might have—depending on her mood.

"So where is she?" Richard repeated his question, letting the screen door slam behind him and lowering himself down onto his favorite Adirondack chair next to her.

"Went to Des Moines to meet with Katie," Gracie answered without changing her focus.

"You seem pensive."

"Yeah." She shook herself out of her stupor and smiled at him. "Sorry. I just don't know what I did wrong with that girl. She doesn't exactly hate me, but I don't know what other emotion I can ascribe to her."

"Narcissistic. Spoiled. Maybe those ring a bell," Richard said.

"Characteristics, not emotions."

"So, what's the point? Are you surprised she didn't stick around tonight? Did you really expect her to?"

"Wouldn't you?" The setting sun was shining directly into Gracie's eyes. She stood up and moved her chair around to where she was looking at the back of the house instead of her untended backyard.

"I don't know your daughter that well," said Richard, slowly, as if carefully choosing his words. "But I have come to expect very little from her that I would call emotional attachment or compassion."

Gracie thought about that for a moment. It was true that Janice seemed to have very little concern or compassion for the homeless people she was helping shelter in Chicago through her real estate duties. She complained about their bad hygiene, their sense of entitlement, their "disgusting" presence at public hearings.

"Do you think I raised her badly? Is that why she's that way?" Gracie asked.

"Who knows? Nature, nurture," Richard said. "The debate is hardly settled. I don't think it's one thing. But maybe she was just born without an empathy gene. You know that was probably developed fairly late in human evolution."

"Yeah, maybe that's why she's still not married."

"Boyfriends?"

"How would I know?" Gracie attempted a chuckle, but failed to bring it up from her chest. She was surprised at how much she was hurt by Janice's behavior that afternoon. "I hardly talk to her. As far as she's concerned, I am here just to make her bed and wait on her. I guess that's what I'm good for."

"Jesus, Gracie. When are you going to deal with this?" Richard said. He put his wineglass on a redwood plank of the deck, and pulled his chair closer. He reached out for Gracie's hands. "You have never let other people determine your happiness. I don't know why you don't come to terms with her. Tell her to respect you or stay away."

Gracie smiled with one side of her mouth. It was a kind of smirk, but she didn't mean it that way. She just found it ironic that the one love she could trust these days was the one that she couldn't cop to in public: Richard's.

"I know," she said. "Thank you. I'm working on it."

Richard leaned forward and kissed her lightly on the lips.

"So, is there a shower here tomorrow?"

Gracie nodded. "Two o'clock. I'm invited. I guess I should feel honored."

Richard frowned at that, and Gracie waved her hand in the air, as if to dismiss those last words. That was exactly the kind of self-deprecation that drove Richard nuts.

"I'd skip it," Richard said. "Come with me. I'm not going to Minneapolis, but there's a sheepdog trial over by Boone. It would be a lot more fun than listening to the snarky comments of a bunch of overdressed, narcissistic young women all day."

"Probably."

Gracie slipped back into her reverie. Ever since Janice left that afternoon, she'd been overcome by melancholy. It wasn't unusual to be disappointed by Janice. Every time she came home, Gracie's hopes for some kind of connection with her daughter were smashed by reality. But this time, she couldn't brush it off or tell herself it didn't matter.

It did matter.

࿓

Gracie and Richard didn't make love every night he stayed over, but when they did, she wondered why they didn't do it every time.

Lying awake a couple of hours later, Gracie listened to Richard snore and reached over to encourage him to turn over onto his side. They were amazingly compatible in bed, much more than she and Jens had been, more than she expected when Richard made the first move toward their love affair.

She shouldn't have been surprised at the easy connection, given their history.

Jens had joined Richard's law practice when they moved

to Johnson Station thirty years before. Richard's wife had died in an airplane disaster in Chicago in the 1970s, and he had raised his son alone, never remarrying. Gracie had assumed he didn't remarry because he was still mourning for his wife, but three years after Jens died, he admitted that he had been in love with her for years.

He told her one starry night on the back deck of her home. The four other friends Gracie had invited to supper that night had gone home, but Richard had stayed and suggested they open another bottle of wine.

"I don't think I need any more wine," she said, "but I'd be glad to open one for you. What would you like? Red or white?"

"Champagne? Do you have any?"

"Sure, but that seems a little odd."

"Yes, but I have something to celebrate," he said with a wink. "Where is it? I'll open it."

After he popped the cork and poured the bubbly wine into their big wineglasses, he proposed a toast.

"To love, wherever you find it." He raised his glass.

"Sure." Gracie wrinkled her eyebrows in confusion. "Whatever you're talking about."

Richard took a big swig from his glass, holding her quizzical gaze.

"Gracie, there's no way you don't know how I feel about you," he said. "I have been in love with you since, oh, about nineteen eighty. Tonight, I decided I'm not going to hide it any longer. Jens has been gone for a couple of years, and I think it's time for me to come clean. So, here's to me professing it: I love you."

He raised his glass toward hers again.

"What?" Gracie feigned surprise. Over the previous few months, she'd noticed how close he stood to her, how intently he listened to even her most trite comments, how quick he was to open a door or pull out a chair for her.

Richard just smiled and waited for her response. Was she in love with him? Definitely. But could she ever get over the feeling that the whole town would be watching and clucking their tongues, whispering—if not saying it out loud—"I knew it!"

"You remember what happened." She couldn't imagine that he'd forgotten, but she was stalling.

"Yes," he said. "But obviously, I don't give a shit. And you shouldn't either."

"I just hate the idea that people will think . . ." Gracie couldn't finish her sentence. It seemed so ridiculous.

Richard stepped closer and put his hand on the back of her neck. He pulled her toward him and kissed her. It wasn't a friendly kiss; it was hungry, and destroyed any reservations she had.

It was so different from the last kisses she had shared with Jens. It had been a long time since she felt desire in a man's lips, and it made her heart race.

Jens had engaged in a low-intensity war of petty slights for the last twenty of their twenty-two years of marriage: laughing hysterically when she misplaced her glasses or keys, suggesting that she was eating too much, and expressing undue alarm if she spilled a little wine, as if she was drinking too much.

Gracie met Jens in Chicago, where she had plied her international business degree from the University of Iowa into a job as a clerk on the floor of the Chicago Mercantile Exchange. It was a wild, male-dominated mash pit of a workplace, where women were still required to wear skirts, sexism and racism were rampant, and a trader's highest achievement, besides making the most lucrative trades, was to come up with the most tasteless and cruel joke of the day. Natural disasters, massacres, airplane crashes, and political gaffes were all fair game.

Working there required a kind of thick skin and fortitude

that few women could sustain for long. Keeping her head down and letting the inappropriate and sexist remarks roll off her back, Gracie managed to hang on long enough to learn the ropes. After a couple of years, a seat on the exchange came up for rent, and using the money her parents had left her, she dived into the frenzied maelstrom of the futures pits.

City life appealed to her with its free-flowing waves of friendships that changed with every job promotion or new apartment acquired by the young urban professionals she and Jens hung out with. They traveled to Europe and Hawaii for vacations, and talked about going someday to South America and New Zealand. Even when she discovered she was pregnant, she didn't intend to change her lifestyle, except for making the necessary housing and childcare adjustments, which she and Jens could easily afford.

But when she was six months pregnant, she started to worry about the jostling in the trading pits. Jens took advantage of her ambivalence and pleaded with her to move to Johnson Station. He wanted to return to his hometown to practice law and raise a family. "My mom will be right there to help with the baby," he said. "And it will be so much easier to raise a child in a small town. Remember? You used to walk to school as a kid, didn't you? Kids can't do that in Chicago."

Finally, Gracie had agreed.

"But we'll still come to the city once in a while, and we'll still travel, right?" She begged him to promise, and he did.

It didn't happen that way. His early ardor vanished once they were settled in Johnson Station, their Victorian home only a block from his parents' house. The plans they had made to explore the world no longer interested him. The baby was his excuse, even when Janice was old enough to go along. Then, after a few years, he refused to even discuss Gracie's wanderlust. He ran for county judge and then for the state's court of appeals. His work was clearly his greatest love, and Gracie learned there was no point in fighting it.

Richard had been Jens's partner when they first moved to Johnson Station, and he and Gracie clicked immediately. When the three of them went out to dinner or for evening cocktails, Richard and Gracie gravitated toward each other. They shared a certain rhythm of thought and sense of humor, and blurted out the same comments at the same time. They debated books and movies and politics, and frequently, they ended up sitting off somewhere by themselves, engrossed in conversation and oblivious to everyone else in the room.

It was innocent, Gracie remembered. They were simply two like-minded people who enjoyed each other's company. If they'd been the same gender, no one would have noticed.

Then one afternoon, Marcia rushed into the library from the bank and closed Gracie's office door behind her. "Did you know that you are sleeping with your husband's partner?" she asked. "That's what Karen told me. She said Nancy told her, and apparently, Nancy said it like it was the truth. Not even a rumor. Like she'd been there to see it herself."

"Nancy?" Gracie barely knew Nancy. She was a hairdresser whose cuts came with liberal doses of gossip. "Does anyone believe anything she says?"

"Well, I'm not sure Karen did, but she got on the phone and called me about it pretty quick. You know how things spread around here."

Gracie knew she was right. If two people heard something today, two hundred would hear about it tomorrow.

She never talked with Richard or Jens about it, but without explanation, the two partners quit socializing. Shortly after that, Jens left the law practice for the justice's bench. Gracie and Richard saw each other only from a distance for more than a decade. Still, when she spied him across the church, the town square, or the café, she felt her heart jump a little. All the more reason to avoid him. And one more reason to regret living in a small town like Johnson Station.

Jens died of a heart attack on the bench shortly after his

election as an appeals court judge. After a while, Gracie and Richard began seeing each other socially again, but only as part of larger groups. Then a year ago, here on this deck, Richard had apparently decided they'd waited long enough.

"I am a little shocked at you," she had said after finally surrendering to Richard's passionate kiss, her heart pounding. "I had you pegged as happy alone."

"Oh, I'm happy enough. But being close to you makes me happier, and I can't wait to see how close we can get."

Gracie felt her face grow hot with a blush, and she gulped her champagne.

Richard nodded his approval. "Drink up, Gracie, and then let's go upstairs."

~5~

It was warm for an afternoon in October, but Gracie didn't turn the library's air conditioner on. She had turned it off in September, the first night of fall, when a cold front finally pushed out the late summer heat, and the last stubborn humidity solidified into tiny icicles, glistening like tiny daggers on scraggly lawns. Once the old cooling system was serviced and tucked away for the winter, she avoided jinxing the aging monster by waking it back up again.

It wasn't unusual for summer to return for a bright, if brief, encore in October. The late afternoon sun beat through the west-facing windows, the library's ancient carpeting collecting its heat and sending it wafting back through the stacks in oxygen-deprived waves. At her desk, Gracie nodded off briefly, her fingers still hovering over her keyboard.

The main entrance door opened slowly and then closed with a thud, and Gracie jerked awake. She peered out the window of her small office into the main library room and watched a teenage girl slink back toward the shelves that held the historical romances. The girl tossed her backpack on a table and flopped down in a chair as if exhausted by the warm, three-block walk from school.

Gracie knew her. Ísabel was one of only a couple of Hispanic teenagers in the town's high school. Her father was an illegal immigrant who had worked at the poultry-processing plant until his deportation with twenty other Mexicans in the INS sweep—the raid Caroline had talked about. Gracie wondered how Ísabel and her mother were supporting themselves now.

Up until the last couple of weeks, Ísabel had been an

infrequent visitor to the library. She stopped in only every now and then, looking for books to help with her school essays. Gracie figured she didn't have internet access at home. She probably didn't have a personal computer either.

"Let me know if you need anything," Gracie called back to Ísabel. The girl looked up and waved somewhat dismissively, barely looking up from her homework.

Gracie turned back to the online order form on her computer. What was she doing again? She glanced back at the latest issue of *Kirkus Reviews* on her desk. She had circled the titles of two novels whose reviews indicated they might interest her rural Iowa readership, and farther back in the volume, a couple of new cookbooks that might interest Liz.

But what about *The Intern's Travels*, the book Caroline had asked about? Should she order it, or should she wait until after the next board meeting to decide? She decided to postpone the order, although she wasn't happy about it. She hated the idea of ceding any authority over book selection to Gregory and his board.

It took a good thirty minutes for Gracie to complete the order form and dig up the library's new PayPal account information to finish the order. She pushed "send" and looked up. Still the lone customer in the stacks, Ísabel had stopped doing homework and had pulled down one of the historical romances she favored. She checked out a couple of them every now and then, always returning them only two or three days later. Apparently, she was a pretty fast reader.

Gracie watched the young girl turn a few pages and tried to imagine what her life was like. She clearly wasn't one of the popular kids. Although Gracie wasn't tuned into the cliques in the local high school anymore—she had been when Janice was in school—she still had a sense for who was "in" and who wasn't. The popular kids roamed in packs, loudly taunting each other with snarky comments and the latest slang. They dressed in the right clothes and seemed to have a second sense about how many tattoos and piercings were just enough, and how many were too few or how many were overdoing it. The not-so-popular made the mistake of either trying too hard or not trying hard enough.

It had been that way since Gracie was in school in Thomasville and probably before. But Ísabel didn't seem particularly unhappy, considering the general melancholy teenage girls tended to wallow in. She was short and slight with thick black hair she wore in a messy ponytail. Her clothes were simple: classic jeans and T-shirts—attire unlikely to elicit attention from her classmates. Most of them probably didn't even see her coming and going.

For two weeks, Gracie had left the girl alone, squelching her curiosity about why she was coming in every day. She remembered how Sara, her visitor a couple of weeks ago, had jealously guarded her privacy. But today the puzzle of Ísabel— and the need to get up and move around—got the best of Gracie.

Her steps were muted by the carpeting, and she surprised Ísabel, who looked up with a start.

"What are you reading?" Gracie smiled broadly.

"Uh, nothing." Ísabel sat up straight and closed the book with the cover facing down. "Just a book."

"Right. I can see it's a book," Gracie said. "I want you to know that there isn't a book in this entire library that I would disapprove of you reading. I was asking only because I was curious."

"Oh." The girl kept her gaze on the book in front of her, avoiding Gracie's eyes.

"I've seen you around here a lot lately." Gracie sat down across the table. "Are things okay at home?"

"Didn't you hear?" Ísabel barely whispered. "Everyone else in town seems to know."

"About your father? Yes, I did hear. You and your mom getting along okay?"

"What are you? Some kind of social worker?" Ísabel still refused to raise her eyes.

"No."

"Then it's none of your business." Even though she wasn't one of the popular kids, Ísabel had adopted their sassy manner of speaking to elders. But, then, she seemed to regret it. Her voice softened. "If it's a problem, me coming in here, let me know, and I'll go somewhere else."

"Certainly not." Gracie attempted a little laugh. "I enjoy the company. It gets plenty lonely in here in the afternoons. Most of my customers come in around noon, and the rest of the day, it's quiet as a cemetery."

"Mmm." Ísabel continued to stare at the back of the book.

"Well," Gracie said, standing up. "Let me know if there's anything I can help you find."

She thought she saw Ísabel nod a little. Gracie would try again the next time she came in. If there was anyone in this town who could use an extra friend, even one as old as Gracie, it was probably Ísabel.

⁊

Gracie couldn't get Ísabel off her mind that evening, and Richard noticed.

"Something bugging you, hon?" he asked as they washed the dishes after a late supper.

"Hmm . . . what?" Gracie shook her head and pulled her mind back to the present.

"What's got you so pensive tonight?"

"Oh, nothing. Just this young girl who's been coming into the library lately. Her father was one of the Mexicans they pulled out of the chicken factory last month and sent home. She's been coming in about every day after school to study and read some crappy Victorian romances."

"So that sounds like a good thing. Why are you worried?"

"I'm not worried. I'm glad she's coming in. But I do wonder why all of a sudden the library has become her second home."

"Probably third home. School is probably her second."

"Sheeeeesh! Is everything a debate with you?" Although there was some truth to her question, Gracie said it with a laugh. "Anyway, I got a sense today that she could use some help."

"What kind of help?"

"I don't know. Someone to listen to her. Someone to care about her."

Richard shook out the dishtowel he had been drying dishes with and folded it over the towel rack by the refrigerator. "You really need to remodel this kitchen."

The change in subject surprised Gracie. "What? Where did that come from? You and your digressions. I thought we were talking about Janice—I mean Ísabel."

"Right. I wonder why you think Ísabel needs you."

"Well, not necessarily me. Just somebody."

"But maybe you. I wonder if this could have something to do with how Janice treated you this past weekend." Richard sat down at the kitchen table and poured himself the last wine from the bottle they'd opened for supper.

"Hey! Maybe I wanted that!" Gracie snapped her dishtowel at him and put it back over her shoulder.

"Open another bottle," Richard said. "But stick to the subject. Maybe you're taking on some surrogate daughter to replace the affection you don't get from Janice."

Gracie pulled the plug from the sink, turned, and wiped her hands dry with the towel on her shoulder.

"I suppose there might be some truth to that." Gracie thought back to what Janice was like in high school. She could count on one hand the number of times her daughter had come into the library after school. Janice had seemed embarrassed of her mother's position at the library, as if it gave Janice a nerdy patina she didn't want. Remembering her own embarrassment at the sex seminars her mother gave at school assemblies when she was in high school, Gracie was quick to forgive her for that.

"Ísabel, though, seems so different from Janice," Gracie said. "Janice hardly seemed like she needed me at all. Ísabel wasn't particularly nice to me today, but even in her sass, I felt a vulnerability that I never saw in Janice."

"Well, Janice does approach life a little bit entitled," Richard said. "It's hard to act vulnerable if you think the world owes you deference."

"Well, what do you think I should do?"

"Should do? You mean for Ísabel? Keep the library open. You'll be killing two birds with one stone: keeping your job and being there for her if she needs you."

"You make things seem so simple." Gracie reached over and tousled the little bit of hair Richard still had on his head. "It must be nice to be a guy."

"But there is something that's bugging me," Richard said. Gracie couldn't help but note the change in his tone.

"Not this again," Gracie said. "We have been over this a hundred times."

"Yes, but let's go over it again. Who are you protecting by pretending we're just friends? You think I don't realize this is why you keep canceling plans to go out of town with me?"

"I need to set a good example." It was her usual answer, and she meant it. To her, it came with being a town librarian.

"For whom?"

"Everyone. The kids in town. Teenagers like Ísabel."

"Ísabel has probably had as much sex in her short little life as you had by the time you were thirty," Richard said. "I think she can handle it." He rose and reached for another wine bottle.

"Don't drink too much or you won't stay asleep. You

know how too much wine wakes you up at night."

"Maybe I'll think of something to do when I'm lying there awake." He wagged his eyebrows up and down suggestively.

"Oh, quit it!" Gracie couldn't help but chuckle. "But I think you're wrong about Isabel. She seems so innocent."

"She seems that way because young girls these days grow up in a world where premarital sex and babies born out of wedlock are norms. For her, there's no reason to chastise herself. Everyone's doing it, like they say."

"Maybe."

"Yes, probably. And I hope you can drop this secrecy thing. I'd like you to go to New York with me at Christmas to see Ronnie."

Ronnie was Richard's son from the marriage that had ended when his wife died, before he moved to Johnson Station.

Gracie shook her head. "What if Janice wants to come home for Christmas? Or probably, I'll go to Chicago again to spend it with her."

"Oh, you mean so you can wait on her? Come on, Gracie. You said it yourself. She doesn't seem to care about you a bit. Maybe letting her celebrate Christmas by herself once would do her good."

Under their patina of Protestant virtue, the townspeople of Johnson Station were pretty much like people anywhere, Gracie figured: full of contradictions, not perfect, not always good. However, some people seemed to think it was a kind of Garden of Eden, where sin had yet to be introduced and innocence was preserved.

Like Gregory. How could he be so naïve? Gracie wondered as she opened the heavy library door the next morning. Or maybe he wasn't and his whole political platform was a cynical strategy to convince people it could still be 1950 if the town, the county, the entire state would live as if it were.

Wasn't the point of history to learn from it, not to repeat it?

Nothing had been settled between Richard and her the night before. Richard still wanted Gracie to go with him to New York for Christmas, and she was still demurring, although it was getting harder and harder for even her to understand why. Did she really care what the people in this town thought?

Gregory's heavy hand at the library wasn't helping. He wanted returning to yesterday's mores and standards of behavior the goal of every institution in town, including her library. He wanted to counter the "lies of the liberal media." He wanted to turn back the clock.

And here she was, pretending to live according to his rules. It was a lie.

So, why did she keep up the charade?

She was pulled in two directions: worried about what Gregory thought and worried that Richard would grow tired of her moral pretense and end their relationship. If he had to keep sneaking around, and if they couldn't travel together, his patience might run out.

Gracie let the heavy front door close behind her, turned up the thermostat by the entrance, and ran through her usual routine of checking the stacks and the bathrooms, and starting a pot of coffee. She had barely sat down at her desk when Armand Oleson appeared at her office door.

"Hi, Gracie," he said, making her jump. He had a way of sneaking up on her that she attributed to the fact that he had less of a problem opening the big front door than most of her regulars, and that he wore rubber-soled walking shoes that made no noise.

"Oh, Armand, you surprised me. What's up?"

"Can I come in?" He was one of the few regulars who

always asked permission to come into her little office rather than just sitting down to talk. Most of the women had been doing it so long, they assumed they were welcome. And, of course, Gregory never asked—he just barged in like he owned the place.

"Of course!" Gracie waved Armand in and handed him a heavy book. "Here's that new history book you were waiting for. *Out of Ashes.* That one about Europe in the twentieth century."

"Super!" Armand sat down, set the thick volume on the edge of Gracie's desk, and began thumbing through it. "I need to get up to speed on European issues. You know, this migrant crisis, the financial mess—they all have roots in the two world wars and the colonial legacy of European empires."

Gracie watched Armand skim the table of contents. Books like this humbled her. When it arrived, she held it, feeling its heft, a metaphor for its weighty topic and worthy enquiry. The book's global viewpoint and the questions it raised reminded her of three other books she had ordered for Armand: *The Sixth Extinction*; *Guns, Germs, and Steel*; and *the Better Angels of Our Nature*.

Those books triggered not only humility but also regret in Gracie. Why hadn't she become a scholar, an expert, a world-renowned thinker instead of a small-town librarian battling politicians with parochial, xenophobic agendas? She had once thought she was capable of anything, but then it turned out her concept of "anything" had been too limited and unambitious.

Armand closed the book and looked up smiling.

"Oh, I almost forgot." Gracie shook herself out of her self-critical reverie. "I ordered another book for you the other day. The new Follett. You haven't read it already, have you?"

"No, no. I look forward to it." Follett was one of the historical fiction authors that Armand seemed to respect.

"So how did you like *The Bloodletter's Daughter*?"

"Silly."

"How?"

"Girls didn't think like that in the Middle Ages," Armand said. "There would have been no inspiration for her to have those thoughts about being a doctor back then. Also, the word 'science' hadn't been coined yet, but she talks about it all the way through."

It was typical. Armand was a quiet man, except when he was ripping some historical novel apart for its inaccuracies or anachronisms. When he first started coming to the library a decade before, she wondered why he continued to read historical fiction books if their minor faults bothered him so much. Now she realized that he read them *in order* to find their errors. It may not have been a need to feel superior as much as it was his need to stay busy.

Armand had retired as the high school history teacher a decade before, and he stayed active by attending football games on Friday nights, coaching the school's golf team as a volunteer, and participating in the school's annual fundraisers.

"Have you been out with the golf team lately?" Gracie asked.

"Yes. Some promising youngsters."

"Any girls?" Gracie had been one of the townsfolk who had argued for a girls' golf team when Title IX was first enacted, but it didn't happen.

"No, but I'd love to have some join the team," Armand said. "They'd probably help motivate the boys."

Gracie made a note to ask Ísabel if she might have an interest in golf. Gracie still had an old set of clubs in the garage, and she wondered if they were modern enough to get a beginner started in the game. Perhaps she'd even go out with her once or twice and see if she could get some of her old swing back.

~6~

It was clear that Ísabel was bright. And she was a good storyteller. After a couple of weeks, she started talking in complete sentences instead of the monosyllables and text-speak Gracie had come to expect from teenagers who came to the library.

Eventually they settled into the same routine each afternoon Ísabel came to the library. The girl would come in, sit at the same table back in the stacks, and work on her homework for about thirty minutes. Then, she'd pull a novel off a shelf, and spend anywhere from a half hour to an hour with it. Finally, she'd look up across the room at Gracie and say "hey." That was Gracie's signal that it was time to come over and talk.

At first, they talked about what Ísabel was studying in school, and the other kids, and one time, Gracie brought up golf. Ísabel wrinkled up her nose.

"Isn't that for old guys?" she asked.

Gracie chuckled. It probably looked that way to a young girl in Johnson Station. The town's nine-hole course was frequently flooded, always infested with mosquitos, and only patronized on any regular basis by a small cadre of old retired guys—the same ones who gathered at the café's back table with the town's businessmen every morning.

Gracie let the subject drop. Perhaps once she got to know the girl better, she could bring it up again, maybe even suggest an outing with her next year once the river had receded from its spring floods.

Eventually, Ísabel grew comfortable enough to share her modest goals with Gracie. A four-year degree was as far as she wanted to go in college, and becoming a teacher or maybe a nurse was about as adventurous a career as she seemed able to imagine. Gracie encouraged her to think bigger.

"How about a corporate CEO?"

"Too much work!" Ísabel laughed. "You can't do that and have babies!"

"Oh, yes you can," Gracie said. "Look at Carly Fiorina. Sheryl Sandberg."

"Who?" Ísabel swiped a dismissive wave in front of her face. "I have no idea who that is. And if I graduate from high school, it will be a miracle. My mom and dad never did."

After that, Gracie pulled back a little, afraid to push too hard. She decided it was better to listen to Ísabel than give her advice. Advice is what the school counselors were there for, although Gracie doubted they were overly concerned about a shy Hispanic student whose parents never showed up to demand their daughter get more attention. They were busy tending to the kids whose helicopter parents buzzed overhead.

"One time I went to Mexico to see where my dad lived," Ísabel started their conversation one afternoon. Gracie sat down across the table from her, sensing the girl had a story she wanted to tell. "He went there to take care of Grandma, who was dying. He was going to come back after she died."

"How did he get back and forth without papers?" It was the kind of question Gracie would never have considered asking three weeks before, when she and the girl had just started talking. Now it seemed that Ísabel appreciated the chance to talk about the difficult things she couldn't share with kids at school.

"Oh, he had a usual guy. A coyote, they call them. He took the same route each time. I guess it was dangerous, but he said he knew what to watch out for, he'd done it so many times."

"How did you get there?"

"I flew." Ísabel said rolled her eyes at what she clearly

found to be a silly question. "I'm a U.S. citizen, you know. I have a passport. Dad bought me a ticket."

"And you went down to see him?"

"Yeah, and to meet my grandma before she died, although it wasn't really like meeting a real person. She wasn't really there, if you know what I mean. She was real sick."

"What did you think?"

"About Grandma?"

"No, I mean about Mexico."

"Oh, my God, I hated it."

"Why?"

"I guess I had a different idea of what it would be like," Ísabel said. "I always felt so out of place here in Johnson Station, and I was sure I'd be, like, much happier there. I thought I would fit in better."

"And you didn't?"

"Well, at first, everything felt so strange. The streets aren't paved, and the neighbors just walked into each other's houses, and no one could speak any English. When I walked around the first day, I couldn't imagine my dad growing up there."

"But you speak Spanish, right?"

"Yeah," Ísabel said. "I do. But it was, like, as soon as I got down there, I wanted to speak English. I wanted to be American. I wanted everyone to know I was an American. I didn't want to be like those people. Everyone was so old. Either a kid or old."

Gracie said nothing. She couldn't imagine what it must feel like to be caught between two cultures, not fully comfortable in either.

"And I didn't expect it to look like that," Ísabel added after a long silence.

"What? Look like what?"

"Well, the dirt streets, you know. And Grandma's cupboards were, like, made out of this really old wood, and you had to clean the floor with a big ol' brush, and it never got clean anyway. And the sink was disgusting. I don't know. It was just something I wasn't used to, I guess."

"What did you expect? Hadn't your dad told you he came from a poor town?"

"Yeah, but poor there isn't anything like poor here. We're poor here, but at least it's nicer than that. I mean, we have a bathroom indoors, and we can wash the kitchen floor."

"So what did you do?"

"I tried to get used to it. I kept telling myself that it was authentic Mexico, my roots, you know. So, I thought if I talked to dad, we could, like, fix it up to look more like home and then maybe I could stay there for a while. But he laughed at me. He wouldn't tell me why he thought that was so funny."

"How long did you stay?"

"Two weeks."

"Do you think you gave it enough time?"

"It was so hot and dusty." Ísabel looked past Gracie out the library's big front window and squinted as if she were imagining Main Street turned into the dirt road in front of her grandmother's house. "I wanted to get back to Mama, but mostly, I just wanted to get out of there. I told dad I had to get back early to get ready for school."

"Do you think he's back there now?"

"I have no idea."

"Haven't you heard from him?"

Ísabel shook her head.

"Has your mom heard from him?"

Ísabel stared straight ahead, and Gracie thought she might be trying to decide how much to share with her.

"I don't know," she said after a long pause. "I don't know."

She stood up, pulled her books together, and slid them into her backpack. She avoided meeting Gracie's eyes.

"Hey, I'm sorry," Gracie said softly. "I guess I was prying."

"Yeah, well, maybe there's some things you don't need to know," Ísabel said icily as she walked away. Something had abruptly changed her mood. "You're not my mom, you know. I don't have to tell you everything."

Gracie watched her pull the heavy door open and slip around it into the darkening evening. She'd have to be careful to not overstep the boundaries Ísabel felt comfortable with if she was going to keep her talking. Listening to the girl and ratifying her feelings was something her mother wasn't doing, something that Ísabel needed from Gracie.

Even if she wasn't her mother, even if she was just a librarian, she didn't want to fail her.

❧

When Gracie called Janice that evening, she intended to do her best to mend fences with her daughter. She wouldn't beg for information; she would just apologize for being so angry at Janice about the bridal party. Her daughter had ignored her all weekend, and then got ready to leave without cleaning up the party mess. Gracie yelled, Janice yelled, and they parted badly.

On the phone, Gracie skipped her usual questions about how Janice's work was going, what was new. She wanted a clean slate, and she'd decided to eat crow to get it.

"I'm sorry about how we ended your last visit," she said immediately after Janice answered the phone. "I don't want that to be how we are."

"Whatever," Janice said. "You don't have to be so critical, you know."

"Right. I get it. I'm apologizing."

Janice said nothing. But neither did she cut off the call, so Gracie ventured on.

"You know, I've been thinking lately that I would really like us to develop a new kind of relationship. I want to get to know you as an adult. Right now, I think we're still stuck in these mom and daughter roles, and frankly, I think they aren't working for us anymore."

"Perhaps if you weren't so judgmental," Janice repeated.

"Yes, I'm sorry about that."

Gracie's contrite attitude seemed to soften Janice for once. She didn't overtly accept her mother's apology, but she did something even more auspicious: she asked Gracie what was new. It was the first time Gracie remembered that Janice actually asked about her life.

"Oh, not much." Gracie was taken off guard. She wasn't sure what to share; she didn't want to choose a topic that would jeopardize this precarious détente. "There was an INS raid in town a few weeks ago, and this girl whose father was deported has started to come into the library nearly every day. I'm trying to figure out if there's something I can do for her without hurting her pride."

"Oh, Mom." Apparently, Gracie hadn't chosen a topic that was neutral enough. "Don't go all soft on this girl. You know how they are."

"Who?"

"Those people. The illegal immigrants. They will take advantage of everything they can get their hands on, including your sympathy."

"Janice, I can't believe you would say that. You don't know this girl."

"I work with these people all the time, Mother. And you aren't some social services agency. Let the authorities take care of it."

"The authorities are nowhere in sight, whoever they are."

"Then call someone. What? Is she sleeping on the streets? Is she starving? Skipping school? You can call the county, and they'll take care of it."

Gracie paused before reacting. *Engage brain before starting mouth.* But it did little good. She still said the wrong thing.

"I can't believe how little compassion you have for the very people your business purports to serve."

"You mean the homeless? The girl is homeless?"

"No, I mean it more generally. People who didn't happen to be born in the U.S. to parents who had no problem providing a nice roof and good food as well as a private school education and a law school degree."

"Oh, now *I'm* the problem." Janice's voice had risen to a high pitch again. "You regret what you provided for me? Where is this coming from, Mother?"

"Never mind," Gracie said. "I really don't know how to talk with you anymore, Janice. Everything is about you. You, you, you. I think you should learn to open your heart and ears a little bit and hear some of what you're saying."

Janice said nothing. Gracie waited until the dial tone confirmed what she feared. Janice had hung up on her.

~7~

Gracie woke up early, long before dawn and couldn't get back to sleep. How did she suddenly find herself facing so many conundrums?

Did Ísabel need her help, and if so, in what way? Was Janice right? Was she getting involved in problems that belonged to someone else? Did it make sense to keep fighting Gregory, who was most likely to win anyway? Were she and Janice always going to be at odds? Was her insistence on keeping her love affair with Richard secret jeopardizing her relationship with him?

Some of her questions had easy answers: stay away from Ísabel's problems, accept the inevitability of censorship, and quit hiding her relationship with Richard. However, those answers each carried its own risks. Staying away from Ísabel would be accepting Janice's "it isn't my problem" attitude toward the world. Not fighting Gregory was a betrayal to her profession. And coming out, so to speak, about her relationship with Richard would mean giving up an image of herself that she was afraid to lose.

What petty problems she had, and how miserably she let them tie her in knots. Petty or not, Gracie needed answers, and she decided to do what she always did when she needed a good listener and a wise mind to help her noodle a problem: she went to church.

Gracie wasn't religious; she was pretty sure she didn't believe in God, although only pretty sure. She went to church most Sundays, mainly to see her friends and neighbors, and to hear the pastor, Terry Milton, make sense of things.

Terry's sermons were based as much on worldly philosophers as they were on religious dogma. He appeared to draw considerable erudition from honest, deliberate introspection, a quality that Gracie found reassuring. Conversations with him could be lengthy and required some patience, but Gracie always found them helpful.

"Gracie! What a pleasure! Do come in!" Terry stood up and enthusiastically spread his arms for a hug when she walked through his open door.

His tiny, sunny office was her favorite corner of the church. Otherwise, she found the blonde wood and minimal decoration of the modernistic church and its towering nave a bit hard and cold, like Scandinavian furniture. But Terry had warmed his space with a love seat covered in a colorful Navajo-inspired upholstery, overlapping rugs from the Middle East and Asia, and several pieces of framed street art.

Gracie accepted his embrace and smiled. She felt better already.

"What brings you in?" Terry back down behind his desk and leaned toward her as she settled into the love seat. "Want some coffee?"

The bitter odor of hours-old brew filled the office from a small Mr. Coffee in the corner behind his desk, and Gracie declined.

"Do you have a few minutes to hear my petty problems?"

"Of course." He smiled indulgently. "And no problems are petty if they bring you here."

Gracie smiled her appreciation and waded through her litany of insomnia-producing issues with him: Ísabel, Janice, Gregory, and *The Intern's Travels*. Terry listened and nodded, and when she was finished, he sat back and intertwined his fingers behind his head.

"You bring me such interesting snippets of real life," he said. "I don't think they're petty questions. They all get to the core question of 'who is Gracie?' Don't they?"

"How did I get to be nearly sixty and not know myself any better than this?"

"Don't be hard on yourself," the minister said, as she expected he would. "Most people just go through life tripping over themselves and never examining what they do, let alone what's in their hearts."

Gracie couldn't help but think of Janice when he said that. How had her daughter ended up so resistant to self-reflection?

Terry closed his eyes, and seemed to sink deep into thought. Watching him, Gracie found herself thinking of him in a new way—as a man, a fallible, human, imperfect creature. He wore his hair a bit too short for her taste; as a child of the sixties and seventies, she still appreciated a little unruliness. His unlined, handsome face, manicured nails, and smooth hands were obviously those of an intellectual, not a laborer.

Terry opened his eyes and leaned forward again, "I think I have an idea of how you can think through these issues."

"Good."

"Kierkegaard was a Christian whose philosophy was based on introspection. I think that's the one skill you have, whether you know it or not. The fact you are in here talking with me is proof of your willingness to do the hard work to understand who you are."

"Okay." Neither brevity nor alacrity was his strong suit.

"Well, Kierkegaard believed that if you look in the mirror and see the person you want to be, then you are on the right track. If you look in the mirror and don't like what you see, then you need to become the person you want to be. To be precise," he said, "the most common form of despair is not being who you really are."

"And that means?"

"You won't know if you've made the right decisions until you make them and then look into your soul and like the person you've become. As Kierkegaard said, life can only be understood looking backward, but it must be lived forward."

Gracie sat and thought about that. Life was a bit risky, but what's the alternative?

"Gracie, the answers to your questions lie inside your own heart. I don't think you need my advice. You need to answer each of them in terms of the person you want to be."

"Well, that makes sense," she said, although she wasn't sure how looking back later would help her move forward right then. She nodded and sat thinking about what kind of person she wanted to be with Ísabel. Loving, caring, responsible, she answered herself. How about with Gregory? Respectful but strong in her commitment to free speech and her patrons' right to decide what they wanted to read. How about with Richard? Honest, transparent, loving, and intrepid.

"Well, okay. I'm going home to look in a mirror," she said.

"Good," Terry said. "And good luck. Remember, virtue is not the absence of sin. It's an effort to live a meaningful and loving life." She was sure that he wanted to add "faithful" to his adjectives of life, but he had always respected her agnosticism. Telling her to have faith in God would only dilute his good advice.

ᙏ

Gracie didn't want to limit anyone's access to any of the library's materials, but she accepted a paradox: she wanted Ísabel to start reading some better literature.

The two dozen old Victorian romances the girl had found in the stacks didn't contain anything Gracie could imagine the girl didn't already know about sex. But their plot lines did suggest something that Gracie wanted to steer the girl away from: the idea that whatever woes a young woman was experiencing, they would all be resolved when the right arrestingly handsome man swept her off her feet and carried her away to a life of everlasting love and happiness.

But what were the alternatives? The girl was too old for Nancy Drew novels, and she turned her nose up at sci-fi. She wasn't even crazy about the vampire and fantasy novels that were popular with most of the girls her age. It was romance that interested her, and nothing else.

Gracie's solution was to try to steer her toward some quality literature that still spoke to her romantic nature. She made a list of possible candidates: *Far from the Madding Crowd, Love in the Time of Cholera, The House of Spirits, Wuthering Heights, Jane Eyre, Dona Flor and Her Two Husbands, Pride and Prejudice, Désirée.* Gracie was sure that Gregory probably would not approve of a couple of them, but he wasn't going to be consulted.

She worked down the list, locating the books on the shelves. The last book she retrieved was a dusty and tattered old copy of *Désirée.* Gracie had first read it as a teenager, younger then than Ísabel was now. She smiled at the memory of her young self, huddled with the book in her bedroom, ignoring neighbor kids playing outside her window. What was it that enthralled and thrilled her about it back then? She stuck the book in her own book bag. Before she gave it to Ísabel, she wanted to see if she could revisit that wild, excited feeling and be sure it was appropriate for the girl.

Starting with the Bronte novels, Gracie left the other books out—one and two at a time—for Ísabel to find when she arrived at the library over the next couple of weeks. Ísabel took the bait without arguing, and either read them quickly or tried them and gave up, but she returned each one after only three or four days. Gracie then upped the ante, leaving the books by South American authors.

"What is this all about?" Ísabel stood in the doorway of Gracie's office one afternoon and waved the copy of *Love in the Time of Cholera* at her. "Are these meant for me, too?"

"Yes, they are, and I hope you enjoy them," said Gracie. "Come in and sit down. Tell me what's happening."

Ísabel plopped down in her usual slouchy teenage manner, trying not to look excited about talking to an old person. But her voice betrayed her.

"Do you know about this really great program we've got going in school?" she asked. "It's this speech thing, where we try to make different kinds of speeches, or read things out loud. It's like drama class and debate class all rolled into one. Not that we have those. But anyway, this guy comes at noon and if you go to it, you don't have to eat your lunch in the lunchroom with the other kids."

Gracie cringed inside, but kept her face as neutral as possible. "You mean the program Gregory Thungaard is leading?"

Ísabel grinned broadly and sat up. "Yup, that's it! Well, we're going to Des Moines for this contest in two weeks, and I get to go stay in a hotel room."

"Oh, really?"

"Yes, me and a bunch of other kids, of course. Gregory is taking us. I'm doing expository reading. That's when you read a story, but you make it really interesting."

"Gregory? Don't you call him Mr. Thungaard?" Gracie was instantly worried. Was Ísabel's teenage excitement strictly with the program or did Gracie sense something else?

"Whatever," Ísabel said with no apparent embarrassment. "Mr. Thungaard, then. Anyway, I'm reading this story by this French guy. I can't even pronounce his name, but it's part of this book called *The Little Prince*. Have you heard of it?"

"Yes, Antoine de Saint-Exupéry," Gracie recalled the author's name aloud.

"Right!" Ísabel looked both pleased and surprised. "That's him."

"It seems like a good choice." Gracie nodded approvingly. "Do you want to read it to me?"

"No, thanks," she said, a little too quickly. "I'm getting coached by Greg—I mean Mr. Thungaard—already. He's really helping me expand my range."

"Expand your range?" Gracie knitted her eyebrows. "What does that mean?"

Ísabel stood up, straightened her shoulders and placed her hand flat against her abdomen.

"See, like this," she said, her voice suddenly taking on a much richer, more mature quality.

"I see what you mean!" Gracie couldn't help but smile. Ísabel was clearly learning something from Gregory, if only a little comportment. "Well, I'm impressed."

Ísabel sat back down, smiling. "Anyway, I can't wait to go."

"What does your mom think?" Gracie asked. "She's okay with you going? Are there other chaperones?"

"No, just Mr. Thungaard." Ísabel nailed the right address this time. "But no, she wouldn't mind. We're in good hands."

"Yes, I'm guessing you are," Gracie said. "But have you asked your mom?"

"She's been too busy," Ísabel said. Her eyes shifted back and forth in a way that worried Gracie.

"Don't you think you should ask her before you plan on going?"

"Ah, sure." Ísabel nodded an exaggerated gesture of agreement. "I will. But I'm sure she'll think it's fine."

"Well, okay then," Gracie said. She glanced at the bills on her desk that she'd been working to pay and record. "I'd better get back to work. Let me know what you think of Gabriel García Márquez."

As Ísabel walked back to the stacks, Gracie looked up to watch. Maybe she was wrong about Gregory, at least in one respect. Maybe he really did have the kids' interests at heart. Maybe it wasn't all about gaining community support for his political campaigns.

He sure seemed to have captured the admiration of Ísabel, anyway.

≈

Not a soul came into the library the next day, giving Gracie time to catch up on paperwork and finish paying the monthly bills.

Just as Gracie finished signing the last check, stuffed it into the envelope, and attached stamps and return address labels to the pile she'd accumulated, Ísabel stepped through the door.

"Hey, sweetie," Gracie called out to her. "Could you run these down to the post office for me?"

Ísabel tossed her backpack on Gracie's guest chair and grabbed the stack of envelopes haughtily.

"What? Am I your slave now?" she said. "It's really cold out there, you know."

"Well, you don't have to," Gracie hated the defensive tone in her voice. It sounded like something she would have said to Janice back when Janice was a sulking teenager. "I mean"—she corrected her tone—"I would think you would be happy to do something for me. We've become pretty good friends, haven't we?"

"I guess." Ísabel tossed her head from side to side and stomped back out the door with the envelopes. The post office was only a block away and she was back in five minutes.

"I'm sorry I was sassy." Ísabel picked up her backpack and turned to go back into the stacks. "I'm just having a little trouble getting warm these days. It's so cold out."

"Does your mom keep your apartment pretty cold?" Gracie asked. She imagined Ísabel's mother needed to skimp on heating bills with her husband gone.

Ísabel stopped and turned back to Gracie.

"Can I tell you a secret?" All the sudden, she looked more like twelve years old than sixteen. She looked down shyly as she had when Gracie first spoke to her back in the stacks and let the backpack drop to the floor.

"Sure. Come on in and sit down." Gracie was worried. Were Ísabel and her mother not getting along? Certainly, she wasn't abusing the girl!

Ísabel slumped down in the chair and stuck her feet out in front of her.

"Promise you won't tell anyone?"

"I'm not sure I can do that," Gracie said. "It depends on what it is."

"Well then, I can't—"

"Okay, I promise," Gracie said. Better to ask for forgiveness later than not be able to help the girl at all.

"Mom's gone."

Gracie frowned and tried to figure out what the girl was saying. Certainly, her mom wasn't dead, was she? Then she realized why Ísabel had started to come to the library the month before. No one else was home. The girl was lonely.

"You mean she left?"

Ísabel nodded.

"Mexico?"

The girl nodded again and looked up.

"But if you tell anyone, they'll put me in some foster home somewhere and I'll have to leave school. And I won't ever get to work with Gregory—I mean Mr. Thungaard—again."

"Is that the worst thing that could happen?"

Ísabel glared at Gracie. How quickly the girl's temper could rise! Again, not unlike Janice.

"Yes," Ísabel spat. "I can't think of anything worse. I like it here. I have friends."

"Yes, I know." Gracie backtracked a bit.

"Well, not many friends." Ísabel's voice returned to normal. "But I have this library and you. And Greg— I mean Mr. Thungaard. And I can walk to school, and I don't have to take a bus. I don't want to end up in some big school in Des Moines where I don't know anyone."

"No, of course not.," Gracie didn't like being grouped in a category—even a good one—with Gregory, but at least Ísabel had mentioned her before him. She let the quiet ambiance of the library settle back around them before asking, "How are you paying the rent? The gas bill? Is this why you can't get warm?"

Ísabel nodded and looked away, embarrassed.

"Well, look, that's not a biggie. I'll call the gas company and take care of it."

The girl nodded again, but still wouldn't meet Gracie's eye.

"Are you safe there?" Gracie asked. "I mean in the apartment. Do you feel safe?"

"Yes." Ísabel looked back at Gracie. "I'm not a child, you know."

Oh, yes, she was. At least here in the middle of the United States of America, she was. There may have been places—perhaps many places—in the world where a sixteen-year-old girl couldn't expect to have a parent, a warm home, food on the table. Places where she would be expected to fend for herself. Maybe even in the town where Ísabel's father and mother were now. But here in the Midwest, right in the middle of the nation's bucolic breadbasket, yes, she was still a child.

"Well, look, I'll take care of the gas bill and the rent," Gracie said. "Bring the bills to me. You are getting bills in the mail, aren't you?"

"Yes." Ísabel looked embarrassed again. "Mom left money but it's gone. I think she thought she'd just be gone a couple of weeks."

"Have you heard from her?"

"Yes. She called last week. She said she was coming back as soon as she can. You know, she's, like, not legal here."

"And, I guess she's not as practiced at getting back and forth as your father was?"

"Nope."

"Okay, then!" Gracie adopted the most cheerful tone she could muster. "You get back to your homework, and tomorrow, we'll take care of those bills."

"You know I'll pay you back," Ísabel said. "Or mom will. As soon as she gets back."

"I'm sure she will," Gracie said. "Now get to work and we'll close up together tonight."

≈

Gracie didn't sleep well that night. She was glad it wasn't one of the nights of the week that Richard usually stayed over. She tossed from side to side, a nagging pain shifting from one hip to the other as she flipped and flopped.

She lay awake, staring into the dark grayness of her stuffy bedroom, embarrassed for her comfort every time the furnace came on.

Her thoughts were guilty ones. Here she had a huge house, more money than she'd ever spend, and no needs that she couldn't fulfill tomorrow if she wanted to. Meanwhile, Ísabel was sleeping alone in a chemically infused apartment over the dry cleaners without adequate heat. And food? Did the girl have enough food? Was she eating lunch at school?

Still, Gracie felt a little jealous of Ísabel. Maybe it didn't feel like it to the girl, but to Gracie, it seemed like Ísabel was living an adventure. A little uncertainty, a little discomfort, but with a lot of independence and a long, long future to look forward to. It reminded her of the envy she had felt as a child when she read the adventures of *The Boxcar Children*.

Of course, it didn't feel like that to Ísabel, Gracie chastised herself. Gracie was lying in bed, warm, safe, and satiated; it was easy to fantasize about adventure.

~8~

The next day, Gracie wished she could see Ísabel that afternoon and get the bills she had promised to pay for her. However, Gregory had scheduled an extra afternoon session for the teenagers in his speech group in preparation for the upcoming contest in Des Moines. Gracie would have to wait another day to start to work on Ísabel's financial problems.

The morning passed excruciatingly slowly, and Gracie decided to close the library for the noon hour and have lunch at the café. She rarely left the building for lunch, and when she did, it seemed that inevitably one of her customers would come to the café to find her, professing some urgent need for a book.

However, the bitter cold December weather had put a damper on any activity in town, and Gracie had plenty of time to consume her grilled cheese sandwich and chicken noodle soup in peace. While she relaxed in a booth, only two other customers came in to draw Betty away from her crossword puzzle, one of several she devoured at the counter when she wasn't waiting on tables.

Returning to the library, Gracie had tucked her head down into the collar of her coat to keep her cheeks warm, so she didn't notice Caroline waiting for her until she was just steps from the library's big door.

"Oh, Caroline!" she said. "I'm so sorry! It's way too cold for you to be standing out here!"

"No, I'm fine," Caroline said. "I grew up here. I'm used to cold Decembers."

Gracie fumbled with her keys, finally having to take her gloves off to unlock the door. Once inside, she pushed the thermostat up a couple of degrees to heat up the cold air they'd just let in.

"Can I make you some coffee?" Gracie wanted to make up for her absence any way she could, even if it meant breaking her one-pot-a-day rule.

"Sure," Caroline said. "I have absolutely nothing going on today."

"You're not working?"

"Tuesdays off."

"Ah," Gracie said. "I should have remembered that." She stepped back into her kitchenette. "I'll just be a minute," she shouted back over her shoulder.

She returned with two cups of steaming coffee and handed one to Caroline, who had made herself at home in the guest chair in Gracie's office. The woman took the cup with two hands and lifted it to her nose, breathing in the pungent vapor.

"So, did you get *The Intern's Travels* yet?" Caroline asked before taking a sip.

"No," Gracie said. "I decided I had better take it before the board, and then we tabled the discussion."

"So, aren't you going to order it?"

"I probably will." Gracie hesitated. She remembered how Caroline had expressed adoration for Gregory the last time she was in the library. Would she be pressing her luck if she tried to get Caroline on her side?

"You see, Gregory Thungaard"—she refrained from calling him "your friend"—"doesn't think it's proper material for Johnson Station readers. He wants me to hold off ordering it until we have developed a policy on what kind of books we will have in our library."

"Hmm." Caroline thoughtfully sipped her coffee. "And what would that policy say?"

"I'm not sure." Gracie realized that was the truth. She hadn't written one yet, and she hadn't reread the policies

Gregory had copied in his package the month before to refresh her memory. "Something about limiting certain controversial topics, sexual depictions, bad language, those kinds of things."

"I'm surprised," Caroline said. "I like Gregory. I thought I liked what he stands for. I've been thinking about signing up to help with his county supervisor campaign. But I don't know if I like that idea. I don't want him to tell me what I can read."

"Well, that seems to be where he's headed." Gracie let Caroline think about it a bit.

What did Caroline see in him?. Gracie knew that some women—perhaps some men, too—were attracted to power. And easy answers, like kicking out immigrants to solve unemployment, banning books to quell rebellions.

Maybe that's what it was, Gracie surmised. Gregory told

"Anyway, that's what I came for." Caroline pulled herself out of her reverie. "If you order it, let me know. If not, I may just have to buy it and live with my sister's condemnation."

"I still have a copy of *Fifty Shades of Grey*," Gracie said. "Have you read that?"

"Everyone's read that." Caroline waved off the suggestion. "And it was horrible. I hope this *Intern* book will be better."

Gracie knew it wasn't going to please Gregory, but she had to do something to counter the barrage of pro-censorship propaganda he'd sent to the library board members. Moreover, if she didn't do it right away, she'd soon be laboring under the policy he was pushing her to write for the library.

She spent much of the week before the December board meeting gathering information that she could use to reverse the sentiment that had resulted in Gregory's resolution. She copied sections of the American Library Association's Library

Bill of Rights, and wrote a letter to the board members, restating her point of view.

Then, partly as an intellectual exercise, and partly so she could argue that she was trying to follow Gregory's advice, she tried to compose a policy that she could live with and that would satisfy him.

She started a draft, erased it, started again. After another four attempts, she decided it was impossible and gave up. If her package made a strong enough impression on the board, perhaps she'd never have to write it.

She had just abandoned the project when Liz struggled through the big front door and glanced at her reflection in Gracie's window before stopping in her office doorway.

"Hey, what's up?" Gracie said, happy to be interrupted. It would be another two hours before Ísabel showed up, brightening her day.

"I was wondering if the library has a copy of an Anthony Bourdain book I want to read. It's been out for a while, but I missed it."

"What is it?" Gracie asked, launching the card catalog program on her computer.

"It's called *Medium Raw: A Bloody Valentine to the World of Food and the People Who Cook (P.S.)*," Liz said, reading the title off a slip of paper she pulled out of her purse.

Gracie typed the title into the search form. "No entries found," the computer responded.

"No, it looks like we don't have it," she said. "Hold on, let me see if it's available."

Gracie pulled up one of her distributor's software programs and plugged in *Medium Raw*. She turned back to Liz while she waited for her slow modem to connect and conduct a search.

"So, what made you so interested in food and cookbooks?" Gracie asked.

"Oh, it was Anthony Bourdain," Liz said, nodding

seriously. "At first, I was just fascinated by his travels, all of the places he goes and the exotic foods. Then, I started to see how foods themselves can transport you to those places: New York, Vietnam, India, Romania, Brazil. I think it's less about cooking than it is about the cultures and the way they let me travel to exotic places in my mind."

"Oh," Gracie said, nodding. So that was why the books always came back unused; in the case of the Bourdain books, at least, it really wasn't about cooking, it was about adventure to Liz.

"You always wanted to travel?" Gracie asked.

"Oh yes." Liz suddenly seemed sixteen years old; the sparkle in her eyes lit up her face. "I was going to join Doctors Without Borders—I was a physical therapist once, you know—and travel the world with them. I used to read atlases when I was a kid like I read cookbooks now."

"What happened?"

"Marriage. Kids. This town. I gave up my career and ended up here with George and two girls. Don't get me wrong: it's a fine trade-off," she said, but her voice wasn't convincing.

"Do you still read atlases?"

"No. Atlases are for people who plan on going somewhere," Liz said. "When I read *A Cook's Tour*, I realized that from now on, I'll just have to travel vicariously, and cookbooks were the way to go. It's a lot cheaper than real travel anyway."

She leaned back and smoothed the front of her slacks over her flat belly. "And I know it may not look like it, but I do like to cook."

Gracie smiled and ignored the comment; articulating any kind of agreement or disagreement to it was a losing proposition, as Liz's husband probably had learned. Instead, Gracie reflected on her own path. "I always planned to travel, too," she commiserated. "I got an international business degree. I was going to work for the IMF or the World Bank.

Then, I ended up in the trading pits in Chicago . . . and then here. I would still . . ."

Shaking off her melancholy, Gracie turned back to her computer. On the screen, Gracie saw the book Liz wanted listed as available from one of her distributors. "I see *Medium Raw* is out in paperback. Not expensive. I'll put it on my next order. We should have it in a week."

"I think the reviews were pretty mixed, but I'm needing some excitement in my life, and this one isn't just about food, it's about celebrities and food," Liz said. "Two of my favorite subjects." She sank back in the chair across from Gracie.

"Let me see." Gracie glanced through the reviews posted on Amazon.com. Liz sat patiently. "Oh, here, let me read this to you. It's from a review from *Booklist*: *On seeing himself through the eyes of a hungry young chef who still has to actually cook just to barely survive, he says, 'Look at me and my nice fucking jacket, standing there all famous and shit.'"*

Gracie pulled her computer glasses down on her nose and looked from her computer over to Liz. "Oh, I think our friend Gregory's going to have a field day with this one, if he ever sees it." She laughed.

"You mean, he won't let you order it? Does he review the books first?"

"Oh, he doesn't have that authority," Gracie said.

Just then, Gracie realized something she hadn't grasped before: Liz and her other regular customers were her allies in her battle with Gregory. The last thing book lovers wanted was Gregory telling them what they should read or not read. Caroline and the *Intern's Travels*, for example.

She put down her glasses and added, "Yet."

"What do you mean, 'yet'?"

"I don't know if I should tell you this, but then again, why not?" Gracie thought out loud. "Our board meetings are public and anything that happens in them is public record."

"What are you talking about?"

"At our next board meeting, Gregory is asking the board to pass a resolution that would set a policy on what books can be ordered and who can have access to what books in the library," Gracie said. "If this policy turns out restricting me from buying books with language that would be considered inappropriate for kids, I might not be able to buy this book."

"You're kidding." Liz looked sideways at Gracie, as if she were checking the door to make sure Gregory himself wasn't walking in. "What gives him the right?"

"Exactly." There. Gracie had planted the seed of community dissent. Liz loved being able to find whatever books she wanted at the Johnson Station Library, and Gracie figured she wasn't going to let Gregory or anyone else take that away. And she wasn't the only one.

Gracie had opened a new battlefront in her war with Gregory—a clandestine, stealthy one, one she would work on over the next few weeks, every time one of her regular customers walked through that heavy front door, assuming the right to pick out any book they wanted to and read it without someone looking over their shoulder.

Once Caroline left, Gracie glanced at the clock. It was only two, and she knew the next three hours before her evening-shift assistant arrived were going to crawl by. She grabbed a dust rag and a can of Endust from the kitchenette and walked back into the stacks. She had hired a cleaning service, but at times like this, with too much on her mind to concentrate on bookkeeping, she liked the physical task of dusting shelves.

It also gave her a chance to notice misplaced volumes. She and her assistant were meticulous about correctly shelving books, but sometimes, a patron would remove a few books at a time, and then put them all back in one place, regardless of where they belonged.

Gracie had started a special section for contemporary fiction a few years earlier so that her patrons could find the latest releases they were looking for more quickly, and she headed there first. She usually kept the books in that section for a year—two if they were popular—and then moved them into the regular shelves with their aging brethren.

She sprayed some Endust on her rag and climbed up onto a small stepstool to reach the top shelf of the section. She pulled the books out, two or three at a time, wiped the tops of the pages off and then swiped the rag over the shelf where they'd been. Working about a foot at a time, she stepped on and off the stool, maintaining a syncopated rhythm.

Up, pull, wipe, wipe, return; pull, wipe, wipe, return; pull, wipe, wipe, return. Down. Move. Up, pull, wipe, wipe, return; pull, wipe, wipe, return; pull, wipe, wipe, return. Down. Move.

It was better than aerobics. At least she was not wasting time while burning off fat. She was accomplishing something.

She reached the end of the top row, and started on the second row down. It was faster; she didn't need the footstool to reach the books or the dust.

As she started in on the *J*'s she decided to look for *Fifty Shades of Grey*. She'd never read it, and with the library so quiet this afternoon, perhaps she'd take a minute to read a couple of pages and see what everyone was talking about. Why did Caroline think it was horrible?

The book should have been one of the first in the *J*'s— for the author, E.L. James. But it was missing.

Funny, thought Gracie. She usually knew every book that was checked out of the library at any time, and she didn't remember anyone taking out *Fifty Shades of Grey* for quite some time. She put down the rag and the Endust and went back into her office. She waited for her computer to boot, typed *Fifty Shades of Grey* into the search field, and looked at its history. Sure enough. It indicated the book was in the library, not checked out.

"Hmm," she said aloud. "I wonder if it was mis-shelved."

Either that or someone had walked out with it, not wanting anyone to know he or she was reading it. Probably a teenager.

Who would it have been? There weren't too many of them who frequented the library, and she knew them all by name. Certainly, not Ísabel! She had told Ísabel that there wasn't a single book in the library that she would disapprove of her reading.

Maybe it was Sara! She had forgotten whether the woman had stopped in this area when she last visited the library, back three weeks ago. But why would a grown woman, well past the age of majority, steal the book instead of just checking it out?

Gracie picked up the dust rag and got back to work. Perhaps she'd find the book farther down the stacks, misplaced by some teenager who had been trying to read it way in the back of the library and put it back in the closest place he or she could reach before Gracie noticed.

By the time she'd finished dusting the contemporary fiction section, Gracie's thoughts had returned to Ísabel and her near-homelessness. Even if Gracie paid her rent and her electricity, the girl shouldn't be living in that apartment by herself.

At home later that evening, Gracie told Richard about Ísabel being alone.

"What if I asked Ísabel to stay here for a while?"

"I think that would be fine if you got permission from her parents," he said. "But are you sure you want to take on a youngster at this point in your life?"

"Well, she's not exactly still in diapers," Gracie said. "She's doing pretty well on her own already, so I don't think she'll be much of a burden."

"Right, but being a mother is something you've done before, right? I would think maybe you'd be looking forward to some new adventures."

Gracie knew what he meant. He'd been asking her for some time to travel abroad, maybe even live in a foreign city for a while, rediscover her intrepid spirit, the one he said he could see lurking under her prim librarian persona.

"I'm not expecting to take care of her the rest of her life," Gracie said. "Just until her mother gets back."

"Then fine," he said. "It's actually very nice of you. I hope you aren't trying to replace Janice, though."

Gracie said nothing.

"You shouldn't think that somehow having another young woman in your house is going to resolve your issues with your daughter," Richard continued. "Don't put that burden on Ísabel. That's all I'm saying."

Gracie thought about that for a moment. Was she trying to do that? Had she arrived at the idea because she wasn't getting anywhere trying to build a relationship with Janice?

"No," she said aloud.

"No, what?" Richard looked confused.

"No, I'm not trying to replace Janice. I was just thinking I have this great big house and three empty bedrooms—at least when Janice isn't home. And here Ísabel is practically homeless. It makes no sense. I'd like to help her out," she said. "As long as I won't get in trouble for it."

Sunday morning Gracie woke up next to Richard and couldn't get out of bed. She had promised to go to church with him, but as she rolled over and looked at the alarm clock, she couldn't do it.

Richard was almost dressed when she told him.

"What's wrong?" He bent down and put his palm on her forehead. "You don't feel good?"

Gracie pushed his hand away.

"No!" She didn't try to hide the irritation in her voice. "I just don't feel like going. I'd rather have some time to myself."

"Oh, well." Richard looked hurt. He backed away. "I'll leave you alone then."

"Yes, please," she said, not even attempting to undo whatever injury she'd done to his ego.

The day before had put her in this mood. She had spent much of Saturday morning preparing to call Janice to talk about Ísabel, and then an hour on the phone arguing with her.

Saturday night was even worse. They had been invited to supper at Marcia and Bob's big Cape Cod-style house; Bob wanted to pick Richard's legal brain about something. All evening, Gracie sat uncomfortably and watched as her friend struggled—mostly unsuccessfully—to be cordial to Bob. The strain in Marcia's behavior was so obvious to Gracie that she couldn't imagine how Bob didn't notice.

Bob and Richard insisted on doing the dishes while the women sat at the dining room table and continued to work on the extravagant magnum of Châteauneuf-du-Pape that Richard had bought in Des Moines.

"How can we turn down an offer like that?" Gracie had accepted their dishwashing offer cheerfully, hoping it covered for Marcia's stony silence. "Just don't break anything."

Richard threw her a look that signaled he was happy to get out of the dining room; apparently, he too felt the tension between their hosts.

"Doesn't Bob have a clue?" Gracie dropped her voice to a near whisper, as the men finished clearing the table, and the swinging door between the rooms closed.

"I think so, but it's his way of dealing with stuff." Marcia matched her quiet tone. "It was the same way when the girls were young and misbehaving. He thinks that if he ignores problems, they'll just go away."

Gracie had gone to bed upset and depressed by what she'd witnessed, and now she'd awakened with the same irritating sense of discomfort. Richard would have to forgive her for being grouchy. She needed some time alone.

As she waited for the coffee to finish dripping into the stained carafe in her quiet kitchen, Gracie glanced out her kitchen window toward the church two blocks down the street. The last of the fall leaves had faded to brown, and their rotting corpses plastered the sidewalks and edges of the gutterless streets. The gray December clouds hung so low over the town that they hid the pointed pinnacle of the steeple.

She poured herself some coffee, and left the refrigerator door open while she struggled to twist the top off a new jug of milk and dribble a few tablespoons into her cup. The refrigerator beeped, impatient for her to close the door.

"Ah, shut up!" she yelled at it. She shoved the milk jug back inside and slammed the door closed. "Can't you leave me alone either?"

She sat down hard on a kitchen chair, nearly spilling the hot coffee. She considered going outside in her nightgown and slippers to retrieve the Sunday *Des Moines Register*, but it looked cold outside; she figured the front-page news would only make her more miserable. She sat still and let her rotten temper sink into her bones, preferring to wallow in it for a while than to try to shake it off. Sometimes things just had to stew before they could be worked out.

Her eyes landed on the small pile of books she'd brought home from the library. On the top was *Désirée*, which she intended to suggest to Ísabel and had brought home to reconfirm as appropriate.

Gracie opened it, letting her thumb release the pages until the fan stopped on page 230. She let her eye pick a random spot to start reading.

> *We kept looking right at each other. There he sat, the ermine collar practically up to his ears and the heavy crown on his shorn hair; and yet for a moment he looked just as he once had.*

Gracie didn't need to look forward or back to know just where the story was: Napoleon had just violated all decency and custom of his time and, grabbing the crown of the empire from the Pope's trembling hands, had placed it on his own head. He had crowned himself Emperor of the Holy Roman Empire, the royal equivalent of Julius Caesar and Charlemagne. And Désirée saw it for what it was: an astonishing transformation of a small, ambitious young cadet in the French army into a small, self-aggrandizing totem, poised for glory and then a great fall, one of the greatest human stories of all time.

Gracie let the big volume snap closed and dropped it on the table. She closed her eyes and saw herself in her mother's house, curled up in a corner of her bed with her messy sheets and covers tangled under her bare legs, where in the light of the old double-hung windows, she had been transported to Notre Dame, the early eighteen-hundreds, and the coronation of Napoleon.

She remembered—felt—the same excited stirring in her gut that she had sensed when she first read the story of Napoleon's first love. She remembered the book had unleashed: a passionate desire—no, *need*—to escape. To get away from Iowa and farmland and dreary school lunchrooms and the hand-me-down clothing and the foul-mouthed, dirty neighbor boys whose aspirations would never rise to the level of even *reading* about Napoleon, let alone emulating him.

What happened to that restlessness, that promise to herself that she would go to France, go to India, go to the other side of the world and see Notre Dame and Angkor Wat and the Amazon, and live the adventures she read about? How could she have been so brave, so ambitious at twelve, and now so timid and guarded and constrained at sixty? If anything, she should now have been more brave, more experienced, more capable of embracing adventure and novelty.

She let out a resounding sigh, one tinged with sadness and near panic. Life never turned out the way little girls imagined it would as they read of great heroes and heroines whose lives were first glamorized, then sanitized, packaged, and made safe by history and great storytellers. She knew that. She certainly wasn't the first sixty-year-old woman to look back on her life and wonder where all the time went. Where all the plans went. Where all the dreams went.

She stood up, rinsed the coffee cup out in the sink and set it upside down on the dish drainer. She wiped her hands and headed upstairs to change into clothes.

Tomorrow, she told herself as she climbed the stairs, ignoring the ache in her ankles, she would invite Ísabel to stay with her. That would be a start. Then she'd see what else she could do to reawaken her spirit.

the current amount and two months of unpaid bills. The rent bill was for two hundred fifty dollars a month, and likewise, was three months in arrears.

At twelve hundred dollars, total, it wasn't a huge amount of money and would make only a tiny dent in Gracie's savings, but it wasn't insubstantial, either.

Gracie tucked the bills into her purse. She would pay them that evening, and if necessary, she would call the phone company to get Ísabel's phone service reinstated. Without a cell phone, a teenager in middle-class town like Johnson Station would be either pitied or ridiculed by her classmates.

She waited a while before going back to talk with the girl, giving her time to finish her homework. Meanwhile, she imagined a few more ways to broach the subject of Ísabel staying with her. Everything seemed hokey, too practiced, too studied, and finally, she decided to wing it. If she came out sounding too motherly, well, that might be what she was—too motherly. Better that Ísabel knew that from the beginning.

"How's the homework going?" She approached Ísabel after about an hour.

"All done."

"What are you reading now?"

Ísabel closed the book she was reading and pointed its cover at Gracie. *Showdown,* by Jorge Amado.

"Really?" Gracie didn't try to hide her surprise. The novel was one of Gracie's favorites, but she hadn't considered that a young woman who so recently was devouring Victorian romances would have chosen it out of all of those she'd offered. "That's great! You must have really liked *Dona Flor.*"

"I did." Ísabel nodded. "This one's much more intense. Not as much of that magic stuff. But I like the way they talk about all of the different kinds of people there were."

"Right!" That's what had fascinated Gracie, too, but she refrained from saying it. She wanted the girl to discover something new all on her own. "I have something to ask you."

"What?" Ísabel acted exasperated, putting her book back down with an exaggerated sigh that made Gracie smile. She wasn't so different from Janice in some ways.

"I wonder if you would consider coming to stay with me for a while."

Ísabel let her finger slip out of the book where it had been holding her place and sat up straight in her chair.

"Is that legal?"

Gracie was surprised. She had expected Ísabel to either reject the idea immediately or ask her things like "how long?" or "why?" or even "do I have to?" She might have anticipated that adults like herself would raise the legal question, but not a sixteen-year-old.

"I'm not sure," Gracie answered truthfully. "But my lawyer friend Richard thinks if your mom approves it, it would be fine."

"Oh." Ísabel looked down at the back cover of *Showdown*, and then shifted her gaze down the stacks and out the front window. "But what would people think?"

"Of you?"

"No. Of you."

"What difference does that make?" Raising the legal question was surprising enough, but Ísabel really surprised Gracie now. How could she be concerned about Gracie's reputation when she was practically homeless?

"You know I'm Hispanic." Ísabel tucked in her chin and looked at Gracie as if she were peering over nonexistent reading glasses, a gesture that was wildly beyond her age.

"Yes, I'm quite aware of that, Ísabel."

"You know what people around here think of us."

Gracie searched her brain for a way to answer that truthfully without adding to the prejudice. "I know that Gregory apparently thinks enough of you to include you in his tutoring. Isn't that a sign of acceptance?"

A sly smile crept across Ísabel's face, one that Gracie

couldn't interpret.

"What are you thinking?" Gracie asked.

"Gregory likes all of the girls." Ísabel winked.

"You don't mean that," Gracie tried not to show her shock, but she reflexively pulled back in her chair and frowned.

"No," Ísabel said. "Sorry, I was just teasing."

Gracie let out her breath and tried to regain her equilibrium and direction. She wasn't convinced Ísabel was "just teasing."

"So back to my question. Could you come and stay with me for a while? Just until your mom gets back?"

"But what would happen to our apartment?"

"It will still be there, and anytime you want to go back, you can. I just thought you might feel a bit safer at my house. And I promise it will be warm."

Ísabel turned again to stare out the front windows. Gracie let her think without interrupting. She had nothing more pressing to do.

Finally, the girl turned back to her and grinned. "Can we get a cat?"

Gracie chuckled. How many surprises could Ísabel pull off in one sitting?

"I guess, but I'd rather have a dog," she answered truthfully.

"Me too." Ísabel laughed. "But I thought that might be pushing my luck."

✍

Ísabel had been living with her only a couple of days when Gregory called Gracie at the library one afternoon.

"What exactly were you trying to prove?" he asked, skipping any kind of salutation.

"Excuse me?" She bought some time by pretending to

not recognize his voice. "Who is this?"

"Gregory Thungaard, the chairman of the board that pays your salary."

"Oh." She felt a little cheeky that morning. "I thought the city paid my salary. Hmm . . . all this time—"

Gregory cut her off. "You know what I mean!"

"I guess you didn't like the package I sent to you."

"And to the other board members," he said sternly. "I think it was totally out of line."

Gracie paused for a moment. She was glad this phone call hadn't come last week when she was feeling low and vulnerable. Ever since she decided to ask Ísabel to move in, and the girl had done so, she was feeling much better. She could handle this, too, she told herself, nodding at the receiver in her hand.

"I believe it is appropriate for our board members to have materials that allow them to see both sides of the issue." She forced herself to remain calm.

"They can do that by themselves." Gregory's voice was nearly trembling. "What is *inappropriate* is for you, staff and not a board member, to express your opinion in the matter. Policy is a subject for the board, not for the staff."

"I totally disagree with you," she said, adding quickly, "respectfully."

"I can see tha—"

"And I am the only one of us with extensive experience running a library, and I have lived in this community most of my adult life. I would think you would be pleased to take advantage of my expertise."

"You interrupted me."

"Yes, and you interrupted me earlier. Further, you are interrupting my workday, and I'd like to get back to what I was doing. If you have anything else constructive to say, let me know. Otherwise, I'm thinking we should take this conversation up at the board meeting."

"As chairman of the board that employs you and pays your salary, I believe it's my duty to discuss your behavior with you whenever it becomes an issue." His voice had lost its tremble and taken on considerably more volume. He was practically shouting into the phone.

"But who decides it's become an issue?" she asked, sounding as rational and calm as she could with Gregory yelling at her. She heard the front door open and looked up to see Armand walk toward her office.

"I do," he insisted. "I set the agenda for this board, and I think it is an issue."

"Just a second, Gregory, there's someone at my office door." Gracie pulled the receiver away from her face and greeted Armand. "I'll be with you in just a second. Could you please close the door for me?"

"Okay, where were we?" She returned to Gregory's call as if it were a casual conversation about the weather.

"We're discussing your insubordination."

Insubordination? Now it was clear what he thought their relationship was. She was his subordinate. Not the head librarian in this town for twenty-five years, but an employee.

She felt her heart start to pound in her chest, and it was her own reaction that made her mad. He had no right to try to intimidate her or treat her as if she were one of his farmhands, but she shouldn't let him do it, either. She needed to get control of her emotions.

"Well, the letters have been sent," she said, concentrating on keeping her voice steady and low. "And now I believe it will be up to the rest of the board to discuss both my behavior and the issue of censorship at the next meeting. I can't get the letters back."

Gregory said nothing, and Gracie tried to end the call.

"But right now, I have a patron who needs some help finding a book."

"Wait a minute!" Gregory commanded.

"Yes?" Again, Gracie sounded pleasantly expectant, as if he might be asking her to tea.

"I also heard that you may be illegally housing one of our minorities. Is that true?"

"What do you mean?" It took Gracie a moment to realize he was referring to Ísabel. Word of her move to Gracie's house had traveled fast. But, did he think she was a "minority" or that there was something illegal about her staying with Gracie?

"You realize that girl's father was deported to Mexico. He was here illegally."

"That doesn't mean it's illegal for her to stay at my house, does it?" Gracie was more surprised than angry at the turn in the conversation. What exactly was he getting at?

"You are sending the wrong message to the community about the sanctity of our borders and the laws of this land." He sounded like one of several candidates who had passed through Iowa in the presidential campaign, pushing their anti-immigration views in every stump speech.

"By giving a girl a place to sleep?"

"By harboring an illegal alien."

"You mean Ísabel?"

"Yes. Or are there others?"

"How do you know about Ísabel?"

"I make it my business to know what's going on in our communities," Gregory said. Gracie could imagine him puffing out his chest as he said that.

"By spying?"

"I don't have to spy."

Oh, don't get so full of yourself, Gracie thought. Johnson Station was a very small town. Everybody would know where Ísabel was staying within the week.

"Look." She was ready to hang up on him. "I've got to get back to work. We can discuss all of this at the next meeting. If you think it's appropriate. Which I don't." She hung up the receiver without saying good-bye.

She sat for a moment, giving her heart a moment to slow back down. She wasn't going to let Gregory imperil her health, giving her a heart attack. But why did he say Ísabel was an illegal alien? Didn't he know her well enough to know she was born in the United States? And hadn't he accepted her as one of his pupils, inviting her into his speech program and even taking her to Des Moines with the other kids? Why would he turn his back on her now?

She shook off the thoughts and stood up to open her door.

"Armand," she called across the stacks. He was in the contemporary fiction section, looking for something. "What can I help you find?"

"Do you have that new book they're all talking about, that intern book?" he asked.

Gracie stifled a laugh. It certainly wasn't historical fiction. However, who was she to decide what Armand should be interested in?

"Not yet," she said. "But I'm going to order some copies this afternoon. I'll put your name on the list of people wanting to read it. I just warn you, it's a long list already."

~10~

Once Ísabel had moved in, Richard moved some of his clothes into Janice's old bedroom, and took some of them back to his house. Gracie called him that night after Ísabel had gone to bed.

"I wasn't asking you to move out," Gracie said. "This is just a temporary thing. Just until her mom gets back or until I figure out how to make it work with you here."

"Right," Richard said, not convincingly. "But why don't I give the two of you the weekend to get settled, and I'll come over for supper sometime next week."

On Saturday, Gracie woke up earlier than usual so she would have time with Ísabel on their first weekend together. She had heard the TV in the guest room—now Ísabel's room—murmuring late into the night, but she assumed that the girl had fallen asleep with the TV on. Surely, she hadn't stayed awake that late.

Gracie usually didn't make breakfast on Saturdays, but she was going to start things out the right way with Ísabel. She wanted to offer her the same stable home life she had provided for Janice, starting with real breakfasts, not the grab-and-run shakes and pastries marketed to "busy moms" on TV. She pulled out a fry pan; set out the eggs, ham, and cheese for omelets; and reached up into the cupboard for a mixing bowl.

Did Ísabel like eggs? There was so much Gracie didn't yet know about her, and she felt a nervous twinge at the possibility of a difficult adjustment. She hoped the girl would be easier to live with than Janice had been as a teenager.

"Hey." Ísabel's voice in the kitchen doorway surprised her.

Gracie twirled around to see the girl standing in a long wrinkled T-shirt, her thick black hair hanging in messy waves, the skin of her slender legs tight and luminous. How perfect the girl looked straight out of bed, Gracie thought. How long had it been since she had been able to look fresh and rested so effortlessly, only seconds after getting up?

"What are these?" Ísabel held a handful of ties in her outstretched hand.

Gracie caught her breath. Richard had apparently left them behind when he moved his few things out of the guest closet into Janice's room.

"Where did you find those?" Gracie asked.

"I asked first." A sly smile spread across Ísabel's face.

"Those are ties." Gracie turned back toward the stove and flipped on a burner under the fry pan. "Would you like some breakfast?"

"Whose ties?"

"Maybe it's none of your business," Gracie tried to mask the irritation in her voice, but the words still came out a little harsh. This was no way to start their first weekend.

"But, they were in my room."

Your room! Gracie was pleased the girl felt that the guest bedroom was hers already. But she hadn't expected to feel her privacy violated so soon.

"Were these your husband's?" Ísabel casually leaned against the doorjamb, wrapping the silk lengths together into a neat coil. "Or are they your boyfriend's?"

Gracie was startled.

"You mean Richard?" She steadied herself against the countertop. "He's just a friend."

Gracie studied the girl's face to see if she was fooled.

"Oh, I just figured he must be a boyfriend." Ísabel laughed. "Don't look so shocked. You must be the most desirable old lady in town. I mean, like you own this mansion and all."

So, she was just guessing. Gracie let out the breath she hadn't realized she was holding. She shook her head and turned back toward the stove.

"Yes, I'm probably the most eligible widow in town," Gracie said over her shoulder, "although I'm not so sure about the 'old' label. And this isn't a mansion. Now, do you eat eggs for breakfast?"

☙

Gregory came over the next night for dinner, and Gracie was happy to see him. She needed his advice.

"You know, I'm thinking this argument with Gregory over censorship is building to some fever pitch," she said. "I wish I knew what I could do to stop it."

"Why don't you see if the American Library Association can help you in some way?" Richard suggested. "Maybe they could send in someone to talk with the board."

"I don't know," she answered. "I worry that people won't like the idea of a group of what they'll call 'liberal atheist outsiders' coming into our community to tell us how to raise our children."

"Hmm." He started chopping an onion for the chili they were making. "Maybe you're right."

"And I don't want to escalate the matter and draw too much attention until I see if I can't somehow convince one more board member to take my side. I think Paul is the weak link on Gregory's side. I'm hoping I can turn him with the materials I sent. Even if Gregory didn't like me sending them."

"What doesn't Gregory like?" Ísabel came into the kitchen and stole a chunk of onion off the cutting board where Richard was chopping, nearly endangering her fingers. She popped it in her mouth.

"You mean Mr. Thungaard." Gracie corrected her, pointing the wooden spoon she was holding at Ísabel.

"Right. Mr. Thungaard." Ísabel parroted her, smiling broadly. "I keep forgetting." She stood next to Richard, a little closer than Gracie would have liked. The girl was quite the flirt, Gracie realized.

"How're you liking it here, Ísabel?" He looked at her while he continued to chop onions. Gracie turned back to the stove and stirred a cup of water into the tomato sauce. If Richard was going to cut off his finger, she wasn't going to watch.

"I like it," Ísabel told Richard. "It's sure quieter here than above the dry cleaners. You don't mind, do you? I found some of your ties in my bedroom. Does that mean she makes you sleep in another room when you stay over?"

"Ahem!" Gracie interrupted. She turned around and waved her spoon at the girl again. "You don't know whose ties they are."

Richard backed away from the cutting board and winked at Gracie. "Well, I hope they're not your other boyfriend's." He laughed. He turned back to Ísabel. "You should be more respectful of other people's privacy," he said. "Maybe Gracie doesn't want you to know whose ties those are."

"Clearly." The girl pulled out one of the kitchen table chairs and plopped down. "Why do you think that is?"

However shy Ísabel had been when Gracie first talked to her in the library, she seemed to have lost that timidity quickly. Maybe she was more comfortable around men. How could that be? When Gracie was Ísabel's age, she could hardly talk to any man who wasn't her father.

"I'm glad you two are getting along so well," Gracie said.

"Yeah," Ísabel said. "Guys like me. I don't know why, but they do. They're much easier to please than women, I think."

Oh, Christ! What kind of trouble had she gotten herself into, taking this fireball under her wing?

"That's because you're a very attractive young woman," Richard said.

Gracie liked the way he sounded—more like a father than a man interested in Ísabel's charms. Maybe it was going to be helpful to have him around after all.

"You need to realize that and don't let it lead you into trouble," Richard continued.

"Oh man, that sounds like a Bible verse, or one of the Ten Commandments!" Ísabel laughed seductively, and Gracie saw Richard turn around and shoot her a disapproving glance.

"I'm serious," he said. "You have too many other talents that you need to hone and develop, and if you decide to rely flirting, you will mess up your future."

Gracie watched Ísabel grimace. The girl turned to her and rolled her eyes. "I had no idea you guys were going to treat me like a child!"

"No." Richard responded before Gracie had a chance. "If you were a child, we wouldn't have to have this kind of conversation. There would be nothing to worry about. Yet."

"Hey, let's change the subject," Gracie interrupted, cheerfully. She looked at Richard. He nodded and turned back to his onions.

"I am planning to go to Chicago for Christmas to see my daughter." Gracie hadn't talked with Richard about that yet, and she trusted he wouldn't choose this time to argue with her. He was still hoping she'd go to New York with him to see his son. Now with Ísabel in the house, he had to understand that wasn't possible. "Have you ever been there? Would you like to go with me? Or do you have plans for Christmas?"

"We usually go over to my *tio's* house for Christmas," Ísabel said. "But he was deported, too. Him and his wife, my *tia*. So, I don't know what I will do. It depends on if my mom gets back by then."

"Right," Gracie said. "If she gets back, obviously, you will want to spend the holidays with her. But if not, you can come with me. When do you guys get Christmas break?"

୰

By the end of the next week, Richard was staying overnight again. It was clear that if anyone needed to be shielded from what the movies called "adult situations," it wasn't Ísabel. The young girl was far more worldly than Janice had been at her age, and leaps ahead of where Gracie had been at sixteen.

How could she not be? It wasn't just books, magazines, movies, and on TV, but also advertising that made constant references to sex and sexual identity. If parents wanted to protect their kids from suggestive material these days, they'd have to raise them in a cave.

To Gracie's surprise, though, much of Ísabel's casualness about sex wasn't influenced by TV sitcoms like *Modern Family*, *Girls*, and *The Goldbergs* as she thought. It came from old movies.

Ísabel had spent a summer when she was fourteen babysitting every night for a family in town that had a satellite dish, and while the kids slept at night, she watched old movie classics made from the forties to the seventies. Watching them with Ísabel after supper that week, Gracie discovered that even though sex and nudity was portrayed more subtly back then, many of the old classics' adult themes weren't much different from modern ones.

At first, she tried to steer Ísabel away from what she considered risqué.

"Oh! *The Apartment!*" Ísabel shouted excitedly from the TV room one night while Gracie was putting the last of the supper dishes away in the kitchen. "I love that movie! Let's watch that tonight."

Gracie stood still for a moment and tried to remember the movie. Wasn't that the one where Jack Lemmon let all the executives at his company use his apartment for rendezvous with their mistresses? Gracie grimaced. She didn't want to watch that with Ísabel. That movie made it look like everyone and his brother was having sex behind their wives' backs. Sure, the innocent Jack Lemmon got the girl at the end—a good message there—but, *whew!* The movie still depicted an awful lot of sexual misbehavior.

"Oh, you've already seen it," Gracie called across the house toward the TV room. "Good, then let's watch something else. I thought maybe we'd watch *Wall-E* tonight."

Suddenly, Ísabel was standing in the kitchen doorway, leaning against the doorjamb suggestively. "Why?" She wiggled her eyebrows up and down. "Is Richard coming over tonight? Don't want to get him too excited?"

"Ísabel!" Gracie was embarrassed, and she responded more formally than she usually did. "That is a violation of my privacy. I would appreciate it if you would exercise a bit more discretion when you reference my relationship with Richard."

Ísabel shook her head as if she was trying to comprehend what Gracie had said.

"Ísabel." Gracie started again, but more calmly this time. "I think that my relationship with Richard is my private matter, and I'd appreciate you not talking about it like it's your personal joke. Okay?"

"Yeah, okay," Ísabel said. "I got it the first time. You just didn't sound like yourself. You sounded like my English teacher when she's trying to talk about something that she's embarrassed about. But let's watch the movie, can we?"

They did watch the movie, although Gracie found herself eyeing Ísabel more than focusing on the movie itself. It was clear from the girl's reactions that she fully understood what was going on, and that it didn't faze her a bit. Gracie realized right then how things had changed over the years, and she wasn't going to be able to change them back.

After that first movie, they dove into Gracie's pile of old DVDs and watched a different one every night. They saw *A Touch of Class, An Affair to Remember,* and *It Happened One Night.*

Ísabel had seen them all, but she obviously enjoyed them. By Thursday, Gracie started to think she was more likely to be corrupted by Ísabel than the other way around.

"I think you can stay tonight, if you want," Gracie whispered to Richard Friday night when he arrived to have supper with her and Ísabel.

"What?" Richard's smile told her how pleased he was that they had cleared that phase of Ísabel's stay so quickly. "Did you girls talk about it?"

"No, I just realized how much more worldly and aware teenagers are these days," Gracie said. "We're not going to be able to pull any wool over her eyes."

Richard's presence in the evening quickly had a salutary effect on Ísabel that Gracie hadn't foreseen: with him around, Ísabel was much more willing to watch movies that weren't focused on romance and "adult situations." The next week, they watched *North by Northwest*, *Under the Volcano*, and *Treasure of the Sierra Madre*. It turned out that Ísabel and Richard were both movie buffs. They traded film industry trivia back and forth, quickly cementing a bond that Gracie hadn't expected and found herself envying.

Now that the three of them were comfortable with each other, Gracie faced the daunting prospect of telling Janice that Ísabel had moved in. She decided to wait until Christmas, when she and Ísabel could tell her in person. It probably wasn't going to be any easier, but she expected that Janice would temper her behavior if Gracie had the girl in tow.

~11~

Gracie turned on the ancient copy machine in her office and let it warm up while she made a pot of coffee. Her board members were due in about fifteen minutes, and she needed to make copies of the agenda. A couple of them never showed up with the ones she sent in the mail.

As the crotchety printer coughed out the copies, she read the agenda again to refresh her memory, and a nervous dread rose up from her stomach to her shoulders. This was not going to be an easy evening. Not knowing how vigorously Gregory would argue for a new policy on "appropriate reading material," she had no choice but to plan for the worst.

But how would she counter his religious and political arguments? She wished she had spent more time thinking about the issue. So many other things had taken her mind off the subject since Gregory sent his package of news clippings and book lists.

Not too long ago, Gracie simply wished that Gregory would go away and leave her alone. It was the same silly nostalgia she had felt during the last presidential election, when she remembered thinking she couldn't wait until the whole thing was over.

Now she knew that, like Trump, Gregory would eventually go away—but only as his political ambitions were realized. He would move from Johnson Station and grandly ensconce himself in the governor's mansion in Des Moines. Yes, he would still mess around in affairs of the state in ways that pissed her off, but one thing Gracie had come to realize about politics a long time ago was that the farther from your home a politician worked, the less he controlled your life, even if his global power increased. Having to face an abhorrent foe on the street or across a table was far more painful and disruptive than a change in state taxes or federal regulations.

Caitlin pushed open the heavy front door, and Gracie watched her walk to the portable conference table she'd set up earlier that afternoon to accommodate the meeting. Caitlin was the youngest member of the board, and the quietest. Three years ago, Gracie had recommended her as a board member because she had a degree in literature from the University of Iowa and worked at a bookstore. She had started her career in publishing in New York City, but had given that up when she moved to Johnson Station with her husband, who had worked at the window factory on the outskirts of town until they divorced and he left. Now she commuted daily to run a store in Des Moines.

Gracie knew she would be an advocate for books and for free speech, but she also knew that the woman was probably too shy to speak up, even if Gregory challenged her most fundamental beliefs.

"Hi!" Gracie greeted her. "Should be an interesting meeting tonight."

"Yes." Caitlin sat down primly at the table and opened the folder she brought to every meeting. It contained the original letter from the mayor naming her to the board, and a copy of the library's charter.

"Do you have a copy of the agenda?"

"No, I forgot it. I'm sorry." Caitlin reached out for the paper Gracie offered her and began studying it in silence.

"Hey, I met a friend of yours recently," Gracie said. She remembered that Sara had mentioned coming to town to go to dinner with Caitlin.

"Who?" Caitlin's expression was as wary as Sara's had been. Her face went from surprised to worried quickly.

"Sara."

"Oh, yes," Caitlin looked down and busied herself with

the papers she had brought. "Sara. Yes, she is a friend."

Gracie got the hint. If Caitlin and Sara didn't want her to pry into their business, she would respect that.

As if to present a study in contrasts, Tony Jacobson burst through the door, making about as much noise as possible. Even though the library's carpeting and books did a good job of absorbing noise, they were no match for Tony's boisterous personality.

Tony was also new to the board, having been nominated by Gregory six months before. He had been the town's pharmacist since the early eighties when, fresh out of medical school, he inherited the struggling Main Street drugstore from his father, and he was a faithful attendee of the back-of-the-café community table on weekday mornings.

"Tony," Gracie said, "good to see you."

"And you!" Tony enthusiastically reached toward her for a hug. Gracie hated embraces from people she didn't like, especially board members, and she imagined that Tony was disappointed, as always, with her stiff acquiescence.

Not only was Tony overly effusive in Gracie's estimation, he was also a sycophant of Gregory's. He was helping raise money for Gregory's run for county supervisor, even though the election was still eleven months away. Gracie had seen the "Thungaard for Supervisor" flyers prominently displayed on the drugstore counters and adorning its windows. Gracie imagined Tony was vying for a post on Gregory's cabinet when he eventually became governor.

Gracie recognized the package Tony carried under his arm as the one Gregory had sent a month earlier with the news clippings and banned-book lists. He wasn't carrying a copy of her package. She handed him a copy of the agenda.

"No, thanks," he said. "I've got mine."

Gregory arrived next, soon followed by Lorena and Paul. Gregory and Tony quickly moved off into the stacks to talk out of earshot of the other board members. Lorena, a full-time mother of six children and one of the few Catholics in town, and Paul, a recently retired mechanic with the state's department of transportation, accepted copies of the agenda and Gracie's offer of a cup of coffee and sat down.

Only Jacob, the oldest member of the board and the one who had been with the body the longest, wasn't planning to attend. He was spending a few weeks in Illinois with his ailing sister before heading to Arizona for a couple of months, and said he would miss what he predicted would be "a lively discussion." It was a blow to Gracie's hopes for balance; he was the only member of the board she could depend on to speak up in defense of the library. Caitlin might agree with her, but she was unlikely to say much.

Once settled around the table, Gregory quickly led the board through a cursory discussion of basic building maintenance. Gracie could tell he was in a hurry to get to his topic: the policy he wanted the board to adopt. It was the second to the last topic on the agenda, and suddenly Gracie realized she'd made a mistake leaving the question of *The Intern's Travels* as the final item for discussion. She had already ordered the book. Three copies, in fact.

"I'm hoping you all had time to read the materials I sent last month," Gregory said when they reached his agenda item. Tony nodded vigorously, making Gracie wince. "Now I think you have a better understanding of what I was getting at in our last meeting. What I'd like to see come out of our discussion tonight is a meeting of minds on what kind of policy we should have regarding what reading materials we provide at our library and who should have access to them."

"But it kind of seems like censorship or book burning," said Paul. He sounded tentative, as if he wasn't sure he really wanted to get involved in the discussion.

"I'm not suggesting we ban books." Gregory's tone quickly became pedantic, as if he needed to explain things very carefully for Gracie and Paul to understand him. "I'm arguing that we should only limit access to vulnerable members of our population. Our town."

"And who are those vulnerable members?" Tony asked. He added a bit too much sincerity to his voice, making it sound very much like he'd been waiting to deliver a predetermined question that Gregory wanted to respond to.

"Children, in particular," Gregory answered without pause. "But others with religious or philosophical views that could be challenged or degraded by sensitive material. We need to protect them as well."

"And what is sensitive material?" Tony prodded him to continue. Had the two of them actually prepared this dialectic for the evening? Gracie wondered. It sure sounded like it.

"Sexually explicit material, offensive language, unsuitable material for children, homosexuality, objectionable religious views, nudity, racism, and sexual education, among others." Gregory read the list off a piece of paper. "And that comes from the American Library Association, not exactly a radically right-leaning group."

"But that's out of context," Gracie countered. "The ALA put that list together to educate the public about threats to free speech, not to argue for it!"

"I'm only saying the list is theirs," Gregory said. "Each one of us can decide why they put it together. I happen to think it's a fairly helpful way of determining what kind of materials we should be careful in owning and distributing."

"But who are these people whose views are in danger, the people other than our children?" Gracie said. "And who decides this?"

"I think that is part of the question we would ask you to consider as you put together this policy," Gregory said.

Smart. He was pretending to include Gracie in the process of enacting his censorship. Possibly he thought by giving her a chance to make these kinds of decisions, she would go along with it. But any policy they devised would require her to segregate the books in the library to keep them away from Gregory's "vulnerable" population. Soon her patrons would start avoiding that section, not wanting to implicate themselves as interested in controversial or salacious books.

"I don't think it's my place or anyone else's to decide what adults are quote-unquote vulnerable," she said. She felt her anger take hold, and her face harden. "And, further, I thought challenging old ideas was why we encourage free speech in this country. You seem to argue that people are better off never exploring alternatives."

"I'm just suggesting it's not always a good thing," Gregory said, his calm voice an obvious attempt to make himself seem the more reasonable one. "Challenging someone's religious beliefs can lead to substantial discomfort and unhappiness."

"Or to a more considered and nuanced view of their religion." Gracie voice rose. "How can you argue against that?"

Tony put his hands up, as if trying to keep Gracie and Gregory from going at each other's throats.

"Look!" It came out louder than he intended, judging from his chagrined expression. He paused and let a few seconds pass. "I think the best approach here is to try to develop a policy and then see if we like how it turns out," he said with a more controlled tone. "We don't have to adopt anything that we think will limit free speech or deprive our townspeople of books they want to read. Let's just give it a try, Gracie. Where's the harm in that?"

"The harm is . . . I know how these things progress." Gracie struggled to tamp down her anger and stay articulate. "We write a policy. We tinker with the policy. We edit the policy. But in the end, we have a policy that still contains the intent of censorship, and I don't think we want that. I don't think we should change anything about the way we've gone about buying books and providing access to them over the past twenty-five years."

She looked over at Gregory. He was frowning.

"Let me tell you something about the job of a librarian," Gracie said. "I'm not just here to order books that the community wants to read, books that will go out of fashion and be forgotten in a couple of years. In the scheme of things, this debate isn't over one book or another that I might order. What's important is that I'm here to help people get information, information they need to navigate their lives. Your list of so-called 'bad' books might contain just what someone needs to learn in order to do that."

Gracie knew it sounded a bit grandiose. But, for the second time that night, she thought of Sara. The woman's two brief appearances at the library over the past couple of weeks had reminded her of the duty she felt to Sara, and to Ísabel, too. The young girl had reminded her of the joy of discovery, the adventure into literature that librarians were privileged enough to guide people on.

She looked around the table. Tony and Gregory were already on the side of censorship, and she knew that Caitlin was against it. With Jacob absent, she needed to get both Lorena and Paul on her side. So far, she couldn't tell how they were taking Gregory's proposal.

Looking from Paul to Lorena and back, she delivered the three sentences she had practiced in anticipation of the discussion. "We should keep in mind these kinds of supposedly innocuous policies have led to banning such books as *Huckleberry Finn, Brave New World,* and *I Know Why the Caged Bird Sings.* We're not talking about *Fifty Shades of Grey,* here. We're talking about books that explore topics of racism, sexism, and mind-control—topics our children need to come to terms with to be responsible citizens."

"Well, I think you are wrong." Gregory slowly enunciated each word. He looked around the table. "And, I think this board agrees with me. We need to take this issue seriously, and we can't do that until we look at some alternative policies. Now"—he looked sternly at Gracie—"do you think you're *up to* drafting something for us, or do we need to have one of us do it for you?"

The phrase "up to" was condescending, and the way he emphasized it, Gracie knew it was deliberately so. It might be an early salvo in the next battle: over whether she was still "up to" doing her job. She felt her palms moisten and her heart race.

"I think we have discussed this enough," Tony interrupted. He pulled a piece of paper out of his file that looked like some kind of typed statement. He started reading.

"I move that this board direct Gracie to develop a policy that provides guidance regarding the purchase and distribution of potentially controversial literature and texts. This policy will determine when the librarian will involve the board in decisions regarding purchases, and it will propose systems to ensure that the books and texts the library owns will be distributed only to those patrons for whom those materials are appropriate."

"I second the motion," Gregory quickly added, to no one's surprise. "All in favor, say aye."

"Aye!" at least three voices intoned in unison.

Gracie watched Lorena and Paul. Lorena met her eyes, Paul averted his. That was all she needed to know. Lorena was on her side; Paul had aligned himself with Gregory. Gracie didn't have a vote on the board, except in ties.

"The ayes are Tony, Paul and me. The motion carries," Gregory said. "Now let's get through this last item and call it a night. Gracie, do you want to explain what you're asking here?"

"No, I don't," she replied. "Given the vote you have just taken, I'd like to table this item for now."

"Does that mean you've decided not to buy this book— what is it? *The Intern's Travels*—for the library?" Tony asked.

"I don't know." Gracie wished she could skip the topic and adjourn. "Until a policy is established that gives the board oversight over book purchases, it appears it was unnecessary for me to include the purchase of any book on the agenda."

"In light of the vote we just took, I'm thinking that it's appropriate to have a discussion about this," Gregory said. "Why would you want the library to have this book?"

"Well, for one, the whole nation is talking about the book, and more people have asked for it than for any other book in the twenty-five years I've been librarian here," she explained. "I don't see why the residents of Johnson Station shouldn't have access to a book that everyone else in the country has."

"How do you know that other libraries haven't decided to reject popular—and might I say, reprehensible—tastes? Do you know if all other libraries are ordering it?"

Gracie was at a loss for an answer. She didn't know if the book was being banned by other libraries, but it seemed unlikely, given the hefty sales numbers it was racking up.

"Definitely they're ordering it," she said. "Everybody is asking about it."

"You see, this is exactly what I'm talking about, Gracie," Gregory said. "Once that book is in our library, children will want to read it. They've all heard about it too, and their parents will think that if the library bought it, it must be okay. This is exactly why we need a policy. In fact, perhaps we should move to suspend all new book purchases until such a policy is established."

"I don't think we can do that," said Caitlin softly, surprising everyone. Five heads around the table whipped around to look at her. It was the first time she had spoken up all evening. "It is not part of the library charter for the board to approve what materials the librarian purchases," she said, pointing to the copy of the charter she'd pulled from her folder. "Until we change the charter to adopt this new policy, if we ever do, I believe it is inappropriate for the board to discuss these matters."

Gregory's mouth opened to respond, but nothing came out. Gracie didn't know if he was so surprised he couldn't talk, or if he realized that Caitlin was right and didn't want to get into an argument he couldn't win.

"Okay," he said finally. "I guess that is correct. But Gracie, I would hope that you would consider the sentiments of this board, evidenced by our vote tonight. I know we have no authority to prevent it—yet—but we are your advisors, and I would hope you will take our advice and postpone buying."

He waited, looking like he expected Gracie to agree with him, but she didn't. She said nothing. She was being obstinate, she knew, but when she looked in the mirror later that night, she wanted to see someone who stuck to her guns.

"Then, we're adjourned." Gregory pushed his chair back and stood up, his earlier victory of the evening deflated by her refusal to bend on this last item.

"Our next board meeting isn't until February," Gracie said. "We take January off, as you know."

"That will give everyone a chance to think about our policy some more, and it'll give you time to write a draft," Gregory said cheerfully, as if everyone was as excited about it as he was.

Gracie ignored that comment. She mustered up the sweetest voice she could. "Have a great Christmas."

The Johnson Station Library's three new copies of *The Intern's Travels* arrived in a box with Anthony Bourdain's *Medium Raw* for Liz, and the book on Ritalin-free child-rearing for Caroline, just in time for Christmas.

The cover on *The Intern's Travels* was quite nice, she realized with a surprise. She didn't know what she'd expected, and she hadn't focused on the book jacket when she ordered it. Of course, you can't judge a book by its cover, but perhaps this was a good sign; maybe the book was going to be a better read than *Fifty Shades of Grey*. That cover was awful.

Gracie thumbed through one of the copies of the much-requested book, stopping on a few pages to read a paragraph or two. The prose flowed smoothly enough, and the dialogue seemed realistic. Then her eyes fell on a paragraph describing a bedroom scene—although it wasn't really happening in a bedroom. She read a page and a half and felt her heart racing.

She was too old for this! She slapped the book closed. The last thing she needed was a how-to book on sex. She'd made love hundreds of times with Jens and now Richard, although never in a way like the scene she had just read. On the other hand, maybe it wasn't too late to learn some new tricks.

"Oh Christ, Gracie," she said aloud. "Get back to work and stop being such an idiot."

She opened the old-fashioned Rolodex she kept on her desk and looked up numbers for Caroline and Liz, whom she'd moved to the top of her *Intern's* list. Now she was going to have the pleasure of calling them to tell them their books had arrived.

It was one of Gracie's favorite things. Whenever she got a book shipment in and started to make calls, she wondered if there were a job in this world that would be like that—a job that entailed only calling people with good news. Nothing else. Just calling with good news.

It would be easy to get up in the morning and go to work if you had that to look forward to every day.

What she wasn't looking forward to was the call she expected to receive as soon as Gregory heard that *The Intern's Travels* was now on the loose in his community. She didn't know how he would find out, but she knew he would. She needed to prepare for that call.

The other thing she needed to prepare for was telling

Janice that Ísabel was coming with her to Chicago for Christmas. She would wait until she was in the city to tell her daughter that Ísabel had moved in. However, she knew even telling her that Ísabel would be with her at Christmas could elicit a screaming fit.

It was a good thing that she never stayed with Janice in Chicago. She always rented a room in a Magnificent Mile hotel so that she could enjoy the shopping and the bustle of the city that she remembered from her life there thirty years before.

She made the hotel reservation at the Loews as soon as Ísabel agreed to go with her. She chose it because it was close to the river, close to Magnificent Mile shopping, and across the street from Navy Pier. It was likely to be too cold to spend much time on the pier at the end of December, but it still would be good to have it as an option. The hotel also had a spa, and Gracie planned to treat Ísabel to her first massage and facial as a Christmas present.

She waited until seven days before she and Ísabel were flying into town and checking into their hotel to call Janice.

"Hi, Mom, I'm really busy," Janice answered her phone at work in her usual brusque manner. "You're still coming, aren't you?"

"Yes, dear," Gracie said, "and I am calling to tell you I'm bringing someone along."

"Richard?"

"No. Ísabel."

Silence. The only way Gracie could tell that Janice hadn't hung up on her was the office chatter in the background. She waited to give Janice a chance to respond, but her daughter said nothing.

"Janice?"

"Why, Mom?"

"Well, she has no one here to celebrate Christmas with, and I thought it would be nice for you to meet her."

"Why do you have to ruin Christmas this way?" Her

daughter's whine reminded Gracie of her mother's.

"Why do you think it will ruin Christmas?" she asked. "We will still have supper and go shopping and go out for drinks. We'll open presents on Christmas Eve in the hotel like we always do. It won't ruin anything to have Ísabel along. She's really a nice girl and quite sophisticated. I think you'll like her."

"Mom," Janice said. "Don't do this."

"What?"

"Don't bring this girl into my life. Into your life either. You'll be sorry. There's no way this is going to end well."

"Well, we're coming, so you'll have to meet her," Gracie said. "We'll be there on the twenty-second and meet you at Les Nomades. I know you love French food, so I made reservations for the three of us at seven-thirty."

Janice didn't respond, and Gracie could no longer hear office noise in the background. Her daughter had hung up.

Gracie held her cell phone away from her ear and watched the home screen return. She considered calling Janice back, but she knew Janice wouldn't answer her call. And she'd be doing exactly what Janice wanted her to do: beg. It had taken her this long to recognize it. Her daughter wanted her to beg for her love.

She wasn't going to do it. She would call again before she left for the airport to tell her they were on their way, but she wasn't going to beg her daughter to treat her with respect.

~12~

When Gracie was Ísabel's age, she had never flown in an airplane and wouldn't fly in one for another seven years. However, Ísabel had flown to Mexico and back, so Gracie expected she would think of it as old hat when they got ready to go to Chicago.

She was wrong. For all her sophistication about the ways of the world, Ísabel was still young enough to crave adventure and get excited about going somewhere new. In contrast, by the time anyone was even half Gracie's age, very few of their experiences ever turned out as uncompromised and pleasant as anticipated, and no matter how much she tried to temper expectations, reality always had a way of tamping them down further.

Ísabel didn't know that yet. Usually as slouchy and shuffling and afraid of showing too much enthusiasm as any teenager—God knew why they were so afraid to look alive!—Ísabel was as jittery and spastic as a Jack Russell Terrier on the way to the airport. Gracie had no patience for it back when Janice was sixteen, but now she got a kick out of it.

Richard had left the day before for New York, and as it had been a Saturday, Gracie and Ísabel had driven him to the airport and then gone shopping for some new clothes for Ísabel. At first Ísabel had protested the expense.

"Mom will want to pay you back, and she really can't afford that," she argued.

"She doesn't have to pay me back," Gracie said. "It's your Christmas present." Gracie hadn't told her she was planning to give her the spa package on Christmas Eve when they opened presents with Janice, so Ísabel accepted that answer.

"Richard wasn't happy, was he?" Ísabel asked after they dropped him off at the airport and headed to the mall on the edge of the city.

"No, he really wanted me to go with him," Gracie said. "Very astute of you."

"Did you decide not to go because of me?" Ísabel asked.

"No, I made this decision before you came to live with me. I don't like to go out of town with a man, any man that isn't my husband."

"Why not? Are you afraid people will talk?"

"No, I'm afraid young people will get the idea that it's okay to do that sort of thing."

Ísabel let a snort escape her nose. "Are you serious?"

"Yes. Absolutely serious. You kids get enough bad ideas from TV and things."

"But is it like your responsibility to save us from sex?"

"Not just sex. I'm just trying to set a good example."

"Whatever." Ísabel sat back in the seat. She said nothing for a couple of minutes.

Gracie thought the conversation was over, but then Ísabel turned to her and put a hand on her shoulder.

"You know, this isn't *The Music Man*, Gracie," she said. "This may be Iowa, but you don't have to be Marian the Librarian all your life."

"Maybe it's more an Iowa thing than a librarian thing," Gracie said. She turned and gave Ísabel a wry smile. "Maybe you can just give me some time. It's not easy to learn new tricks at my age."

"Oh, you're not so old!" Ísabel punched Gracie lightly on the shoulder. "You're not nearly as old as I once thought you were. You're quite the spunky lady!"

Gracie decided to skip trying to figure out why Ísabel had once thought she was old. Or why she had changed her mind. Being called a spunky lady made up for it all.

"Yes, I am spunky," she agreed. "Very spunky indeed."

❧

Pulling into the airport for the second time in two days, Gracie felt a flutter of excitement in her stomach. She hadn't been on a plane in six years, not since she and Jens went to Hawaii for a vacation before he got sick. She and Ísabel were only going to Chicago, a trip that she could easily have made by car, but there was something exotic about getting on a plane.

"I was looking online, and there's a theater close to where we're staying that shows nothing but foreign films and stuff like that," Ísabel said as Gracie drove into one of the airport's huge parking lots. "I wonder if maybe we could go see some while we're there."

"Great idea!" Gracie wasn't faking the enthusiasm; she still hadn't figured out how she was going to keep them occupied for five days, especially if things with Janice fell apart at the beginning. "I used to go there all the time when I lived in Chicago."

"Oh, really?" Movies were clearly Ísabel's favorite subject. "What kinds of things did you see?"

"All of Alan Rudolph's. And Peter Weir's early stuff. You know, *Gallipoli, Picnic at Hanging Rock, The Last Wave.*"

"*Breakfast of Champions?*" Ísabel named one of Rudolph's films.

"No, that came much later. I loved *Trouble in Mind*—Rain City is really Seattle, you know. And *Choose Me.* I think *Choose Me* was my favorite."

"I've never seen those. Let's Netflix them sometime."

"Good idea. It'll be fun for me, too."

"Wow, this is great!" Ísabel exclaimed.

Gracie looked over at the youngster and smiled. Yes, it was. It truly was.

❧

Chicago was cold. Iowa was cold, too, but the Windy City was living up to its name, and Gracie braced herself against the buffeting gusts as she waited for the valet to pull their bags out of the trunk of the taxi. If she were traveling alone, she would have taken the train in from the airport and then walked to the hotel, but now she was glad that she had an excuse not to. Ísabel's suitcase was too heavy for much walking. Gracie had given Ísabel a choice of the suitcases she had stored in the attic, and she was concerned when she chose the biggest one.

"You know, you should never pack a bag that's too heavy to handle yourself," she had admonished the girl that morning.

"I didn't know what to bring!"

Once the valet emptied the trunk and threw their bags onto a luggage cart, Gracie took Ísabel's hand and led her through the big glass doors into the sparkling lobby of the Loews Hotel. She felt Ísabel trying to free her hand and glanced over to see a group of teenagers clustered around the fireplace on one side of the lobby.

She needed to be more sensitive. Ísabel wasn't a child, and Gracie had intended to treat her like the young adult she was on this trip. Chicago was a great place for that: lots of big-city attractions and benefits, but still a safe enough place for a young woman, at least in this neighborhood.

As they approached the registration desk, a slender, well-dressed woman with a briefcase rushed around to get in line in front of them. Ah, yes! She had forgotten what city people could be like. Back in Johnson Station, no one cut in line; they all knew each other, and that would be considered incredibly rude. If someone was in a hurry, he or she asked permission to go ahead, and it was always granted.

"Wow! This is really cool," Ísabel whispered. She turned around and looked up, taking in the high ceilings, the three-dimensional sculptured walls, and the huge chandelier.

"Why are you whispering?" Gracie asked.

Ísabel nodded toward the huddle of teenagers, and Gracie

got the message. It was one thing to admit to Gracie that something impressed her, quite another to show enthusiasm in front of her peers.

Waiting in line for the next receptionist, Gracie tried to remember if it was the same when she was a teen, and she decided it was. How many times had she said "It was okay" to her friends rather than show excitement for something—a family vacation, a movie, whatever. It was cool to go crazy over boy bands or movie actors, but anything or anyone within reach was always just "okay" and never better.

"Nothing has really changed." Gracie realized she had said it aloud when Ísabel looked at her quizzically.

"Nothing's changed to the hotel?"

"Yes. To the hotel." It was easier than trying to explain. Besides, Gracie knew that no young person wanted to be told his or her behavior was typical. They wanted to be "normal" in their friends' eyes, but enigmas to their parents.

They had waited at the front of the registration desk line for ten minutes, and Gracie was growing impatient. The woman who had cut in front of them was taking an inordinate amount of the clerk's attention, in Gracie's estimation. It was cutting into the limited time they were going to have to get ready for supper.

"If she'd get off her cell phone, maybe she could get going," Gracie said loudly enough that she thought the woman might hear her. If she did, she didn't show it.

Looking around, Gracie realized every other person in the lobby was either talking on a cell phone or looking at a screen.

"Doesn't anyone talk to anyone else in person anymore?" she wondered out loud.

Ísabel looked at her like she was crazy.

ﻌ

Janice showed up at the restaurant twenty minutes late.

Ísabel had already finished one Diet Coke, and Gracie had finished her first glass of wine before her daughter rushed in with enough of a flurry to attract the attention of all the diners around them.

"Sorry, Mom." She sounded very much like she wasn't sorry at all. "I'm so busy at work, I wasn't even sure I'd be able to make it."

Janice fussed with her napkin, moved all her silverware to one side of her place setting, and took a long drink of water before finally turning to Ísabel and acknowledging her presence.

"So, you are Ísabel. Nice to meet you." Janice stuck out her hand in such a way that it required Ísabel to lean way out of her seat to reach it, pulling the girl off-balance. Janice looked away from Ísabel immediately and turned her frowning face toward her mother.

"I suppose we aren't going to be able to have a drink." She nodded sideways toward Ísabel.

Gracie countered by lifting her empty wineglass.

"No, it's all right. Ísabel is quite a sophisticated young lady," she said, smiling at the girl. "A little too sophisticated for her own good, sometimes."

Ísabel blushed and looked across the room to avoid her eyes. Janice focused on the wine list, and Gracie waved to catch their waiter's attention. He hustled over, and she ordered another glass of Viognier and another Diet Coke for Ísabel.

"And for you, miss?" the waiter asked Janice.

"I'm not terribly impressed with this wine list." Janice studied the menu without looking up. "Don't you have a Pinot from the Willamette?"

"No, ma'am." The waiter bent forward slightly, an apologetic move that went unnoticed by Janice. "But we have a nice French Burgundy that will perhaps meet your expectations. Would you like to try it?"

"By the glass?"

"Yes."

"How much?"

"I am not sure." He leaned over her shoulder to look at the wine list. "Here it is. It's sixteen dollars."

"For a glass?" Janice looked up into his face, shocked.

"Janice," Gracie interrupted. "It's okay. I'm buying tonight. Order whatever you like."

"But, that's ridiculous," Janice said. "Louis Jadot costs twelve bucks a bottle at the store."

"Bring her a glass of that, please," Gracie told the waiter, who nodded thankfully and slinked away.

"Honestly, what these places get by with!" Janice picked up her menu. She shook her head and began reading.

Gracie looked at Ísabel and winked. She wished she had at least warned her about Janice's temperament. She didn't want Ísabel to think Janice's prickliness was her fault.

They sat in silence until the waiter returned with their drinks and took their orders for supper. Janice asked the waiter for his recommendations, and then argued with everything he said. Gracie began to wonder if her command performance of bitchiness was for her benefit or for Ísabel's.

"So, how are things at the office?" Gracie asked as soon as the waiter turned away.

"Why do you always begin your questions with 'so'?" Janice frowned at her mother critically.

Gracie took a deep breath and peeked at Ísabel. The girl met her glance with fear in her eyes. Gracie had never seen her so unsure of herself. Ísabel was intimidated.

"Is there any possibility, Janice," Gracie turned back to her daughter, "that we could try to enjoy this evening without any more snarky remarks?"

"I don't know, Mom." Janice jerked her head up higher with each word. "Is there any possibility we can spend some adult time together this week?"

That was enough. "What is your problem?" Gracie

snapped back.

"My problem is that this is Christmas, and I don't necessarily like your arbitrary decision to suddenly expand our family."

"Janice!" Gracie hissed and put her hand on the back of Ísabel's chair. "Do you think Ísabel can't hear you or do you just not care?"

Janice opened her mouth to say something, but Ísabel beat her to it.

"I can hear you," she said. "I know you don't want me here. But I really don't have anywhere else to go."

"And you do." Gracie finished Ísabel's thought for her.

"What?" Janice jumped back, an exaggerated look of shock on her face. "You mean you would rather I leave?"

Gracie turned and nodded at Ísabel for confirmation. "I think we both would. I'll ask the waiter to make your food to go for you." Gracie turned in her chair both directions, straining her neck to look for their waiter.

"No, thanks." Janice threw her napkin onto the table and pushed her chair back. The chair legs caught on the carpet and it tipped over backwards. "Merry Christmas, Mother! It'll be a cold day in hell when I invite you again."

"You never did," Gracie said, but Janice was already halfway to the door and out of earshot.

Gracie sat in stunned silence for a moment, looking down at her lap. Ísabel jumped up and turned the chair back upright.

"I'm sorry that happened, Ísabel," Gracie whispered.

"Oh, I thought that went pretty well," Ísabel said. Gracie looked up to see her crooked smile. "Are you sure she's related to you?"

Thank God the girl had a sense of humor.

"Do you think she could be the milkman's daughter?"

"I don't think it works that way."

"Thanks," Gracie rewarded the girl with a big smile. "Thanks for being here."

≈

With nearly two full days before they were supposed to get together with Janice again for Christmas Eve, Gracie was optimistic that Janice would have time to reconsider her behavior and decide to join them to open presents in the hotel, as they had originally planned.

In the meantime, Gracie intended to not let her daughter dampen her fun with Ísabel.

She and Ísabel rode to the top of the Willis Tower— Gracie knew it as the Sears Tower and kept calling it that— took a water-taxi tour of the river, sauntered up and down Michigan Avenue, had lunch at Ed Debevic's, and spent an entire afternoon at the Museum of Science and Industry.

"Hey, are you tired?" she asked Ísabel when they returned to the hotel suite after having lunch on Navy Pier Christmas Eve. Janice had relented and was going to join them for eggnog and exchanging presents, and Gracie expected Ísabel to be anxious about facing her daughter's anger again. However, Ísabel didn't seem anxious; she looked sad. Walking back up the street, she barely looked up from the sidewalk in front of her.

"Yeah, maybe I'll take a nap," Ísabel said. "Can I?"

"Sure," Gracie said. "I'll be happy to sit and read for a while. If we're going to mass later, you're smart to get a little rest."

When Ísabel's nap stretched into a third hour, Gracie started to worry that she might be getting sick. She knocked quietly on the door to the bedroom, opened it slowly, and peeked into the room. Dusk came early to Chicago at Christmastime, and it took Gracie's eyes a moment to adjust to the darkened room.

"Ísabel?"

The girl didn't answer. Gracie walked up to Ísabel's side

of the king-sized bed they had been sharing. Ísabel was wide awake, lying on her back and staring at the ceiling. Her eyes were red and swollen. Gracie sat down beside her and she felt the pillow around her head. It was damp with tears.

"Dear?" she cooed. "What's wrong?"

Ísabel shook her head and refused to meet Gracie's eyes.

"Oh, Ísabel," Gracie said. "Are you thinking of your mom? And your dad?" Striving to keep busy and do as much as they could in their five days in the city, Gracie had totally forgotten that it was the girl's first Christmas without her parents.

Ísabel paused. She nodded slowly, and a sob escaped from her pursed lips.

"I am so sorry," Gracie said. "Let's call them, shall we? Let's call them now."

"But Janice is coming."

"Don't worry about her. You can call them from in here. Use the hotel phone so you get better reception. Don't worry about how much it costs. If Janice gets here before you're done, I'll ply her with eggnog. Maybe she'll even turn into a decent human being before you finish!"

Ísabel smiled a little and nodded again. Gracie stood up and turned on a lamp.

"I'll grab my clothes out of the closet and change in the other room," she said. "Take your time with your mom, and then, when you're ready, come on out and join us."

Gracie closed the door as quietly as she had opened it. Chagrined, she wondered how many times she had been oblivious to Janice's moods as a youngster. Perhaps she hadn't paid enough attention to her daughter's moods either, plowing through life with a stoicism demanded by her own parents. Was that the reason Janice had turned out to be not only independent emotionally, but resentful as well?

Gracie put on the dress she had packed for Christmas Eve mass, and brushed on some eyebrow powder and lipstick. She didn't know if Janice was going to show up or not; she could still have changed her mind and decided to stand her mother up. However, Gracie believed it would not be easy for anyone—even her prickly daughter—to spend the holiday alone. Not knowing anything about who Janice's friends were or how close they were, she couldn't guess what her alternatives might be.

Christmas Eve turned out well, all things considered. Janice did show up, and although she was cold toward Ísabel and Gracie at first, she warmed up by the end of the evening enough to laugh a little and tell a few short stories about her life in Chicago. The eggnog—the version with bourbon, not the virgin version Gracie gave Ísabel—helped improve her attitude. Like mother, like daughter, Gracie realized.

The rest of the trip flew by with a movie, a long trip up to Evanston to see Gracie's last living aunt, and then the Lincoln Park Zoo. Ísabel fairly sparkled with pleasure when she came out of her massage and pedicure appointments, but by the time they took a taxi back to the airport, she appeared exhausted. Back in Johnson Station, she slept in late for a few days, taking advantage of Christmas break from school.

Richard looked happy to see Gracie when she picked him up at the airport the next week. At first, she was surprised by that, remembering how many times she had picked Jens up from a trip and found him so preoccupied with his thoughts he hardly said hello.

She pulled up to the arrivals lane just in time to see him walk out of baggage claim. He hopped into the car, kissed her quickly on the lips, and handed her a fancy gold bag. She peeked: it was a bottle of French wine that he bought at the LaGuardia Airport on his way back to Iowa.

"That's a gift from the civilized world," he joked. "Now,

back to the prairies! Beware the cowboys and Indians!"

Gracie pulled back into the traffic lane and headed toward the exit.

"Does Ronnie miss this wild, wild West?" she asked.

"No, he seems pretty happy there. Broke but happy. How was Janice?" Richard asked.

"Oh, Janice?" Gracie shook her head. "Bitchy."

"So, what else is new?"

"No, I mean it started out really bad. She didn't even last through the first meal with us." Gracie gave a quick version of the disaster at the French restaurant as she drove north through Des Moines and toward the interstate.

When she finished, he groaned. "How embarrassing for Ísabel."

Gracie looked at him and nodded. That was exactly the takeaway she had wanted from him. "She did show up for Christmas Eve, and she stuck around a little longer than I expected."

"Was she nice?"

"Well, she was still frosty, but I got the feeling she was a little jealous of Ísabel at the same time."

"Jealous? Of what?"

"Of my affections for the girl. Can you believe it? Maybe if Janice hadn't been an only child she would have learned to value my attention a little more. Maybe she just needed a little competition."

"Well, despite what her therapist is probably telling her, I don't think it's your fault that she's so narcissistic." Richard shook his head sympathetically and laid a hand on Gracie's shoulder.

"We've been over this before." Gracie chuckled. "It's either nature or nurture, and I'm responsible for both. Or, I mean, Jens and I were. Together. What makes you think she has a therapist?"

"I don't know. I imagine most urban professionals do. It's

a status thing," he said. "Ronnie has one."

"Yes, but he's an actor." She winked at him. "He's supposed to be messed up. But how does he afford it?"

As Gracie drove out of town and headed toward Johnson Station, Richard told her about Ronnie's meager apartment and lifestyle, contrasting then with the dinners and plays he and Ronnie enjoyed on Richard's dime. She found herself getting a little bit jealous of his week in New York; it had been years since she'd been back there, and she suddenly realized how much she missed what had been an annual pilgrimage when she was in her twenties.

"Well, maybe next year we can go there together—both places." She reached for his hand.

He smiled broadly. "Do you mean that? You're not just saying it because it's so far out and you'll change your mind when the time comes?"

"No, I mean it," she said. "But let's not talk about it too much. Maybe we can slip out of town without anyone noticing."

~13~

Johnson Station always seemed incredibly quiet right after Christmas, but this year, during the day, Gracie had the odd feeling that she was the last soul alive in town. By Friday of the first week of the New Year, the town felt downright spooky.

More than once that day, she got up from her desk and walked to the front windows to see if there were any signs of life: a UPS truck cruising slowly past on the icy street; the postman walking past with his post-Christmas bag mercifully light; or even one of the neighbor dogs trotting home after following some kids to the sledding hill. But she saw nothing. Just the still, frozen dullness of the ice-rutted pavement.

Every year, more and more of the town's retirees spent the winters in Arizona or Florida. Gracie worried that at some point they'd quit coming back in the spring. Then, with the population of younger people dwindling and the oldest of the old dying off, it wouldn't take too many more years for Johnson Station to dwindle to a ghost town.

Gracie shook herself out of her dystopian daydream and returned to her desk. Melancholy wasn't healthy. An occasional sadness was part of life, to be embraced and listened to, but extended melancholy was just another name for depression.

When Ísabel pushed through the front door that afternoon, letting in a freezing draft, Gracie was so happy to see her she nearly jumped up for a hug. But the look on Ísabel's face stopped her.

"Hey, what's wrong?" Gracie called out as Ísabel slinked by, dragging her backpack on the floor.

"Nothing."

"Well, it looks like something."

"I just don't feel well," Ísabel called back over her shoulder and threw herself down at her usual table in the back.

"Do you need some Alka-Seltzer or something?"

"No," Ísabel retorted. "I'm fine. I'm just tired." She crossed her arms on the table and put her head down.

As badly as Gracie needed her company, Ísabel wasn't in the mood to give it, so Gracie left her alone to rest until it was time to close the library. They walked home in silence, with Gracie carefully picking the clearest path down the icy sidewalks and Ísabel following several steps behind.

"Teenagers are moody," Richard said as he drove Gracie to Des Moines for supper. Ísabel had begged off eating anything and had gone up to her room as soon as they got home, so Gracie decided it would be a good time for her and Richard to get out of town for the evening.

"So are adults," Gracie mumbled.

"What?"

"I was just saying I'm moody, too. I can't believe how awful this week was. I wanted to close the library, go home, curl up, and take naps all day."

"It's the lack of light."

"Yeah, I know that. But this year it seems like a whole additional layer of malaise."

"Maybe it's just because you had such a good time in Chicago."

Gracie said nothing, and Richard turned and tousled her hair.

"Hey, cheer up," he said. "You have a lot of great things going for you."

"I know, and that makes me feel that much worse about being so depressed."

They drove for a few miles in silence, watching as a light snow started falling, the big flakes illuminated by the headlights of the car.

Rather than driving into the center of town or out to the university district where they typically went for supper, Richard pulled off onto a suburban frontage road lined with chain restaurants. Usually, that would have disappointed Gracie, but she wasn't in the mood for the ambiance or the expense of a fancy meal at a fine restaurant downtown.

"Red Robin or Red Lobster?" Richard slowed down to give her time to make a choice.

"How about Olive Garden?" she said.

"I thought you hated that place."

"Yeah, usually I do, but I'm thinking just a salad and a bowl of soup is all I want."

"Fine. Olive Garden it is." He parked the car next to the restaurant and held her hand as they slipped and slid their way up to the front door. The restaurant was overheated, humid, and packed with customers.

"Gracie!" someone shouted from across the waiting area. She looked up. John, the mayor of Johnson Station, strode across the patterned tile and stuck out his hand. He shook hers vigorously and then noticed Richard standing next to her.

"Hey, Richard!" The mayor pumped his hand next. He was a small man who, even at seventy, shook with nervous energy when he was calm; when he was excited about something, not a cell of his body seemed to be able to sit still.

"Hi, John." Richard wasn't nearly as excited to see the mayor as the mayor seemed to be seeing them. He'd never had a problem with the guy, he told Gracie later. But neither did he find time with him to be very productive or interesting.

"So are you two going to get married?" The mayor rubbed his hands together as if he was cooking up plans for their wedding right on the spot.

"What?" Gracie was shocked. "Where'd that come from?"

"Oh, I've just seen you together a bunch." John ploughed

ahead. "It would be great to see such fine people committing to each other and committing to Johnson Station."

"I'm not sure the two are connected," Richard said. "What if we got married and moved to Barcelona?"

The mayor opened his mouth to say something, and then stopped, confused. He smoothed back the few hairs on his nearly bald head and took out a handkerchief to wipe something off his hand. "Are you thinking of doing that?"

"No!" Gracie said, a little too loudly. The woman next to her laughed nervously and moved back a few steps. Gracie appreciated the extra space.

"We have never discussed marriage, but I'm sure if we ever do, you and everyone else in town will know all about it," Gracie said as calmly as she could while seething inside. "There's no such thing as minding your own business in Johnson Station, is there?"

"Oh, I'm sorry!" The mayor stepped back and stretched his arms out in front of him, palms out. "I just think it would be nice if our citizens have ethical, God-fearing couples setting good examples. I'm a little concerned about what I see happening around us in this world these days."

"What Gracie means is, we'll let you know." Richard reached out and patted the mayor on the shoulder fraternally.

The mayor smiled and nodded at Gracie. "Gregory told me about the policy you are writing for the library," he said, apparently relieved to change the subject. "I think that's a great idea. A good way to establish some moral guidance for our community."

"I thought that was what churches were for," Gracie mumbled. She didn't intend for the mayor to hear her, but he leaned toward her with one ear.

"What?"

"Oh, never mind. Anyway, it seems to me there are much bigger problems in town to work on."

"Like what?"

"Like all those empty storefronts."

"Not Gregory's problem, though."

That was not too different than the point she was trying to make, even if it went over John's head. She let that drop, too.

"When did you talk with Gregory?"

"He was in my office last week," the mayor said. "He was making some suggestions for a new library board member to replace the one we're losing."

"Oh, really?" Gracie didn't know a board member was leaving. As far as she knew, Jacob was intending to come back from Arizona in February, in time for the meeting that month.

"I guess Caitlin isn't going to come back for another term. Didn't you know that?" The mayor looked pleased with himself. His obviously growing relationship with Gregory meant he knew something Gracie didn't—something she should have known.

"Oh yes." She nodded as if she'd just remembered. "Caitlin. Yes."

"Gregory gave me two names," the mayor continued. "Maybe you have one or two?"

"Absolutely. I'll drop them off next week. Are you in the office?"

Gracie was thinking about nothing but the FAC by three o'clock the next Friday afternoon. She was planning what she was going to put out for appetizers, trying to remember what wine she had left in the wine fridge. Did she need to close the library early and a quick trip to Newton for some supplies? Would Gregory find out she closed early, and would that just add to his arguments for getting rid of her?

A little before four, she called Karen and asked her to come in early. Not a soul had come in the library since noon.

Despite her protestations that an open library and a free press were vital to a community's health, it was apparent that not many folks in town were seeking the wisdom of intellectuals and authors on Friday afternoons.

As she pulled her purse and the books she was taking home for the weekend together, the heavy front door opened and closed with a thud. It was the sound the door made when a small person came through who didn't have the strength to guide it to a quiet close.

Ísabel wasn't coming to the library that afternoon, planning to meet with the other students and Gregory to review their performances in the contest in Des Moines last month. Was it Liz?

Gracie stepped out into the main room and nearly ran into the diminutive Sara.

"Oh!" they exclaimed in unison.

Once they backed away from each other and laughed a little at themselves, Sara waved an arm at Gracie's office. "Are you closing? I can come back next week," she offered.

"Absolutely not!" Gracie assured her. "I'm here until the last person leaves. Hopefully by five o'clock or so."

Sara looked down at the list in her hand. Gracie couldn't tell if it was a new one or the same one she had brought in back in the late fall. It had been—what?—five or six weeks since she'd seen her.

"Well," Sara pointed to the paper, "you had offered to help me find some things. I'm not sure these are the right books to get, but Caitlin assured me that you would help. And you would keep this confidential."

"Of course." Gracie motioned for Sara to come into her office. It was more private. In the unlikely chance that anyone else came into the library as they were talking, they at least would have enough warning to lower their voices before being overheard.

"Well, you see I have this person who needs some advice," Sara started as she sat back in the guest chair, more comfortable that she had been on the last visit. "Okay, it's my son. My teenage son. Okay?"

"Sure." Gracie thought it wasn't the first time she'd heard someone disguise a problem they were having as someone else's in seeking a book to help them think it through. But what indication did she have that the problem was Sara's and not her sons? None. She decided to take the woman's word for it.

"Okay, so he told me the other day that he thinks he's gay, and he doesn't know how to know for sure."

"Has he seen a counselor? Is there someone at school he can trust?"

Sara shook her head quickly. "Oh, no. We don't have the money for counseling, and he won't talk to anyone at school."

"Okay, so let's see if I can suggest some reading." Gracie picked up a pen and stretched her hand out. "Let me see that list you have."

It was a good one. The list had some fiction, although it seemed a little old for a teenager, and some non-fiction books that had come out in recent years that Gracie had never considered purchasing. Why? she wondered. Did she think that Johnson Station had no gays or lesbians?

"We have a couple of these." Gracie circled two of the fiction titles. "And I can either put a couple of the others in my next order, or see if I can borrow them from another library."

"Thanks. When would you get them?"

"I'll have to check and let you know. How old is he?"

"Who?"

"Your son."

"Uh, sixteen."

"Hmmm. I'm not sure these are the best novels for him, but I'll go pull them for you." Gracie reached into her desk drawer and pulled out an application form.

"Here, fill this out while I do that so we can get you a library card."

"Can I just use Caitlin's?" Sara reached into her small purse, pulled out her billfold, and extracted a Johnson Station Library card. "She said to tell you they were for her, but we all know better."

"Well, on the internet, no one knows if you're a dog." Gracie smiled. "And at that kiosk over there"—she pointed to the electronic check-out station—"no one knows you're not Caitlin."

Later, Sara walked out with two books and a hug for good luck from Gracie. She turned at the door.

"Thanks for being here for me," she said. Her voice was almost shaking, and Gracie didn't think she'd ever heard such a sincere expression of gratitude in her life.

Sara's visit provided a short-term boost to Gracie's sense of self-worth. It seemed to prove the value of a little town library and librarian. But despite that and the FAC meeting at her house Friday night, Gracie started the next week in a "piss-poor mood," as Richard called it.

On Monday, she could see that Ísabel's mood matched her own, and she started to worry that she was bringing the girl down. They had spent five wonderful days in Chicago over Christmas, and she had been certain that they had created a bond of friendship that would persevere even after Ísabel's mother returned, if she ever did. But maybe Ísabel saw it differently. Maybe talking with her mother from that hotel room, which had seemed to cheer her up at the time, had uncovered a sadness and a loneliness that only her real mother could fix.

"Why don't you call your mom," Gracie said late the next week. Richard had a meeting in Des Moines, and she and Ísabel had the evening to themselves. "Maybe she's got some news about when she'll be back."

"Do you mind?" Ísabel seemed as if she'd been waiting for Gracie to suggest exactly that. Ísabel's cell phone didn't have international calling privileges, so it wasn't something she could do whenever she wanted.

"Not at all. Use the phone in my bedroom. You can have some privacy that way."

Ísabel was on the phone with her mother for an hour, and by the time she'd been on for thirty minutes, Gracie got anxious. At the forty-five-minute mark, she started to wonder what the two were talking about, and when Ísabel finally came downstairs, Gracie was a little peeved.

"Well, that was a long call." She tried to hide the resentment in her voice. It came out snarky.

"I'm sorry," Ísabel said. "It was your idea."

"Yes, but I didn't know you were going to read her *War and Peace.*"

Ísabel's eyes widened, and she looked close to tears.

Gracie had gone too far. "Oh, don't worry. No big deal," she said, trying to recover. That didn't come out right either. Now she sounded petty.

Ísabel turned to run back down the hallway and up the stairs, but Gracie caught her arm.

"Wait," she said. "Don't you want to tell me what you talked about?"

"No."

Ísabel had started to cry. Now there was no way she was ever going to tell Gracie what she had talked about with her mom. After eighteen years with Janice Gracie knew about a teenage girl's stubbornness.

"Okay, fine, it's your business."

"Yes, it is."

"Sit down. It's suppertime. No, it's past supper time."

They ate in silence. "Are you mad at me?" Ísabel asked after a few minutes.

"No," Gracie said. "Let's just drop it, okay?" Again, she knew she sounded angry. As irrational as she knew her anger was, she couldn't seem to pull herself out of it.

Ísabel stopped eating, dropped her spoon into her chili, and stood up. "I'm going to bed," she said quietly.

"Don't you think it's about time you did some dishes and other things around here?" Gracie said. "Does your mom let you act like you're a guest at home? Don't you help *her* out?" She hadn't intended to stress "her," but now it was too late to take it back. If Ísabel hadn't figured it out before, she had to see Gracie's jealousy now.

Without a word, Ísabel picked up her supper dishes and put them by the sink. She rinsed out her bowl, dumped the water left in her glass into the begonia on the windowsill, and opened the dishwasher. When she was done cleaning up after herself, she stood, waiting for Gracie to finish her meal.

"I'll take care of my own, thank you" Gracie didn't look up. "You can go on to bed."

Watching Ísabel leave the kitchen, Gracie felt her stomach sink. The girl didn't deserve this angry treatment. She deserved an apology, but Gracie couldn't drag herself out of her funk to fix things.

"Goodnight," she called halfheartedly after Ísabel. She got no answer.

Richard came in late, well past midnight, but Gracie was still awake, stewing over her own behavior. She gave him a quick synopsis of her argument with Ísabel.

"Well, you didn't take her in so you could get kudos for your kindness, did you?" he asked. "Or to take her from her mom?"

"I know. No, I didn't. I wanted to help her out for no

reason other than I liked her and I worried about her."

"Don't lose sight of that. Maybe it's just winter blues. Maybe you're really not as resentful of her mother as you are of the fact you're stuck in Iowa in the middle of the winter."

"There's some truth to that." Gracie slid over next to Richard's long body and laid her head on his shoulder. "Maybe next winter we should get out of here."

"Arizona? Florida?" Richard sounded pleased.

"How about South America?"

"Why South America?"

"I want to go see Machu Picchu. And they speak Spanish there. Maybe Ísabel can come with us and translate."

"If she's still here then."

"Yes. If I haven't driven her away."

&

The next morning, before she left for her coffee klatch, Gracie knocked on Ísabel's door. She wanted to apologize. When she got no answer, she opened it slightly and peeked in. Ísabel's bed had been made and her backpack was not on the writing desk where she usually kept it. She had dressed and left the house while Gracie was still in the shower.

At coffee, Jackie, Marcia, and Gracie sat moping together. In the back, only three businessmen had shown up at the men's table. The retirees were either home avoiding the icy streets or greeting the morning from their pools in Phoenix. Belinda had quit coming to the café after the argument with Gracie over reading materials, and they agreed that they didn't mind.

"Isn't this depressing?" Jackie looked around at the nearly empty café. "Why does anyone stay in this town in January?"

"Jobs," Marcia and Gracie responded in unison. Marcia elbowed Gracie and they linked pinkie fingers.

"So, what's your excuse?" Marcia asked Jackie. "You're

not working anymore."

"Nils is too cheap to go to Arizona, but I'll tell you, when he's gone, I'm outta here. Maybe for more than the winter. Maybe forever."

Jackie looked at her watch and started to slide out of the booth. "I have a hair appointment this morning," she announced. "Got to run. See you guys on Friday?"

"Yes, twice," Gracie said. "Coffee and FAC."

"Thank God," Jackie buttoned up her coat. "Nils isn't invited to either one."

As she walked out the door, Marcia pushed herself out of the booth and crossed over to the other side to face Gracie.

"Thank God she's gone," she said. "I've got to talk to you privately."

She glanced over Gracie's shoulder, and then leaned down close to the tabletop and whispered, "Carl and I are now officially having an affair."

Gracie didn't know what to say. She sat up straight and tried to keep a poker face. She wasn't ready to congratulate Marcia; she knew how affairs usually ended in Johnson Station, and she didn't wish her friend any of it—rumor mongering, divorce, ruined reputations. On the other hand, Marcia and Bob were clearly not happy with each other anymore. Perhaps it was time for Marcia to move on, but was an affair the right way to do it?

"You don't seem very excited for me," Marcia said, watching Gracie's face go blank.

"Well, I'm glad you've finally found something that . . ." Gracie couldn't think of how to finish her sentence. She started over. "I hope it was good . . ." She stopped again. "I mean the sex, I guess. I mean, why else would you do this?"

Marcia sat back and stared at Gracie. "I can't believe you just said that," she whispered harshly. "Do you think that's all it's about? Sex?"

"Gosh, I don't know," Gracie said. It was the truth.

"What else is it about?"

"Companionship, Gracie. Someone to talk to. You have forgotten how dull your life with Jens had become. But I remember. Now you have Richard, and I can see how much happier you are. Can't you be happy for me, too?"

Gracie paused for a few seconds. She hadn't put any thought into how she would feel or what she would say when Marcia's interest in Carl finally reached this point. She wished she;d thought about it, maybe talked with Richard about it.

"I'm sorry," Gracie finally said. "I just don't want you to get . . ." Again, she couldn't finish a coherent thought.

"Get hurt?" Marcia smirked. "Is that what you were going to say? Well, let me tell you this: Hurt is sitting in that living room with damn sports on TV every night, watching your butt sag and your boobs sag and your chin sag, and doing absolutely nothing to turn things around. I'm not going to spend the rest of my life like this, Gracie. I'm going to move on now. I don't know how it's going to happen, but I am."

Marcia got carried away by her explanation, and her voice rose back up to normal volume. Gracie glanced around. Thankfully, the café was even emptier than it had been before. They were the only two patrons left.

Gracie's eyes caught a glimpse of the big black-and-white clock over the window to the kitchen.

"Oh, yikes!" She started to scoot her butt out of the booth. "I've got to get the library open. It's after ten. Gregory Thungaard is going to have my ass."

Marcia grabbed her forearm and held it.

"Can't we talk?" Her eyes pleaded. "I need to talk to someone, and you're the only one who knows."

"Sure," Gracie said. "I'm at the library all day. Come by."

~14~

Marcia didn't call all day, and by evening, Gracie had forgotten that her friend had wanted to get together. First, Caroline distracted her, and then her mind went back to her argument with Ísabel.

Caroline, the voracious reader of child-rearing books, came in midmorning. It wasn't Tuesday, Caroline's usual day off from her veterinary clinic job, so Gracie was surprised. She was also surprised by the woman's gloomy face.

"Hey, why aren't you at work?" Gracie feared the worst. Had she been fired? Laid off?

"I took a little time off," Caroline said. "I've been feeling a little down—winter stuff, you know. And I decided to put in a few extra hours at the food bank, maybe cheer myself up a little bit by doing something good for someone else."

"Good plan." Gracie admired people like Caroline— people who loved animals and still cared enough about humans to volunteer for things like the food bank.

"Yeah, but then I get hit with the news that we're closing and moving all the food over to the county seat."

"What?" Gracie had heard nothing about that.

"The town council voted last week to end its subsidy. That ten thousand dollars a year was keeping us afloat. Without it, no chance."

"I had no idea the city was contributing that much," Gracie admitted.

"Apparently, a lot of people didn't," Caroline said. "And when Gregory found out, he had a fit. He argued that the city had no business being in the welfare business. At least that's what Amy told me."

Amy was a good friend of Terry's, Gracie's minister, and she had run the food bank for the past ten years, taking it from a simple closet in Terry's parsonage to a nice space in the town's empty industrial park. The industrial park had been the former mayor's brainchild, considered the town's best bet to pull itself out of the agricultural depression of the mid-eighties, but it had failed to attract a single business in thirty years. The food bank was its only occupant.

"I'm not surprised." Gracie had overheard Gregory talking about the industrial park at the back table in the café. If could kill the food bank, then he had the town council in his pocket, too, not just the mayor. If so, even her library funds were at risk.

"Anyway, now I'm bummed," Caroline said. "That food bank was the one thing that made me feel good about my life here. You know I have a degree in architecture I've never used? I will never be married, never have children, and most my clients are sunning themselves in Phoenix with their precious little dogs, and I'm here . . ." She ran out of steam.

Caroline sat in Gracie's office and sulked a little while longer, but eventually she seemed to get the hint that Gracie had things to do. Perhaps it was the way Gracie turned to her computer and got online, the dial-up connection screeching loudly enough to stop their conversation. When she left, Gracie turned the computer back off. She really had no need to be online.

What else did Gregory have his thumb on?

Armand was standing in front of her, looking down with sympathy when Gracie lifted her head off her desk. As usual, he'd snuck up on her—not on purpose, but by his quiet manner.

"Hey, what's wrong, Gracie?"

"Oh, just catching a quick nap." She lied, embarrassed for getting caught moping. She hadn't been sleeping; she'd been head-down, lamenting her decision thirty years ago to move to Johnson Station.

"I don't think so." Armand chuckled softly. He sat down, folded his hands on the edge of her desk, and looked just like she remembered him when he taught Janice high school history. Compassionate. Kind. Fatherly. He was her age, and yet he made her feel like a kid, a kid who needed his help.

"What is it, Gracie? What's got you down?"

Gracie sat back in her chair and considered the question.

"I don't know how you do it," she said.

"Do what?"

"Stay so happy and so busy."

"Why wouldn't I be?"

"This small town gets me down sometimes. I feel trapped and like I have no privacy. But worse, I feel like a few people pull all of the strings."

"Yes, that's probably true." Armand looked out the window and waved his arm at the street. "Here and in big towns. It's proportional. Here, for our eleven hundred souls, there are probably three or four majordomos. In a small city with ten times as many people, maybe thirty or forty. In Des Moines, maybe three hundred."

"Well, majordomo is a bit of a rose-colored term. Sometimes they're just little dictators and ideologues."

"Yes, sometimes. But these things go in cycles. One year, the guy pulling the strings is the mayor, the next year, maybe it's the pharmacist. But the more important point is that the benefits of living in a small town outweigh the downsides. In how many cities in this country could I get as involved with our young people as here in Johnson Station? Come to think of it, in how many places could you have become the town librarian, even though you don't have a library degree?"

Gracie had to smile at that. Only an old school teacher

could comfort her while bringing her down to size at the same time.

"Oh, I don't disagree." Gracie shook her head and laid it back down on the desk. "Maybe I just wish I lived in a different small town, one with a dictator I like."

"Maybe."

"No. I'm not telling the truth." She raised her head and looked him in the eye. "I have always wanted to be back in Chicago. I wanted to go to work for the International Monetary Fund. I never wanted to end up back here, forty miles from where I grew up, fighting small-town bigotry."

"Maybe you should find a way to fix that." Armand rose to his feet. "But I, for one, would miss you. You understand books, you understand scholarship, you understand people like me. I think we've been lucky to have you, and I consider you a friend."

"Thank you." Gracie managed a smile. "Thanks. You make me feel much better," she lied. "No wonder you were such a great teacher. Now what can I do to help you?"

Ísabel had skipped her usual afternoon stop at the library, and Gracie was worried that she had decided to move back into her mother's apartment. She locked up the library early— only Armand and Caroline had come in all day—and walked by the dry cleaners building. The windows of the apartment on the second floor were dark.

When she got home, Ísabel was upstairs in her room with the door closed.

"Hey, can I come in?" Gracie knocked softly.

"Yeah," the girl answered right away. "Sure."

Ísabel was sitting on her bed in her underwear and a T-shirt, her covers bunched up under her bare legs to hold her knees up. She was reading *Désirée*. She could have been Gracie forty-five years earlier, sitting on top of messy sheets, her head deep into a thick copy of the very same book.

"I am here to apologize." Gracie sat down at the foot of the bed, being careful not to crowd Ísabel's personal space. "I was nasty to you yesterday, and I had no reason to be."

"Was it about my mom?"

Gracie wasn't surprised that Ísabel had seen through her, but she didn't expect her to call it out so plainly.

"Yes, I think largely it was. I've become very fond of you, and I think I am a little jealous. I know she's your mom, and I expect when she returns you'll go back home with her. I will miss you, but that's fine. And I'm sorry I was so mean."

"That's okay." Ísabel looked up at Gracie with sad eyes. "I don't think Mom is coming back for a long time. That's what we were talking about. She was trying to explain. But it's like she is afraid to try to come up again."

"I'm so sorry, Ísabel." Gracie now felt even worse for her behavior the night before. "I know you miss her. Maybe you can go down and visit this summer after school is out."

"Yeah, maybe." It sounded like Ísabel wasn't very excited about the idea. Gracie remembered how Ísabel had described her trip to Mexico years before.

They said nothing for a few minutes, but sat, trancelike. The silence of the room, the house, the neighborhood hung like a cold, dark blanket over Gracie's thoughts.

"I see you're reading *Désirée*." Gracie finally broke the spell. "What do you think?"

"I really like it," Ísabel said, giving a teenager's kind of book review. Four words were enough.

"When I read it, it made me want to go to France and Spain and Sweden. Anywhere that wasn't Iowa."

"Really?" Ísabel seemed surprised. "Why didn't you?"

"Oh, I kind of messed things up, getting married, getting pregnant right away. Coming back to Iowa. And then time passed, and I never got around to it. I never found the time.

Between the library and raising Janice . . ."

"Maybe you should go now."

"Yes, maybe I should. And you definitely should. You should go as soon as you get out of college. Go live abroad. Go see the world!" Gracie found herself worked up by idea.

"Maybe I will," Ísabel said. "I think I want to go to France. Or Spain. Or somewhere. I just want to get out of here."

"Perhaps we can go somewhere this summer. Somewhere exotic." Gracie reached over and patted the girl's bare leg.

"Okay," Ísabel said. "If I haven't already messed things up, too."

Gracie frowned. "What do you mean? Messed up things between us? No, you haven't."

Ísabel shook her head sadly.

"Then what?"

"Oh, nothing." Ísabel looked past Gracie, out the window into the darkness. "Nothing."

Gracie waited for more, but Ísabel reopened her book, and Gracie took the hint that it was time to leave.

Obviously, something was wrong that Ísabel didn't want to talk about. But wasn't that always the case with teenagers?

"Do you have any idea where my wife is?"

Bob had never called the library before, and it took Gracie a moment to recognize his voice over the phone.

"You mean Marcia?"

"Uh, yes. That is the only wife I have, as far as I know." Bob sounded more snarky than worried. If Marcia were missing, Gracie would have expected him to take a different tone, to sound concerned. Maybe he knew more about Marcia's other love life than Gracie thought he did.

"No," Gracie said. "I saw her yesterday morning at

coffee. Didn't she come home after work yesterday?"

"The bank says she came in yesterday, and at noon she told them she wanted to take a few days off. It's so slow right now they let her go. But she didn't say where she was going."

"And she isn't answering her cell phone?"

"Not when I call."

"I don't have a clue." It was almost the truth. Gracie suspected this had something to do with Carl, but as to where Marcia was, she didn't have any idea. "But I'll see if I can find out anything. I'll call our friends."

Bob hung up. He never was one to extend a conversation needlessly. His Scandinavian stoicism was something Gracie recognized in many of the town's long-term residents.

Gracie sat a moment and tried to recall the last thing Marcia had said on Wednesday morning at coffee. Oh, yes. Marcia had asked Gracie if she could come by to talk, but then she didn't. Gracie had let it slip her mind as she focused on her troubles with Ísabel.

Of course, this was about Carl, the farmer, but had they run off together? That seemed unlikely. Carl had a wife and kids at home. An affair he could risk. Disappearing and leaving his family would have been out of the question.

Gracie tried the easiest thing first: calling her. To her surprise, Marcia answered her cell phone on the first ring.

"Hey," Gracie said, unprepared for a conversation. "Uh, Bob just called. He said he doesn't know where you are. He said you're not answering his calls."

"That's right." Marcia's voice was low and sad. "He's called about fifty times. I just can't talk to him right now."

"Where are you?"

"Away."

"Why? I thought you and I were going to talk sometime on Wednesday."

Marcia hissed a long, deep sigh into Gracie's ear. "Yes, but shit happened."

"What? Carl? What happened?"

"Look." Marcia paused for a long moment. "I can't talk about this yet. Not over the phone, anyway. Is there any chance you could come here? I really could use a friend right now."

"Where are you?"

"Iowa City."

"Shouldn't you let Bob know?"

"No, I can't. Maybe you could call him and tell him I'm okay and I'll be home soon."

"What should I tell him happened?"

"Don't tell him anything. When can you get here?"

Gracie wrote down the address of the bed and breakfast where Marcia was staying, and promised to get away as soon as she could. She had to find Karen, her nighttime assistant, and see if she could cover for a day or two at the library. And she had to reach Ísabel and Richard and put them in each other's care, and cancel the Friday FAC. First, she had to call Bob back.

"Where?" Bob asked first when Gracie said she'd reached Marcia.

"I don't know, but she's fine." It was a lie, almost. She didn't know exactly where in Iowa City Marcia was. and she figured it was one of those times it was better than telling the truth. "She just has some things to figure out."

"Is she coming home?"

"I'm sure she is."

"When?"

"I don't know."

This time Gracie cut the conversation off. She would never be able to satisfy Bob with answers, at least not until she got back from Iowa City, perhaps with Marcia in tow.

❧

The winter drive from Johnson Station to Iowa City was a study in dreary. The dry, frozen corn and bean fields stretched back over low hills on either side of the road, broken up by two or three homesteads every mile and an occasional wooded creek bed. Although taking Interstate 80 most of the way would have cut about a half hour off her trip, Gracie still preferred to go by way of the old highway, Highway 6, a two-lane that passed through five or six tiny towns—the number depended on how strictly one defined "town"—until it finally dipped down under the interstate, past the University of Iowa campus, and into Iowa City.

On 6, she was likely to get stuck behind a grain truck going forty miles an hour, hauling corn or soybeans to a local elevator—that's what farmers did in the months when they weren't planting, cultivating, or harvesting. Still, she preferred the bucolic pace and proximity to rural life of the two-lane over the high-speed detachment of the interstate.

About halfway, Gracie passed a couple of picnic tables that sat under a stand of glorious oak trees, their dark branches sketching contrasting jagged lines against the gray skies to the east. A few hundred yards past the dirt lane that led off the highway into the rest stop, she slowed down and turned around. How many years had it been since she and her parents stopped there on their way to her grandparents' house on the other side of Iowa City? At least forty-five, she guessed.

The tables were flaky with peeling paint, and dirty patches of ice in the shade matched the shape of the wide trunks of the trees. As Gracie got out of the car and stretched, she imagined her first German shepherd, Trixie, jumping out after her and heading off to find a squirrel to chase up a tree. She saw her father pull a Coleman cooler out of the trunk of their old Buick and set it on the table. Out would come a big pitcher of ice tea and three glasses, an old bread sack filled with tuna fish sandwiches, and a Tupperware container with carrot and celery sticks.

It was there, decades ago, as she sat chewing her tuna fish sandwich with Trixie waiting patiently at her side for a little bite of it, that Gracie first felt grateful for her parents and her Iowa life. She must have been about eleven or twelve, and the epiphany came from reading *A Tree Grows in Brooklyn*. Up to then, Gracie had assumed that everyone grew up in places like Iowa, with safe, wide-open spaces, because it was all she knew. Reading about Francie—a poor girl in the slums of Brooklyn who knew only one stubborn tree, with leaves that curled around the third-floor balcony of her tenement building—had suddenly expanded and exploded Gracie's concept of the world. It was the book that turned Gracie into a reader, a dreamer, and eventually, a librarian.

The sun had started to break through the clouds, and although it was still only midmorning, Gracie felt the day already warming up and promising to melt the rest of the accumulated ice and hard-packed snow that had laid claim to eastern Iowa since Christmas. Gracie turned her face toward the soft rays, their heat discernible against her skin.

Her mood lifted, and Gracie let out a long sigh. The past few days—no, the past few weeks—had taken a toll on her spirits to an extent that Gracie hadn't even recognized. Sitting on this lonesome highway on a brightening, windless day, she could feel the tension seeping out of her muscles through her skin and into the dry air. She needed to bring Ísabel here. She needed to tell her about growing up in Iowa back when it was the best of all worlds, back when it seemed like she'd drawn the long straw, and she felt sorry for everyone else. Back before she read things like *Désirée* and dreamed of the big world beyond the cornfields.

Marcia had given her the address for a bed and breakfast, and as Gracie pulled up in front of an old Queen Anne home with a broad front porch in Iowa City, Marcia walked down the steps of the sidewalk toward the car. Even from a distance, Gracie could see Marcia had gotten little sleep the night before. Her eyes were pink and swollen, the bags below them dark with smeared mascara.

Gracie felt guilty for showing up a half hour late. She pointed to the B&B, averting her eyes from Marcia's face.

"Wow, nice! This can't be cheap," she said. "Where'd you find this place?"

"Let's go get some coffee," Marcia whispered loudly. "Bed and breakfast guests can be so nosy. I need to get out of here. We can walk."

When Gracie backed out of the parking lot behind the B&B the next morning, she wasn't worried about Marcia any more. They had talked and talked for most of the past twenty hours, and sometimes that's all a person needed to get her head back on straight. Marcia was going to be fine, and if she decided to leave Johnson Station and go live among aboriginal New Zealanders, Gracie would support her all the way. If she came home and figured out how to persevere with the rest of the aging Iowans, that would be fine too.

"Do you think my disappearance will be a big scandal back home?" Marcia had asked her at breakfast. Gracie wasn't sure whether Marcia wanted it to be or not.

"No, as far as I know only your husband, your bank manager, and I know you left. And Jackie."

Gracie drained the rest of her coffee and stood up to head back to Johnson Station. She picked up her purse, and then remembered why it was so heavy.

"Oh, here!" she said, pulling out a book and handing it to Marcia.

"What's this?" Marcia asked, and then, glancing down at the cover, exclaimed, "Oh, *The Intern's Travels!* You bought one!"

"Actually, three," said Gracie. "But you still have to get

this one back in two weeks or it will be overdue."

"No problem," Marcia said. "I'll be back next week."

~15~

It started later in January, the fifth or sixth week after Ísabel moved in with Gracie.

Gracie hadn't been pregnant for nearly thirty years, but she would never forget nor mistake the violent vomiting, the coughing afterwards, and the moaning that came after that for anything other than morning sickness. Three days in a row, Gracie was in the kitchen, drinking her first cup of coffee of the morning, when she heard Ísabel rush to the bathroom they shared upstairs and empty her stomach into the toilet.

The first day, Gracie shook it off. Maybe she was wrong. Perhaps it was something not quite right about the school lunch the day before. And Ísabel looked fine by that evening. A slight case of food poisoning would look just like that, Gracie rationalized.

The second day, Gracie caught her breath at the sound of Ísabel's footsteps hurrying down the upstairs hallway and the repeat performance in the bathroom that followed. Still, Gracie held her tongue, hoping that Ísabel would offer her an explanation that afternoon when she came into the library.

But Ísabel went straight to Gracie's house instead of coming into the library that afternoon, and on the third morning when the girl came out of the bathroom, looking miserable and weak after her vomiting spell, Gracie was there waiting for her.

"What is it, Ísabel?" Seeing the anguish on Ísabel's face altered Gracie's tone from the stern, authoritative voice she intended to use to one soggy with sympathy.

"Nothing." Ísabel ducked her head and tried to skirt around Gracie.

Gracie caught her by the shoulders and pulled her in. At first, Ísabel resisted the gesture, holding her body rigid and staring over Gracie's shoulder, but after just a few seconds, she relented. She leaned against Gracie and her arms went slack at her sides.

"I don't know." Ísabel's voice broke into sobs. "I don't know what's wrong with me."

"I think we both know," Gracie said softly. "Let's go back to your bed and talk about it."

Ísabel let Gracie steer her back to her unmade bed, and she flopped facedown and sobbed, her body shaking violently. Gracie rubbed her back through her T-shirt, and waited a couple of minutes until the girl quieted down before she continued.

"You're pregnant." She made sure no judgmental tone crept into her voice.

Gracie wanted to know so much more: Whose baby was it? How long had Ísabel known? What did she want to do about it? But she held the questions back. Right then, Ísabel needed a supportive adult, not a critical, questioning one. "What can I do to help?"

Ísabel rolled over onto her back and clutched her stomach. She looked up at the ceiling and shook her head back and forth.

"I don't know! I don't know!"

"Okay." Gracie held a steady hand on the girl's shoulder. "Calm down. You'll make yourself sick all over again."

Ísabel took a deep breath and stopped shaking, her body sinking deep into the mattress as if by the sheer weight of her conundrum. Gracie waited until the girl's eyes met hers before asking again.

"What can I do? How can I help?"

"I really love him, but I didn't want this to happen." Another sob escaped along with Ísabel's words.

"Who?" Gracie asked. It sounded like Ísabel would rather

talk about who the father was than what she wanted to do about it. She hadn't had time to consider her options; probably she had been so full of anxiety and uncertainty, she couldn't think ahead yet. "Who is it? A boyfriend?"

"Oh no." Ísabel rocked her head back and forth on the mattress again. "That would be easy. He's so much more than that."

Immediately, Gracie recoiled. More than that? A relative? Could Ísabel have been abused by an uncle—or worse, her own father? Gracie shuddered. But no. Her father had been gone since September. Impossible.

"Why 'so much more than that?'" Gracie wasn't sure what line of questioning would be effective; not sure what she could find out without increasing the girl's anxiety.

"I can't tell you." Ísabel looked at Gracie with determination in her eyes. "I'll never tell you. It would cause so much trouble. It's not worth it. I need to take care of this myself. He doesn't deserve this."

"That's probably—" Gracie started to disagree.

"No one can know!" Ísabel cut her off. She slammed her fist into the mattress.

"Well, then let's not talk about that right now." Gracie backed down. "It's not as important as figuring out how you are going to take care of yourself."

Ísabel looked back at the ceiling and let her tears run down into her ears. Gracie fought the urge to reach over and brush them away. But the last thing the girl needed now was to be treated like a baby.

At the same time, the last thing Gracie needed was this complication. She was already on shaky ground with Gregory because she'd invited the girl to stay with her, a violation of immigration laws in his ill-informed eyes. Now if he saw Ísabel was pregnant, it was going to raise his disapproval to a whole new pitch.

But what if she didn't carry the baby? What if she decided

to get an abortion? How much risk would there be to Gracie if she helped her with that? There didn't seem to be any easy answers.

Gracie shook her head at her own thoughts. Whatever issues this pregnancy raised for her, it was going to be a million times worse for Ísabel.

After a few quiet minutes, Ísabel wiped her face with her hands and turned to Gracie with a wry smile.

"Bet you never thought you'd be dealing with this kind of shit when you invited me to live here," she said.

"It doesn't change how I feel about you at all," Gracie said. "We're in this together, Ísabel. And don't swear so much."

She let Ísabel lie quietly for another minute before nudging her. "Now, you need to get up and wash your face and get off to school. We don't have to figure this out this very minute."

Gracie leaned down and slipped her hands under the girl's shoulders, attempting another hug. What could be more important to Ísabel right then than knowing that Gracie still loved her?

Once again, Ísabel calmed down in Gracie's embrace and lay still. Gracie sat up.

"Don't tell anyone, okay?" Ísabel looked up, her eyes pleading.

"Of course not."

Ísabel held Gracie's eyes for a long moment, and then blinked and nodded.

"I'd better get ready for school then."

All day long, as she sat at the library and tried to work, Gracie thought about Ísabel. She remembered those two or three times in her own adolescence when she'd let things go further with her boyfriend than she had planned to, and she spent a few nervous weeks, hoping that her period would return.

She'd been lucky, but apparently, Ísabel hadn't. It was just like getting a DUI; it wasn't as if she'd never driven after drinking too much. Rather, she'd never been unlucky enough to be caught. She frowned thinking about the number of people who—even today—still saw teenage pregnancy as the result of a moral failing, even though nearly half of America's babies were born out of wedlock, and even though virtually no one she knew had entered marriage as a virgin.

Everyone was a hypocrite in one way or another. Gracie sighed heavily.

In her quiet office, she tried to focus on the latest *Kirkus Reviews*, searching for new books that might interest her audience, especially her regulars. For a few minutes, she succeeded, and she circled the review of another new book by Ken Follett that she expected Armand would be in to ask her about any day now.

But then her mind wandered back to Ísabel, and she imagined the girl sitting in her history or algebra class, distracted and worried that everyone around her could see through her, could see her secret.

While she wished Richard was home to talk to about the situation, she was also glad he had gone to Florida for a retired lawyers' convention that week. She and Ísabel would have time to talk things over and figure out what to do without the embarrassing—for Ísabel, anyway—presence of an unrelated man hanging around the house, listening in on their conversations.

Gracie breathed a sigh of relief when she saw Ísabel walk through the library door after school and make a beeline for the back of the stacks where Gracie had first talked with her three or four months before. How much had changed since then! How different her life had become in such a short time.

By heading straight back to her usual place, Gracie figured that Ísabel was saying: *Leave me alone. I'm glad you're here, and I'm glad I have a place to go, but I need you to leave me alone, too.*

With Ísabel nearby and within view, Gracie found it easier to concentrate on her work, and she thumbed through the rest of the review magazine, choosing two more potential titles for purchase, neither of which was likely to cause Gregory issues.

"Ready to go?" She called back to Ísabel about a quarter to five. "I'm going to close up early. Other than you, I haven't seen a soul all day."

The weather was awful, and most of the library's patrons were still in the desert or staying home. No one was going to miss her.

"Isn't it too early?" Ísabel didn't look up from her homework. "It's not five yet." Gracie realized the girl wanted things to remain as normal as possible—no early exits on her behalf—and she made a mental note to try to make that happen, although she didn't know how they could ignore the elephant in the room.

"I have vegetables for ratatouille for supper tonight, and you know how long that takes to cook," Gracie argued. "I'd like to get home a little early and get started. You can help."

They walked side by side over dark sidewalks toward home. Their breaths turned to little plumes of smoke in the frozen air, and Gracie thought about how gray-brown ugly Iowa could be in the winter. So far this year, they'd had little snow to brighten or soften the landscape, and it had all melted in last week's January thaw. Now, once again, the fields in the country and the yards in town were cold, frozen hardscapes with dry brown tuffs of stubble and dormant grass. Farmers prayed for a good dump of wet snow that would store up moisture for the crops they'd plant in the spring and hold the precious topsoil in place, keeping it from freeze-drying and blowing away.

Back when she was a child, kids prayed for snow so they

could build castles and tunnels and defensive walls for snowball fights. Gracie wondered if kids these days still did those things after school and on the weekends. She hadn't seen a snow castle or a good snowball battleground around town in years. Maybe it was a lack of snow. Or maybe today's kids all sat inside and played video games and watched reruns of prime-time TV shows.

Gracie caught herself holding the back door to her house for Ísabel, who looked at her askance. There was no way Ísabel could understand how differently pregnancy was viewed back when Gracie was carrying Janice. "Her condition" is what Gracie's mother would have called Ísabel's pregnancy, and back then it was still considered a sickness that required everyone to treat her like a fragile dove: carrying things for her, and, of course, opening doors, at least through the first trimester. (Somehow, it never occurred to Jens to relieve her of household duties like vacuuming and lifting laundry baskets, though.)

Now women played tennis and ran marathons while pregnant. It was acceptable to see pregnancy as an illness as far as qualifying for medical coverage was concerned, but it was no longer seen as a particularly fragile condition.

The pregnancy itself wasn't the biggest danger Ísabel faced. Far more dangerous was how it might stymie her education, stall her dreams, and give people like Gregory more reason to dismiss her. He would probably make her drop out of his speech program if she decided to carry the baby. The one extracurricular activity the young woman had that broadened her life would be taken away. Gracie felt herself getting mad just imagining it.

"You know, it's not the worst thing that can happen," Ísabel said. They stood at the kitchen counter a half hour later, cleaning and chopping vegetables for the casserole. "I don't want you to worry about me. Lots of girls have babies on their own. And they still go to college and have jobs and get married."

"How did you know that's what I was thinking about?" Gracie turned to her.

"I just figured. You've been really quiet tonight. None of your usual preaching about taking advantage of opportunities and making the most of my life. Your usual evening speeches."

"Am I that predictable?" Gracie chuckled. "I'm sorry. I would like to be more interesting than that."

"Well then, you might get out of town once in a while and do something other than order books." Ísabel eyes sparkled with tease. "Maybe you'd have something else to talk about."

"I'm surprised you're in such good spirits." Gracie put down the chef's knife and dropped handfuls of the vegetable pieces into a casserole dish. "Have you made some decisions?"

"Actually, I have," Ísabel said. "I really think I should get an abortion."

Gracie was shocked. She stood back and took in the calm countenance of the girl standing next to her. It couldn't be an easy decision, regardless how old you were, what your religion was, or how many parents or other family members you had around to help you get through it.

"Are you sure?" Gracie reached over, lifted the full casserole dish and turned to set it on the stove while the oven heated up.

"Of course not," said Ísabel. "I don't know if anyone ever is. But I don't want Greg—" She stopped.

Gracie dropped the casserole dish on the stove with a bang. She twirled to face Ísabel.

"What did you say?"

Ísabel looked horrified, as if she was just as shocked at what had just escaped from her mouth as Gracie was.

"Were you just going to say Gregory? He did this?" Gracie pointed at Ísabel's stomach. She grabbed the apron she had tied over her skirt and roughly wiped her hands to hide how much they were shaking.

"No!" Ísabel said. "No, I was just—" She stopped again. Her face betrayed her. Suddenly she looked afraid, as if she thought Gracie would hit her.

Gracie took a deep breath and kept her eyes locked on Ísabel's. So, was this why Gregory was so opposed to her living with Gracie? He didn't want Gracie to find out what was going on between him and the girl?

"I need you to tell me the truth." She lowered her voice and spoke slowly. "Sit down. I need you to tell me exactly what happened."

❧

An hour later, Gracie had most of the story—at least the part of the story that she could stomach, and a little bit that she couldn't.

"It wasn't his fault." Ísabel pleaded with her at one point. "I wanted it."

"You didn't know what you wanted!"

"No, I did! I wanted him to touch me. He is so mature, so powerful. I've slept with boys before, but it has always been just a joke. With Gregory . . . I just knew it would be different with him."

Gracie felt ill, but she held her tongue. It wouldn't help to register her disgust at what the girl was saying.

It had happened on their trip to Des Moines for the speech contest he had helped the teenagers enter. He had arranged for Ísabel to have her own room, while the other girls were paired up two to a room. At first, Ísabel thought nothing of it; the trip had an odd number of girls, and someone had to go solo.

After supper, they'd all gone to their rooms, and shortly after she'd changed into the T-shirt she wore to bed as a nightgown, he'd knocked on her door. She'd wondered if she should let him in, but then she'd succumbed to temptation or curiosity, and opened the door.

He first maintained he wanted to hear her recite her expository reading one more time, just to be sure she was ready, but then he had brushed her hair aside while she was reading it, and kissed her on the side of the neck. Gracie grimaced at the picture Ísabel's description painted.

"You don't have to give me any more details." Gracie cut her short. "I get the picture."

To her horror, Ísabel looked positively entranced, recalling that night and describing it. No doubt it brought to life those Victorian bodice-rippers she had devoured before Gracie steered her toward slightly better literature. Gracie knew that Ísabel wasn't reading those lowbrow books for information on sex; she already knew plenty about it. She was reading them for the romance, for the abandonment, for the soaring passages about fate and ecstasy and passion. Gregory was her Mr. Rochester, her Sir Lancelot, her Romeo.

And Ísabel believed she had wanted it? It would have been so much easier if Gregory had overpowered her and forced her to have sex against her will. Gracie recoiled in horror at the thought. Rape? Would rape have been a better thing for Ísabel? How could Gracie have such a thought?

Even if the girl had relented or had asked for it, it didn't absolve Gregory of culpability. It was still rape. Sex with an underage girl, however "consensual," was still rape. She wished Ísabel were angrier about what happened. She wished Ísabel hated Gregory for it the way Gracie did—hated Gregory, period. How could Ísabel see him as sexy? Gracie shivered.

But that was more about her than about Ísabel. She needed to let go of her own emotions if she was going to help Ísabel sort through hers.

Now, how was she going to do that?

~16~

Gracie could think of nothing else the next day at the library. Her mood swung from ear-reddening anger to sadness as she tried to think through Ísabel's options and come to terms with Gregory's culpability.

She had tried to convince Ísabel to go to the police and report the rape right away, first thing that morning. It was already late—probably at least five weeks after the fact—but it was better than waiting any longer.

Ísabel flatly refused to go.

"They don't need to know." Ísabel shook her head violently. She picked up her backpack, ready to walk to school. "I can take care of myself."

"But, Ísabel!" Gracie tried to keep her voice calm, but she was furious. "This is rape. In Iowa, this is a felony. That man can't get by with this!"

"I'm sixteen," Ísabel said. "Sixteen. It's not statutory rape unless I'm fifteen."

"How do you know that?"

"I looked it up. No one can charge him with rape but me, and I'm not going to."

"Ísabel, I can't believe you're defending him," Gracie said. "When you get older you'll understand this better. He's what we call a person in a position of power. That compromises your decision-making and puts you at a disadvantage."

"But I wanted to do it," Ísabel argued. "It's my own fault. And I could have asked him to wear a condom, but I didn't."

"Of course." Gracie put her hands on Ísabel's shoulders. "Of course you think that. But with teenage hormones and the compromising situation, you weren't in a good place to be making decisions, and he knew it. He took advantage of you. Don't you see that?"

Ísabel stood still in her coat with the backpack hanging off one shoulder and looked Gracie in the eye.

"I know you think I'm a child." Her voice barely rose above the hum of the refrigerator. "But I'm not. I'm going to school now. If you want to help, maybe you could figure out where we can go for my abortion."

Once Ísabel left, Gracie sat down at her kitchen table and took a few deep breaths. Maybe Ísabel was right, maybe wise before her years. Maybe going to the police would cause the girl more harm than good. She didn't want or need to be questioned by strangers about what happened—especially male strangers in uniform. How intimidating would that be? Only Ísabel could accuse Gregory of rape. If she didn't want to, no one could force her hand.

What stuck in Gracie's craw was the idea that Gregory was going to get by with this. No one would ever know what he did. He'd never be punished. Worse, he'd be free to continue to pursue more young women. There had to be something she could do to stop him, but what? How could she enforce any kind of sanction against him without Ísabel's cooperation? Unless Ísabel confronted him directly, he had no reason to worry about repercussions for his behavior.

Gracie locked her back door and walked to the library, where she quickly ran through her morning routine and sat down with her coffee. Bill-paying and other mundane library tasks were going to have to take a back seat while Gracie focused on what Ísabel needed. Certainly, she needed to see a doctor. Then, before she would help Ísabel get an abortion, Gracie needed to think about whether she *should* help her get an abortion. Wasn't Ísabel too young, too emotionally immature to make this decision? What if she regretted it later?

Gracie thought back to her own sixteenth year. What

would she have done? Abortion wasn't legal at that time in
Iowa. Yes, two girls in her class got pregnant before they
graduated from high school. Back then, their choices were
limited. They dropped out of school, had their babies, and got
married, just like people in generations before them had.

Marriage wasn't an option for Ísabel. Gregory was
married. Ísabel could have the baby, but she'd have to raise it
on her own, or she'd have to give it up for adoption. Thank
God Ísabel wasn't considering either of those. Either one
would postpone many of the things she wanted for Ísabel and
that Ísabel seemed to want for herself.

Gracie had never really considered the question of
whether she was for or against the right to an abortion, but
now she was glad Ísabel had it as a choice, and she was
surprised how sanguine she was with the girl's decision. But
was it right to let the girl make her own decision? Of course,
Gracie would talk to her about it, just the two of them, as soon
as things settled down, but Gracie was no counselor. Didn't
Ísabel need professional advice?

Maybe Terry could help. He certainly was thoughtful
enough, but his religious convictions and affiliations wouldn't
allow him to discuss abortion as an option, would they? Gracie
couldn't imagine Ísabel would agree to talk with a minister,
anyway.

Gracie looked up the phone number for a women's health
clinic in Iowa City. The clinic provided contraception and
abortion services, and Gracie asked the receptionist if they also
had counselors.

"Are you the one considering an abortion?" the
receptionist asked. She was obviously well-trained. Her phone
manners were impeccable.

"No, a young girl in my care wants to have an abortion,
and I think she should probably talk with someone before she
goes through with it. I'm worried she's too young to make this
decision on her own."

"If she's old enough to get pregnant, chances are she's old enough to decide on her own," the woman answered. "But, we do provide counselors who can talk with her, if you would like to bring her in. We call them client advocates. If the young woman still wants to have an abortion, she can start the process afterwards. Do you want to make an appointment?"

"I think I should let her do this herself," said Gracie. "I think she's the kind of girl who wants to be in control, or at least think she is."

"Very wise. And you know about Iowa's notification rule?"

The receptionist explained that Iowa required that women under the age of eighteen notify a parent at least forty-eight hours before an abortion.

"You mean she needs their permission?" Gracie asked.

"No, we just need proof that she has notified them."

"How does she prove it?"

"We can send the letter for her, and that is proof of notification. But we will have to do that two days before the appointment."

"Oh, okay," Gracie said. "Can you do that right away?"

"Yes."

"Then, I'll have her call you after school today."

That seemed easy enough. If the clinic sent the notification to Ísabel's address, her parents wouldn't even receive it until they got back from Mexico, and Gracie doubted that was going to happen before the abortion took place. And since Ísabel gathered the family mail from the post office box, she would be able to pull the letter before her parents even knew it was there—certified mail or not. In Johnson Station, the post office was a little more loose with the rules than they were in bigger cities.

But was that fair to Ísabel's parents? If Janice had faced the same predicament and was under the same requirement, how would Gracie have felt about someone helping her daughter get around the notification rule?

Well, Gracie wouldn't have abandoned her in the first place. She had harbored no disdain for Ísabel's parents, but now it seemed terribly irresponsible for Ísabel's mom to go back to Mexico without Ísabel. On the other hand, perhaps she'd been trying for months to get back to Johnson Station.

Gracie put that on her mental list of things to talk over with Ísabel: What did Ísabel think her mother would think about getting an abortion? Would the girl consider calling her mother to talk to her about it? It would make Gracie feel much better if she would.

Gracie wrote the Iowa City clinic's number down on a pad of paper for Ísabel. Then she called her own doctor in Des Moines and made an appointment for the next day. It was somewhat ironic. The bad thing about living in Johnson Station was that there was no doctor in town anymore. The last one had retired two months before. The good thing was there was no doctor in town, and therefore, there was no way anyone could see them coming and going, and wonder what was up.

Ísabel came into the library that afternoon a little later than usual, which caused Gracie an hour of peptic consternation. Nevertheless, once she walked in and turned the corner into Gracie's office, all was forgiven.

"How was school?"

"Okay. I stayed afterwards to meet with Greg—I mean, Mr. Thungaard." Ísabel's energy level was as low as Gracie had ever seen it.

"Alone? Ísabel, I don't want you meeting with—"

"No, not alone." Ísabel stopped her. "It was the group. Like all of us who went to Des Moines. He gave us our trophies, and we talked about the next competition."

"Seriously." Gracie felt the heat rising in her face. "You can't be considering doing another thing with him after what happened."

"No, I'm not." Ísabel sighed. "But I didn't know what to tell him. Anyway," she reached down inside her backpack and took out a six-inch gold-colored statue of a girl in front of a microphone. "Here, I think you should have this. For putting up with me."

"You won this?"

"Yup. First place. That is first place in my age thingee for expository reading. I didn't win the overall prize, but Greg—I mean Mr. Thungaard—said I might next year."

"But there's not going to be a next year."

"No." Ísabel said it flatly. She had a good reason to be disappointed, Gracie thought. Here, she had proven that she was good at something, and Gregory had taken it away from her. But she was afraid Ísabel didn't see it that way. The girl would either be blaming herself for what happened or blaming Gracie for making her drop out of the program, which, of course, was what she intended to do.

"How did you feel seeing him again, after all that's happened?" Gracie asked. It was a question she wasn't sure she wanted to get an answer to, but she was sure it was something that Ísabel wanted to talk about. Her sad face telegraphed how hard the afternoon had been.

"I got kind of angry." Ísabel looked distracted, as if she was playing the last hour of her day over again in her head. "You know, he didn't treat me any different than Linda or Karen. He wasn't really nice to me or anything. I started to get, you know, a little angry at him. I mean, like, they didn't sleep with him, did they?"

"Well, I don't know the answer to that, but I'm sure he wouldn't let on that you were special to him in front of the others, would he?"

"No, I guess not." Ísabel stopped to think, and Gracie

sensed that the girl was coming to the right conclusions about Gregory all on her own. "I'm pretty mad about it all."

"I don't blame you."

"I mean, I'm the one carrying this thing"—Ísabel waved at her stomach—"around and throwing up every morning, and he doesn't even know about it, and if he did, he probably wouldn't care."

"I don't know." Gracie could have agreed and used the opportunity to stress what a bad guy Gregory was, but it seemed like a better idea to let Ísabel decide that by herself. It would be more meaningful to her that way.

Gracie changed the subject. "Hey, it's about time to close up, but I wanted to share three things with you. First, I called a clinic in Iowa City today, and they want you to call and talk to them."

"About the abortion?" Ísabel looked up.

Jackie explained the process.

"Okay. But I don't want them to send my mom a letter."

"Well, I expected that. But if you give them your parents' address here, they'll never get it, right?"

"Oh, right!" Ísabel smiled for the first time that afternoon. "Good thinking."

"And when you call them, you can make an appointment for two days later to go into the clinic. They'll talk with you about your options and then you can proceed."

"They're not going to try to talk me out of it, are they?" Ísabel's smile disappeared.

"No, that's not how they operate. But I do think it's good for you to have someone to talk about this other than just me."

"Kinda letting you off the hook, like?"

Gracie couldn't help but smile at that. The girl was damn smart.

"You got me." Gracie nodded. "You know, I just want to make sure you're doing what's right for you, and I'm not your mother, so I think I'm limited in what I can do. I don't know you as well as she does. And she's not here, so, yes. Having someone else to talk to seems to make sense."

"Okay." Ísabel said. "As long as they don't preach at me or something."

"They won't." Gracie was glad she hadn't brought up the idea of talking with Terry, now. "And I made an appointment with my doctor in Des Moines for tomorrow. I think it would be wise to have a check-up."

Ísabel nodded and grimaced. "Do I have to put my feet in those stirrup things?"

"Probably."

"Yuck."

"The price you pay for being a grown-up, Ísabel."

Gracie called the school the next morning to tell the staff that Ísabel wouldn't be in class. Then she walked to the library and went through her morning routine. Karen was coming at noon to relieve her so she could take Ísabel to the doctor.

On the way to Des Moines, Ísabel was jittery. She fiddled with the air vents on her side of the car and changed the radio station six or seven times in the sixty-mile round trip. Gracie said nothing. Usually, such activity would have triggered a sharp rebuke, but she could imagine that Ísabel was struggling with enough emotional turmoil without her nagging.

Sitting at a stoplight on the way to the south end of the capital city, Gracie reached over and turned down the volume on the radio.

"I want to ask you something," she said. "Are you going to tell your mother about this?"

"Yes." Ísabel didn't take offense at the question; she sounded like she expected it.

"Now or later?"

"Later."

"Why not now?"

"She'll like try to talk me into coming down to Mexico and having the baby down there. She's Catholic, you know. She thinks abortion is like a sin. Like murder."

Gracie let that sink in for a moment. Where did that leave things?

"Perhaps you should tell her now, anyway."

"Why?" Ísabel turned sideways in the passenger seat, her knee bouncing nervously against the console between them.

"It just seems like something a mother should know."

"Yeah, well, there's a lot of things she should know, but she's not here, is she?"

"I'm sure it was a very hard decision she made to follow your father to Mexico." Gracie patted the girl's knee. "I once heard a very wise man say that if you look back at something you did in the past and see that you had other options, that doesn't mean you could have chosen any of the others."

"Huh?"

"Well, the point is, I wouldn't be too hard on her. You don't know what someone is going through unless you are wearing their skin."

"Why are you taking her side all of a sudden?" Ísabel sounded confused, even a little perturbed. "I thought you didn't like her."

"I don't know her, Ísabel. How could I not like her? I just want to be sure you've thought this through."

"Yeah, I have. I will tell her afterwards, if she ever comes back. If she doesn't, then I guess she'll just be in the dark."

Once they checked in at the doctor's reception desk, Gracie asked Ísabel if she wanted her to come into the exam room with her. "There will be a nurse in there with you, but if you want me there, I'll—"

"No!" Ísabel shook her head. "No, I'll be too embarrassed. Two people seeing my vagina in broad daylight is bad enough."

Gracie had to smile. That was true. Perhaps this was the girl's first time up in the cold, metal stirrups of a gynecologist's office, but she already had a clear concept on the humiliation that was coming. Gracie was also certain she'd never said the word "vagina" aloud when she was sixteen. She probably didn't even know how to pronounce it.

"Fine, I'll just wait here."

Two days later, allowing for the forty-eight hours the clinic needed to notify her parents, Gracie drove Ísabel the other direction to Iowa City. This time, she took the interstate instead of the old highway, and Ísabel, thanks to the medicine the doctor in Des Moines had given her for morning sickness, looked like she was going to sleep most of the way.

Gracie grasped the steering wheel tightly, seething over the conversation she'd had with the school principal that morning. She had called early to the school office to let them know Ísabel wasn't coming to school; she was sick, Gracie had said. Five minutes later, the principal, Kyle Jennings, called her back.

"Why are you calling us about Ísabel? Where is her mother?" He had a way of making even short sentences sound officious, as if adults as well as students needed to acknowledge his authority.

Gracie wondered just how many of the nation's graduates with education degrees from decent colleges would have wanted his job, running a budget-strapped, rural school system with an enrollment of only two hundred students. Not one of Johnson Station's high school graduates had garnered attention for outstanding academic or athletic achievement over the past thirty years. If he ever left, you could probably count the applicants for his job on one hand and not need the thumb or first three fingers, she concluded. No wonder he exhibited all the classic traits of an insecurity complex.

"Her mother and father are in Mexico," Gracie said. "You remember that raid at the poultry factory last fall?"

"Yes, I knew her father was deported. But her mother wasn't, was she?"

"No, but she went down with him."

"So, why is Ísabel with you?"

"I asked her to stay with me so she wouldn't be alone until her mother got back. Apparently, the INS has no interest in the matter since she is a U.S. citizen."

"But shouldn't you have informed the proper authorities? Shouldn't the state's social services agency decide where she goes?"

"I have a letter from her mother asking me to be her guardian in her absence," Gracie said. It was a lie—another white lie to add to the many she was finding herself telling for Ísabel's sake. Gracie jotted a note on a notepad she kept by the phone: "Get letter from I's mom."

"Is it notarized? Signed by an attorney?"

"No, it is just an informal arrangement."

"Gracie. A note is what you need when your kid is sick and misses school. It's not sufficient for taking custody of a minor child."

"Well, it's not permanent," Gracie countered. "Her mother will be back any day."

"No matter. I am going to bring this up at the school board meeting tonight," the principal said. "In the meantime, I am going to call social services. This isn't right. A girl Ísabel's age should not be deciding on her own where she stays and with who."

Whom! He was so damn officious, and yet he didn't even know simple grammar.

"I think she's probably better off staying in school here in Johnson Station," Gracie argued. "She has friends, and she likes her teachers. Who knows where social services might send her?"

"I'm going to talk with the board, anyway." Gracie was relieved; that sounded like a retreat, like he wouldn't call social services right away. That would give her time to figure out how to keep Ísabel from being sent to foster care and away from her teachers and friends. And away from Gracie.

But then she remembered: Gregory was on the school board, too. In the past year, he had weaseled his way into nearly every institution in town: the library board, the school board, and the church deacons. Apparently, given the town council vote on the food bank, he had managed to engineer some kind of pull there, too. It looked like a grand political strategy to build as much credibility as possible before his run for county supervisor, then state senator, and then governor.

Gregory already knew that Ísabel was staying with her, and he had been clear in his negative opinion of the arrangement. Now he would have an official reason to interfere.

Still, Gracie wondered, why was this a matter for the school board to discuss? It wouldn't have been in any bigger city's school, or in any district big enough to have school board elections where people actually ran for office against other people instead of simply putting their name on the ballot, knowing there'd be no competition. Oh, the pain in the ass living in a small town was getting to be! Everything was everyone else's business, and there was no escaping the big bully in town.

She didn't want to worry Ísabel about it; the poor girl had enough on her mind. She didn't mention it to Ísabel that morning, but Gracie missed having Richard around. He was due back in town from his convention that night, and she couldn't wait to talk to him about all that had happened. He might have some advice about how to protect Ísabel from social services.

By the time Gracie located the one-story building that housed the women's clinic in Iowa City, her stomach was roiling with anxiety. Out in front of the building, a gaggle of abortion protestors sat alongside the public sidewalk. As

Gracie pulled past them to the parking lot behind the building, they stood up, picked up their placards, and started yelling after her car. Gracie was glad Ísabel slept through that. The parking lot and the back entrance were on private property where the protesters couldn't come.

"We're here," She gently shook Ísabel awake. "Are you ready?"

Ísabel slowly sat up. She threw Gracie a wan smile. "As much as I will ever be."

"Now, you know a counsel— I mean, a patient advocate will talk with you first. At any time you change your mind, just let them know."

"I'm not going to change my mind," Ísabel said. "Haven't we already been over this?"

"Okay, then. Grab your coat and let's go."

The reception room looked like the friendly waiting rooms Gracie had visited in mammography clinics: comfortable chairs, bright-green potted plants, and an admissions desk discreetly screened off from the street. Gracie stayed beside Ísabel as she checked in, but she let the girl talk for herself. This was so much more than a learning experience, of course, but Gracie figured the more Ísabel took responsibility and managed things herself, the more she would own the outcome.

Only when the receptionist asked how she was going to cover the cost of the procedure did Gracie step up.

"We will pay with a credit card," Gracie said.

"Would you like to apply for assistance? We have a sliding scale—"

"No. No need. We are happy to cover the entire amount."

Ísabel smiled at Gracie. She looked relieved, and Gracie realized the girl might have been wondering herself how she was going to pay. They hadn't discussed that at all.

~17~

Ísabel took the first of the abortion drugs, called Mifeprex, right away. She would take the second medication, misoprostal, two days later, and that would expel the fetus. Gracie had done her research and knew that, in rare cases, the first medicine alone could induce the abortion.

"I think it would be best if you stay home until the entire process is over," she told Ísabel that night when they got back from Iowa City.

"Yeah, I know," Ísabel said. "That's what Diana told me." Diana was a nurse and so-called advocate who spoke with Ísabel before she met with a doctor at the clinic, and Gracie was grateful the woman had not only been thorough in explaining the procedure, but Ísabel had liked her well enough to refer to her by her first name and often. It relieved Gracie of the burden of being Ísabel's only adult confidante.

Gracie had another reason to keep Ísabel home and out of the public eye: the school board had talked about Ísabel living with Gracie, and Gracie knew that everyone in town would not only know about it, but that some people would have an opinion on the matter that they'd be careless enough to share with the girl herself.

Gracie fixed a quick casserole supper for the two of them, and then left for Des Moines to pick Richard up at the airport.

"Call me if you feel sick or for any other reason," Gracie said. "I'll hook up the Bluetooth so I can answer the phone while I'm driving."

"I'll be fine," Ísabel said. "I am going to go to bed, though. I'm really tired."

❧

When Gracie's phone rang on the way to the airport, it wasn't Ísabel. It was Kyle Jennings.

"We discussed the matter of the minor child who is staying with you at the board meeting last night." He sounded as officious as ever. "The board has instructed me to contact social services. I am calling you to give you notice that I will do that tomorrow. I would expect that you will hear from them forthwith."

"Forthwith?" Where the hell had he come up with that word? Was he trying to impress her? She had been married to a lawyer and judge who, over thirty years, had never felt the need to use such arcane language. Neither had Richard. Oh, how big some fish got when they swam around in tiny ponds!

"Ísabel is safe, happy, and thriving. Isn't that what matters?" said Gracie. "If anything happens to take her away from the only community she's ever known, I hope you realize that is going to be on your shoulders."

"And if anything happens to her while she's in your custody, it will be on yours."

Oh, like impregnation by one of your school board members? She thought it, but she didn't say it. Could anyone think that was more her fault than Gregory's?

Richard was waiting at the arrivals curb when Gracie pulled up. She didn't remember ever being so happy to see someone in her entire life.

"Did you sleep on the plane?" she asked him as he dropped into the passenger seat.

"Yes, why?"

"Do you mind driving? I have so much to tell you, and I don't want to distract myself while I drive."

They switched seats, and Richard drove out of town and back onto the highway to Johnson Station.

"Why didn't you tell me all of this on the phone?" he

asked once she'd finished a long description of the past few days. Since he left a week before, she hadn't told him anything about the pregnancy, the abortion clinic, or the school board's discussion of Ísabel's residence. "That's an awful lot for the two of you to deal with on your own."

"We're okay." Gracie hoped she was right. "I wished many times you were here, but we got through it—so far, anyway—on our own. That is one strong girl, I'll tell you."

"But Gregory? That's despicable! I can't imagine how angry you must be. First, he pretends to be a saint, then tells everyone else how to live, and it turns out he's a pervert and a pedophile!"

"I couldn't have said it better." Gracie sighed deeply. It was a huge relief to share all this with Richard and not be carrying it all on her shoulders alone. She had told no one else. She'd missed the last two coffee klatches. She didn't want to tell Jackie about any of this, and Marcia hadn't come back from Iowa City yet.

"Can you stay home tomorrow with her?" Gracie asked. "I really need to get back to the library, but I don't want her to be alone. There can be complications from these drugs."

"Absolutely," Richard said. "I have nothing I need to do. And I'm tired, anyway. Maybe she and I can rent some movies on Netflix and eat popcorn all day."

Gracie smiled and looked out at the road ahead, illuminated by the headlights. She was a very lucky woman. Most widows in Johnson Station were doomed to a life alone, or to settling for a mediocre companion with whom they shared nothing but a small-town provenance. She and Richard had known each other for thirty years; there was a trust and a comfort in their relationship with more depth than what she had ever experienced with Jens.

"What do you think we can do about the school board?" she asked.

"They have no jurisdiction over the matter. I think all we

have to worry about is the state social services folks. But I don't think this will hit them as an emergency. We'll have some time to figure it out. Did you ask Ísabel to get that letter from her mother?"

"No, I haven't told her about it yet. I didn't want her to have to deal with it until she's done with this procedure."

"Could you call her mom?"

"I think that would make her mother suspicious, like I was trying to take her daughter away from her. I think Ísabel has to do it herself. And her mom doesn't speak much English."

"Well, I don't think we should wait two days," Richard said. "If the state calls, it would be best if we could hold them off with that letter, at least temporarily."

"I'll talk to Ísabel about it tomorrow"

&

Gracie told Ísabel that Richard knew she was pregnant before she left for the library.

"I told him on the way home last night. Is it okay if he stays home with you today?"

"Sure!" Ísabel said, a little more enthusiastically than Gracie had expected. The two of them had built a nice father-daughter friendship over the past couple of months, and now Gracie realized the girl had also missed him while he was gone the past week.

"If you need anything, anything at all, and if Richard can't help, call me. I'm not going to be that busy. Most of the library users are still in Phoenix, so it will be quiet."

It wasn't quite as quiet as Gracie had expected. It was an in-service day at the elementary school that day, and a couple of the larger day-care centers brought a gaggle of kids each to the library to fill a couple of hours of time. The number of their charges bloated by the mid-week break, the day-care owners, and their largely Hispanic staff members had their hands full.

The staff brought their own kids, too. It was the first time in the months since the poultry plant closed that any of the Spanish-speaking children Gracie had bought books for had been in the library, and she happily helped them check out books on the day-care owners' library cards.

The day raced by in a din of cacophony and a blur of zig-zagging children. Gracie wished a few more days a month were like that, if only a few. She thought about proposing a new program to the board—perhaps a Spanish-English reading hour once a week for the kids after school Perhaps Ísabel would be willing to help with that.

Isn't that another way that libraries made communities strong? she thought as she walked home that evening. By turning kids onto books early, especially those who didn't have many books in their homes?

As he had proposed, Richard and Ísabel spent nearly eight hours that day watching movies. They had bounced back and forth between old classics and in-their-lifetime favorites: *It Happened One Night*, *Bull Durham*, *Sunset Boulevard*, and *Moonstruck*.

To Gracie's surprise, they also fixed supper—a comforting pot roast they made in the Crock-Pot. They even baked powder-milk biscuits. It had been a long time since Gracie came home to a meal that she didn't fix herself. She remembered only once or twice that Jens had stayed home for some reason and made the only meal he could cook: spaghetti with meat sauce from a jar.

Gracie was even more shocked when the smell of supper and the proud faces of its aproned cooks brought tears to her eyes. Wasn't she a little old and jaded for such sentimentality?

Ísabel socked her lightly on the arm. "I figured you for a sort of tough-love kind of gal." Ísabel mimicked the voice and vernacular of the movie classics they'd just finished watching.

"Aw, Gracie." Richard pulled her into his arms. "Don't get all mushy on us. We're just thankful for everything you do for us. Right, Ísabel?"

"Yup." Ísabel looked away. She seemed a little embarrassed at Richard's show of emotion. It was tough being a teenager, inching along an emotional high wire, doubting her own strengths and building defenses against her weaknesses. Ísabel could watch mushy movie scenes one after another, distant as they were from reality, but up close and personal, they were a little raw for the girl's sensibilities, especially now.

Two of Ísabel's teachers had sent online homework assignments for her to complete when she "felt well enough," and as soon as she was finished eating, Gracie suggested she head up to her room and do what she could before falling asleep.

"Richard and I will do the dishes tonight," Gracie said.

As soon as she heard Ísabel's bedroom door close upstairs, Gracie whispered to Richard, "The Department of Human Services called today. They wanted to know what the situation was."

"Wow, that was quick," Richard said. "What did you tell them?"

"Basically, that Ísabel's parents were in Mexico and that they asked if we would take care of Ísabel while they were gone."

"That's it?"

"Well, they asked a lot more questions, but I begged off. I told them I was busy at my job and perhaps we could set up a meeting next week sometime. Maybe they could come to the house and see where Ísabel and I are living. I figured that they just want to know that things are nice for her here."

"And they were okay with that?"

"Well, at first, no. She read me this legalese about how Child Emergency Services was required to assign so-called 'targeted' children to either approved foster families, relatives, or some kind of juvenile shelter. I argued that taking Ísabel out of her school and away from her friends, even temporarily, seemed like unnecessary interference with her life."

"Good. I like where you went with that."

"Yes, but then the social worker told me that not only had Kyle Jennings called with concerns about Ísabel's welfare, but apparently, some other man had made an anonymous call to report that Ísabel was being kept in what he called an 'unhealthy environment' with two unmarried adults."

"Gregory?"

"That would be my guess." ·

"That guy is unbelievable."

"We don't know it was him, but I can't imagine who else it would be."

"Well, the state can't take a girl from a parent and put her in foster care without a judge ordering it," Richard said. "My guess is that we're probably going to be harassed a bit with this, but I don't think they'll actually make Ísabel leave."

"Then why would Gregory do this?"

"Probably less to raise public suspicion of you and more to grandstand and advance his political agenda," Richard stood up and started gathering dishes and rinsing them off in the sink. "He's gaining some political chips with the 'family first' and anti-immigration folks. I wouldn't doubt if he makes some kind of public show of the whole thing. Maybe at your next board meeting."

"But nobody comes to our board meetings."

"Right. But what if he asks people to come? What if he gets a bunch of his cronies to show up and make a fuss?"

"Oh, shit! I guess he could." She stayed seated at the table and watched Richard put the dishes in the dishwasher. She was exhausted from the past few days of travel to Des Moines and Iowa City.

"Do you think you should quit coming over here?" Gracie asked.

"I think that's giving in to a narrow definition of 'family' and an anachronistic idea of morality," Richard said. "But I know how much it means to you to be able to take care of Ísabel right now. If you think that's best, I will be glad to sleep at home until this is over."

"God, just when I need you the most!" Gracie felt frustrated. "And just when Ísabel needs you most!" She buried her head in her hands and sighed. She felt Richard's hand on her shoulder.

What right did Gregory have to butt into her life like this? Or Ísabel's? Especially Ísabel's, given what damage he'd already done.

☙

The night Ísabel took the second medication, misoprostol, Gracie couldn't sleep. She waited, wide awake, for the girl to get up and head for the bathroom.

Richard had come over for supper with them and then gone home. Gracie thought it would be easier for Ísabel to get through the induced miscarriage if she didn't have to think about Richard being nearby. Yes, he and Ísabel were friends, but there were some things girls didn't want to share with men, even those who were like fathers to them.

Before she went to bed, Gracie knocked on Ísabel's bedroom door and asked to come in.

"You okay?" she asked.

"Yeah." Ísabel was lying on top of her covers, looking at the ceiling. "Just a little nervous. Do you think it's going to hurt a lot?"

Gracie wondered whether it would be better to calm the girl's nerves with assurances that it wouldn't be bad, or prepare her for the worst. She sat down on the bed by Ísabel's side.

"I think it's going to hurt," Gracie said. "You read the brochures that came with the medicine. They said severe cramping, maybe some nausea. I think it will be like a very bad period. The good thing is it shouldn't last as long. Maybe a few hours at the most."

Ísabel nodded, and kept her eyes on the ceiling. Gracie watched as she blinked little rivers of tears down the sides of her face.

"I'm so sorry you are going through this," she whispered.

Ísabel nodded again and swallowed hard. She grimaced as if trying to stop the tears from coming. Gracie reached for her hand, and Ísabel let her hold it. They said nothing for a couple of minutes.

"I'm a little mad right now," Ísabel whispered harshly, breaking the silence. "Why did I let him do this to me? Why didn't he insist on using a condom? He's the adult, isn't he? And why isn't he the one waiting to dump blood all over the toilet?"

"I think those are good questions." Gracie stopped there. She didn't want to take advantage of the pain Ísabel was going to go through to gang up on Gregory. She would wait until it was all over to discuss his behavior with Ísabel, including his attempts to get child welfare to interfere with their lives. For now, she needed to be comforting and helpful, not preachy or manipulative.

Ísabel sniffed. Gracie reached for a tissue and handed it to her.

"I'm going to let you sleep." She squeezed Ísabel's hand and standing up. "If you need me for anything, let me know. This should be over soon."

It was a little after midnight when the waiting ended and the sickness started. Gracie heard the hallway floor creak as Ísabel slipped past her room to the bathroom and closed the door. If she'd wanted help, Gracie thought, she wouldn't have tried to sneak by.

Ísabel made five or six trips to the toilet that night, and Gracie was sure neither of them got much sleep. Finally, about seven in the morning, the bathroom visits stopped, and Gracie dozed off. She woke with a start at eight and jumped out of bed.

"Are you okay?" she asked quietly at Ísabel's closed door. There was no answer, and Gracie opened the door quietly and peeked into the sun-streaked bedroom. Ísabel was sprawled facedown diagonally across her bed, one arm stretched out above her head and the other under her abdomen. She was snoring lightly. Gracie tiptoed across the room and put her hand on the girl's forehead. Infection wasn't unheard of following nonsurgical abortions, but so far, Ísabel's temperature seemed fine.

Gracie backed out of the room and closed the door.

Luckily for Ísabel, it was over in just a matter of hours. Of course, there could be complications from medically induced miscarriages. Gracie couldn't help but wonder what Gregory would have thought about it all. What if she'd suffered one of the possible nasty side effects, like hemorrhaging or infection? Would he have considered them "the wages of sin," even though Ísabel had gotten him out of a nasty jam produced by his own perdition?

But he wouldn't know. And that wasn't fair. Why should he be going his merry way with no concerns about or even awareness of the consequences of his actions?

Gracie asked Karen to cover for her at the library that morning until she was sure that Ísabel was going to be okay. When the girl finally came downstairs and shuffled into the kitchen, Gracie knew she would be fine—physically, anyway. Who knew what emotional trauma might hit Ísabel in the hormone-shifting weeks ahead? Guilt? Regret? Postpartum depression was as much chemical as anything, and a baby didn't have to be carried to term for the reactions to the sudden drop in estrogen and progestin to wreak its havoc.

"Breakfast?" Gracie asked.

"Coffee?" Ísabel asked. "Can I have some coffee? And toast?"

The fact that Ísabel could even think about eating was a huge relief, and Gracie jumped up in her best Edith Bunker imitation, bustling around to fulfill Ísabel's wishes.

"Do you want to talk about it?" She put a cup of coffee and the milk carton down in front of Ísabel.

Ísabel shook her head. Gracie saw both exhaustion and sadness in her haggard face. She wasn't going to pry into the girl's feelings unless Ísabel wanted her to and was ready for it.

"You feel okay?"

Ísabel barely nodded as she leaned down to her coffee cup and sipped noisily. "I'm okay."

"Still bleeding?"

Ísabel nodded again. "But it's not bad."

The toast popped up, and Gracie turned to butter it.

"Thanks for helping me through this." Ísabel sounded ten years older than she had two weeks before. Gracie worried that the pregnancy and abortion had stolen a measure of youth, some innocence from the girl that she'd never be able to recover.

Perhaps that had always been the case, Gracie mused. From the beginning of humanity, girls turned into women overnight, often not by their choice but by the actions of predatory males wielding strength and power.

She set the toast on the table and sat across from Ísabel, trying not to stare at her. It didn't seem the time for small talk, but neither did it seem the time for a heavy discussion.

"I saved some," Ísabel whispered.

"You what?" Gracie thought she heard what Ísabel said, but she was too surprised to believe it.

Ísabel bit into a piece of toast and calmly met Gracie's wide eyes. "I saved some of the tissue."

Gracie felt the blood sink from her head. She imagined for the first time what Ísabel had seen rush from her body into the toilet. She worried she would faint. She breathed deeply and closed her eyes until the sensation passed.

When she opened her eyes, Ísabel was looking at her. The girl chewed slowly and swallowed. She took another sip of coffee.

"Why?" Gracie asked weakly.

"Paternity."

"What do you mean, paternity?"

"Last night," Ísabel started, and then she paused to sip more coffee.

The pace of her delivery wasn't just from exhaustion; it was a bit of a performance. Clearly the girl had thought about this conversation for a long time—probably all night.

"Last night, I realized how angry I am about what happened, and I started to get really angry when I sat on that toilet and felt like my insides were falling out." She paused again to take another bite of her toast.

"I decided that you were right about one thing: We can't let this happen to anyone else. No other girls in school. At least not because of him."

"So, what do you plan to do?"

"I will keep it in the freezer. And I will talk to him and let him know that I kept it. And with your help, I'll figure out what he will have to do to keep me from taking it to the police."

"Oh." Gracie started recovering her composure, but now she was surprised—almost frightened—by the calm, strategic direction of Ísabel's mind. Perhaps she was far more capable of handling Gregory than Gracie was—at least at this end of the ordeal.

"I figure that he won't even know whether I really kept his DNA or not, but that's not important." Ísabel's face brightened with satisfaction in her own thinking. "What's important is that he thinks I did."

"I get it."

"So, what do you think our demands should be?"

"Well." Gracie put up her hands to ask for a moment to think. "I believe we should prohibit him from working with students ever again. I believe we should let him know that if we find out he had sex with any other girl, we will drag out the evidence and help convict him of a pattern of such behavior."

Gracie was surprised at how quickly she was able to list possible demands. She had thought about them more than she realized.

"And, we should demand that he stop trying to interfere with our living arrangement."

Ísabel stopped chewing and looked at Gracie, confused.

"What do you mean, *interfere?*" she asked.

"Well, I didn't want to tell you about this until you were through your ordeal—"

"Abortion, you mean."

"Yes, abortion." Gracie began to think Ísabel had aged twenty years, not ten, in the past two weeks. "Anyway, I didn't want to tell you, but he has been trying to get child welfare involved in where you live."

"Oh, that ass!" Ísabel threw the rest of her toast back on her plate and sat back. Her tired expression turned angry.

"Yesterday, the state called me," Gracie continued, "and I put them off. But apparently, the school board also discussed the fact your mother is gone and that you are staying with me. The principal doesn't think our arrangement is appropriate."

"Why would he care?"

"I don't know, but you know Gregory is on the school board."

"Oh, I see." Ísabel's expression went from angry to worried. She glanced around the kitchen as if taking in the comfortable surroundings. "But what's wrong with me staying here?" A hint of insecurity appropriate to Ísabel's age crept back into her voice.

"Nothing," Gracie said. "Richard said the state can't put you in foster care without a judge's order, and he doesn't think the state will try to get one. Someone from social services is coming to visit next week, and I think once they see us here, they'll realize their time is better spent elsewhere."

"This is just unbelievable," Ísabel said. "Just fucking unbelievable."

"Ísabel!" Gracie had never heard her use that word before. Less offensive words like *damn* and *hell* and *shit*, sure. But never the *f*-word. "Watch your language!"

"Hey!" Ísabel slapped her palms down on the table, making Gracie jump. "If I'm old enough to get pregnant and then messed with by the man who did it, and go through what I went through last night, then I think you ought to let me say 'fuck' once in a while."

Gracie couldn't help it: she smiled. Slowly, Ísabel smiled back. They locked eyes for a moment, and then Ísabel stood up, walked around the table, and wrapped her arms around Gracie's shoulders from the back. Gracie closed her eyes to savor the gesture, and they stayed still for a long minute.

~18~

Gracie went back to work after Richard arrived to stay with Ísabel. They were planning another movie day, and Gracie grimaced in sympathy for Richard. Ísabel, not surprisingly, was in the mood for some sappy emotional fare: *Steel Magnolias* and *The Fisher King*.

Richard gently laid his arm across the girl's shoulders. "Okay, but only if you promise you won't tell anyone if I cry."

"It'll be our secret." Ísabel looked up at him with a big smile.

An hour later, Gracie was paying bills at her desk in the library when the phone rang.

"Gracie?" he asked. "Gregory here."

Immediately Gracie's heart rate took off. She wasn't prepared for his call. Somehow, she had let herself believe she wouldn't have to talk to or face Gregory until the next board meeting at the end of the month, unless she and Ísabel initiated their meeting with him before then. That left her unprepared for what she suddenly realized was a huge challenge: not letting on that she knew anything about his night with Ísabel in Des Moines, and not hinting at the consequences. If she and Ísabel were going to make the most of their meeting with him to discuss their demands, they needed the element of surprise.

"Gracie?"

"Yes. Sorry. I was in the middle of something. You surprised me." She recovered enough to answer.

"Someone told me you bought that book." His voice was a note or two lower than usual, and it sounded like he was trying to ooze authority. "Did you?"

She didn't hesitate with her answer. "No, I bought three copies of that book. At the rate our library consumers are asking for it, it will still take three years to satisfy demand with that many."

Gregory's exaggerated sigh whistled in her ear.

"I simply can't believe this, Gracie!" he yelled. "We talked about this at the last meeting and I thought I made it perfectly clear I didn't want you ordering any more books until we set our new policy."

"But, we tabled that discussion when Caitlin said she thought it was inappropriate given the charter."

"I don't give a shit what the charter says!" Gregory sounded furious. "And Caitlin is leaving the board."

"Why?"

"Because I asked her to."

"Well, who died and made you king?" Gracie was instantly embarrassed for the childish comeback. She was going to have to do better than that if she was going to manage Gregory going forward. But her point was valid. The mayor, not the board chair, was responsible for appointing members to the library board.

"Don't trifle with me, Gracie. We need to establish some rules and some respect, both. As the library board, we are responsible for your appointment, and I think you should keep that in mind when you are tempted to talk to me like that."

Gracie hadn't been scolded since she was a teenager. It took her a couple of seconds to regroup and regain some poise.

She took a deep breath and responded. "I am only saying that so far, the board has not adopted any policy regarding the purchase of books, my purchase of *The Intern's Travels* was not voted on at the last meeting, and I thought the mayor appointed board members, not the chairman. Certainly, those facts don't point to a lack of respect."

Gregory's silence indicated he was at a loss for how to

correct her "facts." Finally, he lowered his voice another notch. "Is it true that you are living with a man you are not married to?"

The low blow was Gracie's second surprise. She had an impulse to hang up, but she squeezed the receiver and gritted her teeth. She wouldn't give him the satisfaction of negating her credibility with innuendo and not being called on it.

"What does that have to do with my operation of the library?"

"We—the board, that is—are concerned about certain standards of behavior in our community, and as the librarian who interacts with both children and adults in this town, we are concerned that your personal behavior befit your position."

"This is not *The Music Man*." Gracie quoted Ísabel. "This is not River City and I'm not Marian, the librarian. I don't think my personal behavior has anything to do with how well I dust these shelves, pay the bills, keep records of books coming in and out, and answer the public's reference questions."

"But it appears to affect what books you choose to buy for our shelves," Gregory said.

"No, I buy books based on what people in the community ask for, not based on what I want to read."

"Furthermore," Gregory continued, as if he hadn't heard what she said, "the school board is very concerned about Ísabel living in that situation."

"What situation?"

"With you and an unmarried man."

"Would you prefer he were married?" Gracie didn't care that it was a bad joke. "What if he were married to someone else? Would that be better?"

"Don't be silly, Gracie!" Gregory now sounded like he was losing his temper. "I am not going to let this slide."

"What slide?" As he lost his temper, Gracie started to feel

like she was gaining the upper hand. The less emotional she was, the more he was losing his composure.

"Your insubordination and keeping that girl."

"I think you should rethink both, Gregory," she said, more calmly than before. "According to our charter, what I have done isn't even close to insubordination, and 'keeping that girl' has nothing to do with my job. Furthermore, as you conflate your duties on the library board and on the school board, I think it might start to look to some people like you are creating some kind of a little fiefdom here. People in small towns don't like that sort of thing. It violates their sense of democracy."

"My service to this community takes many forms." Gregory was now hissing his words. Clearly, she had tripped some emotional trigger by not kowtowing to him. He probably wasn't used to that. For the past few months, his wealth and the body language he used to control situations had granted him near impunity. Whatever he wanted, he got. People were nearly genuflecting in his presence, intimidated by his burgeoning political clout.

Well, when it came to ceding control, he hadn't seen anything yet. Just wait until Ísabel confronted him with her demands.

"Yes, I know," Gracie said. "And I'm sure you are far from done in finding other ways to, as you say, serve the community. But until the board changes the charter or votes on a purchasing policy, which I believe was the subject of your call, I don't see that the impressive power you have amassed so far really matters."

"You bi—" Gregory caught himself.

Gracie imagined him, red-faced, unable to form a civil sentence, and smiled. She had obviously pushed him over the edge. She was a bit surprised at how easy it was to make him lose control. Surprise number three. He was going to have a tough time in big-time politics if he was unnerved so easily.

Without another word, Gracie replaced the receiver. Then, it occurred to her that his quick temper also meant she and Ísabel had to be careful when they confronted him with Ísabel's demands. The last thing she wanted was for Ísabel to have to face a nasty, raging lunatic.

The girl had already been scarred once by Gregory's lack of self-control.

⟁

As the afternoon slowly labored toward the end of her shift, Gracie took more than her usual number of calls from residents looking for a bit of information, an answer to a trivia question, a phone number for a local business. It was part of her job to look things up, regardless of what reason the caller had to ask.

Anything she could find in a reference book, like an almanac, dictionary, encyclopedia, phone book, or the *New York Public Library Desk Reference*, was no problem. However, more recent trivia, like popular songs and musicians or recent world events, required Gracie to get online. With her ploddingly slow connection, each of those requests could eat up fifteen or twenty minutes of her time.

If Gregory really cared about improving the library's service, he could get on board with allowing her to get higher-speed internet service. But so far, he had been the biggest opponent to adding cable or satellite internet to her budget. It went beyond his desire to reduce the budget, which was an expected part of his anti-tax philosophy. Gracie suspected he didn't want people to have access to new information, whether it was lyrics to popular songs or news of the Middle Eastern conflicts. Information was power, and Gracie wondered if it bothered him to have power spread so indiscriminately.

On her walk home that afternoon, Gracie replayed her conversation with Gregory over in her mind. Was she remembering it right? Could he really lose his cool that easily? If so, was it safe for Ísabel to confront him with her demands?

Maybe what really bothered him about Ísabel living with her was that it might limit his opportunities to continue to have sex with the girl. Could he really be so shallow? Was he really such a sanctimonious ass?

A few months before, if someone had told her there were politicians who could preach and behave in such an egregiously contradictory fashion, she would have pooh-poohed the idea. Since then, thanks to the heated environment of the presidential election campaigns and the rise of snoopy social-media sites, examples of exactly that kind of hypocritical behavior had started to appear almost commonplace. Gay-bashers who solicited same-sex encounters. Environmentalists who stole water in the midst of droughts. Born-again evangelists who arranged abortions for their mistresses in foreign countries. Why should she believe it couldn't happen at home in Johnson Station? Little political tyrants like Gregory weren't immune to the same bankrupt ethical compass as the big tyrants.

When she got home, Richard was sticking a couple of big frozen pizzas in the oven, and Ísabel was upstairs, he said, either doing her homework or taking a nap.

"How is she?" Gracie asked after reciprocating Richard's warm kiss.

"Fine. She bawled like a baby at *Steel Magnolias*."

"Probably good for her. Released some emotional tension."

"So did I," Richard said sheepishly. Gracie figured he knew that Ísabel would tell on him if he didn't admit it up front.

"You're such a softy!"

She threw her coat onto the coat rack in the mudroom and slipped off her Sorels. Then she made a beeline for the wine cabinet and pulled out a deep red Syrah.

"Since you're cooking, I'll open the wine," she said. "And if you want some, I'll open some more."

"You planning on drinking the whole bottle yourself?"

"I just might." Gracie sat down at the kitchen table with a glass and the bottle. "You wouldn't believe the conversation I had with Gregory today."

Richard opened five cupboards until he found a wineglass, sat down, helped himself to a pour, and listened.

"Unbelievable," he responded when she was finished. "Fucking unbelievable."

"Hey, so that's where Ísabel is learning to use that word."

"Oh, trust me, she didn't learn it from me." He pointed up at Ísabel's room. "Just because you love her, don't underestimate her worldliness."

"Yeah, I know," Gracie said. "She wasn't a virgin before Gregory got to her. But at times she seems so vulnerable, so childlike. I think it's hard being a kid these days; so much media, so much information—long before they're really emotionally ready to absorb it."

"Or before we are." Richard gave her a crooked, sorrowful smile.

"Right."

"Ísabel told me you have a plan," Richard said. "A plan to confront Gregory."

"Oh, she shared that with you?"

"Yes. But be careful, Gracie. Be sure you know exactly what you're asking from him, and don't step over any boundaries. I mean don't threaten to tell his wife or bring it up at a board meeting. Keep it classy, or it'll come crashing down on you and Ísabel."

"Hard to keep things classy when you're talking about rape, abortion, and perversion, isn't it?"

Richard nodded. He'd said his piece, she gathered, and she'd take his advice. It was her plan anyway—keep it simple, keep it as classy as possible under the circumstances.

"And, just so you know, Ísabel called her mom today and asked for that letter."

"Oh." Gracie had forgotten about it. "How did that come up?"

"She wanted to talk about whether anyone could really make her move out of here," Richard explained. "I guess since I'm a lawyer, she wanted to know what I thought. I told her a letter from her parents probably wasn't definitive, and that the country's policy toward immigration and first-generation citizens was in flux, but that a letter couldn't hurt."

Gracie stood up, pulled a head of lettuce and some tomatoes out of the refrigerator, and started making a salad. She was whipping up oil, vinegar, and spices into an Italian dressing when Ísabel walked into the kitchen.

"Mmm," she said. "I smell pizza!"

"Yes, Richard has graciously cooked for the second day in a row, but this time without you," Gracie said. "Do you think I should keep him?"

"Oh, he's a keeper." Ísabel laughed and socked Richard lightly in the stomach.

Gracie had noticed the girl's tendency lately to express her connection through that kind of physical contact. She remembered Ísabel punching her in the arm from time to time. Was this physical expression of belonging normal? She didn't remember Janice doing anything like it as a child or a teenager. How little she knew about rearing a teenager! Maybe that was how Janice turned out so prickly.

Gracie had failed to pack a lunch that morning, and apparently, Richard and Ísabel had subsisted on popcorn through the day, so the pizza and salad disappeared in a matter of minutes. Patting his still-flat stomach and pushing away from the table, Richard begged off helping with the dishes.

"I really should get home and check my e-mails," he said. "I've totally checked out the past two days, and considering I was away all last week, I'm a bit behind."

"No problem," Ísabel piped up. "I got this. Gracie, you too. Just sit there and drink your wine."

"I will." Gracie lifted her wineglass as if to toast the idea. "See you later, Richard. Supper tomorrow?"

"Let's go out," he suggested, pulling on his parka. "I'll take my two favorite girls to Des Moines. You guys decide where."

Gracie sat and watched Ísabel load the dishwasher and wipe off the counters and the table. A few minutes after Richard had gone, she sat up straighter and reached up for Ísabel's arm.

"Sit down for a minute," she said. "I think we should talk about things."

"What?" Ísabel gave her that "am I in trouble?" look that Gracie remembered from Janice's teenage years.

"We need to plan our visit to Gregory," Gracie said. "And I want to hear how your conversation with your mom went today."

Ísabel closed the dishwasher, wiped her hands on a dishtowel, and sat down. She reached for Gracie's wineglass and took a sip before Gracie could stop her.

"Whoa!" Gracie couldn't help laughing. "You're not legal yet."

"I'm a U.S. citizen, I'll have you know." Ísabel smiled. If she was going to be hit with a postpartum depression from the crash of hormones, it apparently hadn't started yet.

"I meant a legal drinker. You have about five years to go."

"Wow, that's a long way off." Ísabel looked longingly at Gracie's wine. "It seems a bit funny, doesn't it?"

"What?"

"Like, I only have to be eighteen to get an abortion without telling my parents, but to drink, I have to be twenty-one."

"Yes, it's all arbitrary," Gracie agreed. "But not to put too fine a point on it, you're neither eighteen nor twenty-one. And

I'm not bending the rules, not when it seems the whole community is watching us."

"What do you mean?"

"I'll get to that in a minute. How did the conversation with your mom go today?"

"Good. She's sending the letter. I have a feeling she's not coming back soon. She seems really happy that I've got a nice place to stay. She says she remembers your house. Apparently, she helped your maid clean here one week."

"Maid?"

"Housecleaner. Whatever."

"Oh, you mean Lisbeth. Well, that's nice. I'm glad she's happy with you being here. I certainly am."

"Even after all the problems I caused?"

"Yup. Even after all of that. Meanwhile, we need to decide when we're going to go to Gregory and what we're going to say. I think the sooner we let him know what happened, the sooner he will back off. He called again today, threatening to get you out of here."

"Where does he want me to go?" Ísabel raised her hands, questioning. "Move in with him and his wife?"

"Good question," Gracie answered. She stood up and opened the top junk drawer next to the refrigerator, and pulled out a pad of paper and a pen. "Now, let's get down to business."

They sketched out a strategy. First, they would let Gregory—Gracie no longer tried to enforce the "Mr. Thungaard" protocol; he didn't deserve it—know about the pregnancy, the abortion, and the tissue that could prove his paternity. Then they'd lay down their simple demands: no more work with students; obviously, no more sex with schoolgirls; no more interference with their living arrangement.

In return, Ísabel wouldn't go to the police or sue him for injury. What he didn't need to know was that Ísabel wouldn't do that in any case; there was no way she was going to bring anyone else into the conversation about what Gregory and she had done.

"He mustn't know that," Gracie said. "If he senses any hesitation on your part, he'll call our bluff."

"Okay. Okay."

"What I'm worried about most is that he'll get angry and violent," Gracie said. "Do you think it would be okay to bring Richard along? It might feel less threatening."

Ísabel shook her head. "I don't know. Don't you think it should be just us girls?"

~19~

Gregory kept an office on an oak-studded hill on the highway at the outskirts of town, although Gracie didn't know what he actually did in it. She regularly saw his car and two or three others there during the day, so he apparently had staff as well. Was he already building a campaign team for his run for county supervisor?

It had been Ísabel's idea to meet in his office. "And I think we should show up at least fifteen minutes early," she said.

"Why?" Gracie asked.

"He is going to suspect this has something to do with me, since you aren't asking him to meet you at the library. So, he will send his secretary away on some errand so she won't see me come and go," Ísabel said. "If we come early, we'll blow his cover. Then he'll worry that even if we promise not to tell anyone else about this, his secretary is going to wonder what it's all about. He'll have to start screening his mail before she opens it and answering calls before she picks up the phone."

Gracie laughed. "Oh, Ísabel! You have such an imagination."

"But it's like . . . well, like little things that always blow someone's cover. It's never the big obvious shit that's easy to see coming. We can put him on edge, let him know that as much money as he has, he can't control everything. Two people can show up at his office fifteen minutes early and whammo!"

That's when Gracie realized that the girl wasn't just watching those old movies—she was learning from them. Their plots turned not on predictable acts of the main characters, but on the little mistakes, the little hints that told the audience all would not go as planned. A scene might look like it was stuffed with minor characters of no import, but any of those eyes and ears could be the crack in the dam that would eventually lead to the break—the unraveling of some nefarious scheme.

When she called him, Gracie insisted she meet Gregory in his office.

"What's this about?" he asked. "If it's library business, I think we should meet in your office."

"No, it's personal."

"I don't understand. Our only relationship involves the library," he argued.

"How about the school board?"

"You don't have a child in school."

Gracie said nothing. Let him put two and two together, taking a page from Ísabel's playbook—or screenplay. Now he had to know that it was about Ísabel. Now he had to worry that the girl had spilled the beans about their night in Des Moines.

"So, what is it about?" His voice was unsteady. Gracie was sure he knew. *Good.* The first piece in Ísabel's plan was in place.

"Let me just say that what I want to meet with you about is something you'd much rather hear from me than from anyone else in this community," she said. "But it's your choice."

"I don't like playing games."

"No games."

He paused. "Well, okay. How about noon tomorrow? You can take your lunch hour and close the library."

And you can send your secretary out to lunch. How convenient! Ísabel had seen how this was going to play out all the way.

❧

Gracie pulled the Buick up under a big oak tree in front of Gregory's office and turned off the engine. They were twenty minutes early.

She turned to Ísabel. "Are you ready?"

For the first time since they started talking about this meeting with Gregory, Ísabel looked uncertain.

"Are you okay? Honey, we don't have to go through with this."

"No, I want to," Ísabel said, even though tears had started collecting on her lower eyelids. "I just have to keep remembering how much it hurt, how horrible it was."

"I would rather you could put that behind you." Gracie put her hand on Ísabel's shoulder. It was true. But, if they didn't go through with this, Gregory would walk away scot-free, and Gracie would have to put up with his sanctimony until the end of time. Gracie couldn't remember a time when she had felt so conflicted about anything.

"You know, I think I have to talk to him about it." Ísabel slapped her hands on her thighs. Gracie yanked her hand out of the way. "Do you have a Kleenex?"

Gracie gave her time to wipe her eyes and compose herself. Ísabel nodded to her, and they got out of the car.

True to plan again, a woman in the front reception area of the small office building was standing up and dropping her cell phone into her purse when they walked in. She was clearly going out for lunch.

"I'm sorry, but I don't see an appointment on his calendar." She looked at her computer screen when Gracie introduced herself.

"I'm quite sure he's expecting me," Gracie almost added, *and I'm sure you weren't.*

The receptionist opened the door behind her desk just far enough to peer in through the crack. "A Gracie Jensen is here to see you."

"Oh, she's early," Gracie heard Gregory say from behind

the door. He dropped something on the floor—something heavy. "Shit! God damn!" Maybe it landed on his toe, she thought, smiling and winking at Ísabel.

"Do you want me to send her in?"

"No, she'll just have to wait. You don't have to stick around, Marlene. Go on to lunch. I can handle this."

Marlene closed the door gently and turned to pick up her purse. "He'll be with you shortly." She walked around Gracie and nearly ran into Ísabel; she hadn't seen her behind Gracie. "Oh, are you two together?"

"Yes, but he knows," Gracie said quickly. She wanted to keep the element of surprise in their favor.

"Well, enjoy your meeting," Marlene ducked out the door. "He's a very charming man."

"Yeah," Ísabel said, wringing as much sarcasm out of that word as Gracie thought possible. "We know."

"I guess we just sit and wait," Gracie said. Instead of sitting, though, she walked to the window overlooking the golf course below. Suddenly she remembered once wondering if Ísabel would be interested in learning to play golf. So much had happened since then, it seemed like years and layers of innocence in the past.

"Hey, Ísabel," she whispered over her shoulder. "Have you ever wanted to try golf?"

"Uh, no." Ísabel sounded definite about it. "We already talked about this, remember? It's a game for rich old men."

"Well, not necessarily." Gracie stared out at the frozen fairways lined with cottonwood and oak trees. The closer the holes were to the river, the more they were defended by cottonwoods; the higher on the hills, by oaks. It looked beautiful, even in the gray-brown shades of midwinter.

"I played a long time ago, long before Jens died. A bunch of girls and I would play every Tuesday morning in the summertime. The men got Saturdays, you know, because they had to work. Well, most of us women worked during the week, too, but we still managed to get out and play at least nine holes."

"So, what's fun about it?" Ísabel sounded skeptical. "It looks boring."

"I guess it does." Gracie smiled remembering how many times Jens fell asleep on Sunday afternoons watching golf tournaments on TV. "But it's really quite addictive. Promise me you'll go out with me once next spring. Maybe you'll get the bug."

"Sure," Ísabel said, with no enthusiasm. "Whatever."

Gracie turned back to the window. She wasn't nervous about approaching Gregory with Ísabel, but she wasn't sure they were asking enough. How would they monitor Gregory's actions? Even if he agreed to do the things they asked, how would they know he was sticking to it? How would they enforce his agreement to stop working with students? All he would need would be a request from the principal—his buddy—to keep going and he'd simply keep going.

Gregory's door snapped open.

"Gracie." He choked. "Uh, and Ísabel?"

Gracie turned around in time to see Gregory's face morph from surprised to frightened.

"What are you doing here?" He addressed Ísabel directly.

"We came to talk to you." Ísabel turned to Gracie for help. She looked timid, facing him.

Gracie realized she had an opportunity. With Ísabel looking vulnerable and Gregory afraid, she would be the voice of reason, of dispassion. She had the upper hand.

"Let's go into your office," Gracie said. "I'm sure you'd rather no one walked in on us out here."

Gregory held the door open for them, and they slipped into his office. It was at once lavishly appointed and ugly. The leather furniture was too large and too formal for the simple square room and its aluminum windows. The wood-framed diplomas and awards hung on the walls crookedly, and a large inspirational picture of a bald eagle and the single word "Soar" was set in a frame that cost at least fifty times the price of the chintzy poster. Large, thick Asian rugs, overlapping on the floor, smelled of musty wool.

"Nice view of the golf course." Gracie walked over to the window that displayed the same view as the one in the reception area. "Do you play?"

Even with her back to him, Gracie could sense Gregory's discomfort. She was pleased with how things were going and in no hurry to put him at ease.

"Uh, no," he said. "Can—"

"Why not?" Gracie interrupted. "You're so close! I'll bet it would be a great fundraising tool. You could twist arms while you're chasing birdies."

"Um, I don't play that well," he said. "Can we—"

"I find that surprising!" Gracie said, still staring out the window with her back toward him. "A man of your stature? I would have bet you for a collegiate champion!"

"Excuse me, but can we get down to business here?" Gregory sounded like his patience was thinning.

Gracie turned and flashed the sweetest smile she could muster, looking at his creased face. She had heard that he was in Arizona the weekend before, and apparently, he had gotten a bit too much sun. His skin was crinkly, getting ready to shed a dry layer or two, making him look at least ten years older.

"Of course." She put her hand on Ísabel's shoulder and guided her to the deep, nail-studded sofa across from his large walnut desk.

"Now, what can I do for you ladies?" His hands nervously picked at papers on his desk.

"No need to be so nervous!" Gracie laughed. Calling out his nerves was likely to make him even more nervous. That would be to her advantage.

"I'm not—" Gregory stopped and dropped his hands to his lap. He tried to lean back to feign composure, but he leaned too far and had to jerk his legs forward to keep from toppling over backward.

"Ísabel, do you want to start?" Gracie looked at the girl beside her. She reached over and held her hand.

Ísabel looked at Gracie's face for a few seconds and seemed to gain some strength from her composure.

"Sure." She looked at Gregory. "I had an abortion last week. I want you to know because it was yours."

"My what?" Gregory asked. His face was blank.

"Well, your baby, stupid," Ísabel said. Gracie nearly laughed.

"What makes you think so?" Gregory locked his eyes on Ísabel and smiled, as if he thought he could intimidate her, but his lip quivered a bit. Gracie squeezed Ísabel's hand tightly.

"I know. We had sex in Des Moines six weeks before I had the abortion."

"Says who?"

Was he really going to try denying even that? Gracie wondered. If so, it could be a very long conversation.

"Says me and the DNA I have in a bottle in the freezer."

Gregory's face whitened under the peeling skin, and he swallowed hard before forcing another smile.

"Well, who all did you have sex with that week?" Gregory sneered slightly, his dried-up face crinkling as it moved. "Maybe it's not my DNA."

"Oh, don't stoop so low!" Gracie interrupted. "Impugning the girl isn't going to change things."

Gregory flashed an angry look at Gracie. "You should stay out of this!" He was already starting to lose his temper, and that's not what Gracie wanted.

"Okay, look." Gracie pumped one hand, palm down, to tamp down the tension in the room. "You should calm down."

Gregory sat back in his chair again, more carefully this time, and his eyes darted back and forth between Ísabel and Gracie. "What do you want?"

"Ísabel?" Gracie nodded at Ísabel to continue. It was their plan to have Ísabel do most of the talking so that Gregory could see he didn't intimidate her. It would signal to him that if he didn't do as they asked, she wasn't afraid to fight back.

"I could go to the police. I could, like, sue you, I guess," she started, somewhat shakily. "But, I would really not want to. So, I am going to tell you what you have to do."

Ísabel took a piece of paper out of her purse and unfolded it slowly. She was doing a good job of keeping Gregory off-balance, Gracie thought.

"First. You will never have sex with another student again."

"I didn't—"

"Oh, don't be silly!" Gracie stopped him. "Go on, Ísabel."

"Second. You will never tutor students again."

Ísabel looked up, as if she expected Gregory to interrupt again. Instead, he was pursing his lips, staring at his hands in his lap.

"Third. You will quit interfering with Gracie and me. You will stop trying to get me in trouble for staying with her until my mom gets home." Ísabel looked up again, refolded the paper, and put it back in her purse. "And if you don't do these things, I will take my little sample of your nasty DNA and go to an attorney. And I will sue your ass off."

Gracie smiled. Ísabel had promised not to swear, but now Gracie could see that the girl had hit just the right insurrectionist tone. All hose movie scripts had been good training.

"Why should I believe you?" Gregory asked after a long pause. "Why should I believe you have what you say you have?"

"Do you want me to describe what happened to me?" Ísabel asked, her temper rising. "Do you want to know what that felt like? What it looked like? Do you want me to, like, give you details? You are going to get sick if I do. It was nasty. And you're an ass."

"Now, now . . ." Gregory seemed unsure of how to proceed in the face of Ísabel's anger. "No, I don't need your pretty stories."

"Ugly stories, Gregory. Ugly!" Ísabel retorted.

"Okay, whatever, but you still have given me no reason to believe you."

Gracie decided it was time to interrupt. He could try to stonewall a sixteen-year-old, but Gracie wasn't going to let him intimidate her.

"You have no choice but to believe her," Gracie said. "You can't afford to deny this unless you want your political career to end right now—right now when the height of your glory is chairman of the Johnson Station Library and a seat on the school board."

Gregory looked surprised. Clearly, for all his political savvy, he hadn't considered what a scandal involving a pregnant teenager would do to his political chances. Maybe he'd already convinced himself that he was too powerful, invincible. Maybe all he had considered was the possibility of paying the girl to keep her silent, and up to now, he thought he was simply haggling over price.

"I'm still your boss, Gracie," he answered sternly. "I can still get you fired."

"That will take a vote of the entire board. And, in doing that, you risk that Ísabel would come forward in retribution. She's my friend. She'll stand by me."

Gracie looked over to Ísabel for affirmation. Ísabel didn't meet her eye. Perhaps Gracie had gone too far. The girl was never going to come forward and publicly implicate Gregory, and playing this bluff was apparently a bit above her acting ability. Gracie hoped Gregory didn't see the girl's ambivalence.

Lucky for her, he was staring out the window toward the golf course, not watching Ísabel's face.

"Do we have your word?" Gracie demanded. "No more working with students. No travel with students. You will leave Ísabel alone. Right?"

Gregory didn't answer. He kept his head turned toward the window and closed his eyes.

"Okay," he said. "I'm quitting the business of tutoring those brats anyway. I have much more important work to do."

He meant it as an insult to Ísabel, Gracie knew. But Ísabel didn't take the bait. She looked exhausted and ready to get out of that office. It looked like the ordeal had taken more of a toll on her fragile body than Gracie had anticipated.

"We will hold you to your word." Gracie stood up and offered a hand to Ísabel. "And I can promise you, we will be watching you very closely. Ísabel is friends with all of your other students, and she will know."

Gregory said nothing. He opened his eyes, but continued to look away, his jaw set in anger.

Gracie led Ísabel toward his office door. "Have a nice day," she said back over her shoulder as she closed the door. She let her voice drip with sarcasm.

Marlene had already returned when they passed through the reception area. "Did everything go okay?" she asked.

"Just fine!" Gracie said cheerfully. "And he wants to meet with us again next Thursday, same time. Could you mark that down?"

Marlene turned to her computer and clicked enough keys to enter the appointment—an appointment that Gracie and Ísabel had no intention of keeping and Gregory would know nothing about. She imagined how anxious he would be a week from now, wondering what more she and Ísabel were going to demand.

❧

"We're not really going back, are we?" Ísabel asked

timidly once they pulled out of Gregory's parking lot.

"No, absolutely not," Gracie said. "I just wanted to keep him on edge. I'm learning from you."

"Do you think he'll do it? The things we asked?"

"Yes, Ísabel, I think he will. I don't think he has a choice. You were wonderful, by the way. Very calm, very professional."

"Thanks," Ísabel looked out the side window. "I don't know how I let this happen to me. I should never have . . ." She stopped. It appeared that going through the abortion had changed the way she remembered the night in Des Moines with Gregory. Gracie remembered the starry look in the girl's eyes when she first tried to tell Gracie about it, how eager she had been to share the romantic details. Now Ísabel remembered pain and disgust, and that was how she would remember sex with Gregory from that point on.

"Well, I think that a lot of it is behind you now, Ísabel," Gracie said. "You will never forget the pain and the fear, probably. But now you have settled the score as well as you could. We can start looking ahead now instead of looking back."

Richard was waiting for them when they pulled into the driveway. He opened the back door, eagerly searching their faces as if for signs of success or failure.

Gracie waited for Ísabel to get out of the car, and reached for her as they headed up the sidewalk. Ísabel pulled away and hurried through the door and up the stairs to her bedroom.

"What was that all about?" Richard asked. He looked concerned.

"I think it was harder than she thought," Gracie said. "I am pretty sure I couldn't have pulled off what she just did at her age. But it took an awful lot out of her. You know, she's just gotten over a pregnancy. The next few weeks are likely to be touchy."

"But how did it go? Did he agree to her terms?"

"Yes," Gracie said. "But somehow I think she gave up more than she got back. We'll probably never know, really, if he sleeps with other girls or goes on trips with them. The only thing she really got out of the deal was that he won't try to make her leave my house. Meanwhile, she gave up ever really settling the score and seeing him punished for what he did."

"Well, retribution is overrated sometimes."

"Right, but you don't know that unless you get it." Gracie opened the refrigerator and pulled out a loaf of bread and the tuna fish salad she had prepared that morning for their lunch.

"Do you think you should take her somewhere? Go on a little vacation?" Richard took Gracie's coat and turned to hang it up in the mudroom.

"No." Gracie pulled sandwich plates and silverware out of cupboards and drawers. "As nice as I think that would be for both of us, I think she's got to work through this now or it will still be there later. It could still be there when she's married and having a baby she really wants. And postpartum depression isn't something that goes away just because you're on a beach instead of in a classroom."

"What, then?"

"I think therapy. Do you know anybody in Des Moines? I think we're going to need the help of a professional."

As she and Richard ate their sandwiches silently, she couldn't shake the feeling that Gregory's promise was shallow. It left him too much room to maneuver, including room to interfere at the library and room to embarrass Gracie and Richard. They weren't included in the agreement.

Even on the points he had agreed to, unless he was convinced that Ísabel was willing to expose him, he had all the power. Gregory knew Ísabel would never turn him in; Gracie could sense it in his stony stare, his quick acquiescence to her demands.

Moreover, as much as he had seemed knocked off-balance by their visit, Gracie had a feeling that it wouldn't take an egotist like him long to regain his composure. He'd be cocky as ever next time she saw him.

She needed to come up with something else. Something that didn't involve Richard or Ísabel. Some revenge she could extract on her own, or with the help of others who didn't know why she was doing it.

~20~

Having the ordeal of meeting Gregory face-to-face over with was a bigger relief than Gracie realized it was going to be. Whatever the outcome, he hadn't gotten violent, Ísabel had communicated her demands, and he had—nominally, at least —agreed to them. She had plenty of time to figure out what else she could do to punish Gregory; it might just present itself to her someday serendipitously.

Walking to coffee, Gracie was relieved to be getting back to a routine as well. She'd missed enough work that she knew things were piling up at the library. And as companionable as Richard and Ísabel were, she missed her friends. She missed being a part of the community that didn't involve politics and censorship and the complexities of raising a teenager.

It had been two weeks since she'd seen Marcia. Gracie knew she was back from Iowa City, but they hadn't found time to talk, even on the phone. Maybe someday, long after Ísabel had left town and Gregory was in the statehouse in Des Moines, she'd share the story of Ísabel's pregnancy with Marcia. Maybe not. But knowing Marcia would be there to listen was, in itself, comforting.

But then, it turned out maybe she wasn't going to be.

At coffee klatch, the café was exactly the same, and Gracie wondered what else she might have expected. Things hadn't changed in there for the past twenty years. What difference would two weeks make?

The tables in the back were still only half-full of local businessmen. The retirees wouldn't start coming back from the desert until the middle of March, a month away. Other than Gracie, Marcia, and Jackie, the only other patrons in the front were two men who looked like they had just wandered into town after conducting some kind of business out at the chicken plant. Perhaps they were recruiters brought in to find replacements for the deported Mexicans that would allow the plant to reopen.

Marcia leaped up from the booth when Gracie came in the front door and hugged her, nearly lifting Gracie off her feet in her enthusiasm.

"Boy, have I missed you!"

"Well, that's what you get for running off," Gracie laughed. "When did you get back?"

Marcia looked sideways at Jackie in the booth—a silent reminder to Gracie that she needed to be careful about what she said aloud. She had apparently not shared everything with Jackie yet, but Gracie didn't know what parts of the story would be safe. She would have to follow Marcia's lead.

"I got back last week. It was a nice getaway. I got some things figured out. I just got done telling Jackie I've filed for divorce."

"Oh." Gracie sat down quickly to let her butt absorb the shock of the news. "Really? So fast?"

"When I got back from my sabbatical"—apparently that's what she was calling her escape to Iowa City—"I realized how stuck I was in a lifestyle I don't care about any more. But that's not the biggest news."

"Oh no." Gracie wanted to be positive and supportive, but she was afraid that Marcia was acting impulsively. Was it about Carl? "What else did you do?"

"I have applied for an internship with a microfinance charity in Seattle. If I get it, I'll be leaving at the end of March."

"Aren't internships for college kids?"

"Not anymore," Jackie interjected. "Now it's how companies keep costs down. They hire temporary workers as interns so they don't have to pay them."

Gracie looked at Jackie with a puzzled frown. "How do

you know?" Gracie asked her. Jackie was a retired English teacher. What would she know about today's hiring practices?

"I read all about it in the *New Yorker*," Jackie said. "Man, those articles are long!"

"Hmm, sounds like another way to screw the middle class," Gracie said.

"Yes, but if you don't take the internships for no pay, you have no chance to get on as an employee," Marcia argued. "I really want this job. If I get on with this organization, I could be working in Seattle and traveling to Central America three or four times a year. Beats living in Johnson Station all to hell."

"Well, I'm happy for you. Aren't you, Gracie?" Jackie elbowed Gracie.

"Yes, but I need a cup of coffee. Where's Betty?"

As if on cue, Betty walked up behind Gracie and set a full cup on the table in front of her. "You other girls okay?" she asked. Jackie and Marcia nodded.

"Well, if you go, I'll miss you, Marcia," Gracie said. "Maybe it's time for me to get out of here for a while, too."

"Well, where have you been?" Jackie turned back to Gracie. "We haven't seen you for two weeks."

"In Iowa City and Des Moines, helping Ísabel with some health issues."

"Oh, I thought maybe you and Richard had eloped," Jackie said. "Seems like he's over there a lot."

"Well, snoopy, yes, he is," Gracie said. "I think I'd have him move in if I weren't so busy with other things."

"You mean, you guys are sleeping together?"

"Well, duh." Marcia grinned at Gracie. "I guess you've given up on keeping it a secret."

"Yes, I have," Gracie said. "I'm tired of bowing to this town's shaming. Jesus, that rumor is more than fifteen years old, isn't it?"

"I knew it!" Jackie said, proving Gracie had been right all along. People would think they'd been lovers way back when

Jens was still alive. Right then Gracie realized quite calmly that she didn't care anymore. Perhaps facing Gregory's adultery head-on had put her own comparatively benign behavior in perspective. "Well, welcome to the real world, Gracie!"

"Speaking of the real world, how was *The Intern's Travels*?" Gracie asked Marcia.

"What would that have to do with the real world?" Marcia laughed. "It wasn't worth the hype. There was lots of sex, but I think I've had better right here in Iowa."

With Carl or Bob? Gracie refrained from asking.

"Yes, those hot books rarely live up to their billing," Gracie acknowledged. "Bring it back, though. I have a bunch of folks waiting to read it."

Walking the short block from the café to the library, Gracie felt the warmth of the café shielding her from the cold February wind. Friends like Marcia and Jackie were what made small-town living so nice. But was it only in a small town that an older woman could have these kinds of friends? She hoped for Marcia's sake that wasn't the case. She'd never been to Seattle, but she was sure it was no small town.

A caseworker from the social services agency in Des Moines was scheduled to visit the next morning, and once again, Gracie asked her assistant, Karen, to cover for the first couple of hours at the library. Ísabel went on to school. If the social worker decided she needed to talk with the girl, she would call on her at school.

The visit only took about fifteen minutes, and Gracie was at the library only a half hour late. She had welcomed Joan, as the slightly scruffy social worker introduced herself, showed her Ísabel's room, told her about the girl's fascination with classic movies, and invited her to stay for a cup of coffee. Joan thanked her, but said she had too many investigations underway and couldn't afford to take the time.

"Are you going to see Ísabel at school?" Gracie asked.

"The best time would probably be about ten. That's when she has study hall."

"No, I'm quite sure it isn't necessary," Joan said. "I appreciate your time, Mrs. Jensen. I'll be sending you a copy of my report next week." Gracie had a hunch—a strong one—that the report would be brief and inconsequential. Joan knew as well as everyone—except, it appeared, the principal and Gregory—that Ísabel was doing just fine under Gracie's roof.

❧

Nearly every woman—and Armand—who asked to get on the list for *The Intern's Travels* begged Gracie to not tell anyone that she wanted to read it.

"Don't worry!" Gracie told each of them in pretty much the same words. "Your secret is good with me. But you should know just about everyone in town is on my list."

Unanimously, they took that news as a big relief. How little they all really knew about each other. Within their small circles of friends, the older women were no more afraid to talk about these things and admit to reading such books than the younger women were. But across the community, there was still this patina of correctness, this façade of chastity that served as a straightjacket, keeping people apart.

While she believed that what her customers read was private information and no one else's business, Gregory thought otherwise. He had asked for the names of those on her list twice over the past two months, and she refused to give them to him.

When he stopped by the library unexpectedly a week before the board meeting in February, she first thought he had come to ask for the list again. Gracie had been nodding off, lulled to sleep at her desk by the quiet of the afternoon and the overactive furnace. She jerked awake at the sound of the big front door slamming shut.

"Am I interrupting?" A sly smile crossed his face as he peered through the door of her office as if he knew she had been napping.

"Oh no!" she replied, a bit too enthusiastically. "I was having a bit of trouble staying awake. Too little going on here today."

"So, I see," Gregory looked around. Gracie could imagine that he was wondering why they were paying her, given the lack of activity he was witnessing.

"I want to talk," he said. "Do you have a moment?"

Gracie sat up straight at his auspicious tone.

"Sure." She tried to sound enthusiastic. "Come in and sit down! I certainly hope you're not asking for the waiting list for that book again."

He sat down, threw one leg over the other, and shook his head. He leaned back in the chair and crossed his arms over his chest. He had regained his cockiness, apparently having quickly recovered from the humiliation Ísabel had laid on him the week before.

"No," he said. "This is a more general discussion. I don't suppose you have any coffee?"

"Actually, no." Gracie didn't want to encourage him to stay any longer than necessary. But it was also true. As usual, she hadn't made a pot of coffee since she opened the library that morning.

"Well then, I will get right to the point," he said. "I wanted to give you a fair warning that I and some of the other board members have been discussing how to take this library to the next level." He sniffed and lifted his chin.

Gracie cringed at "the next level." It had become such a cliché. Everyone was taking everything to "the next level" these days, whether it was their yoga poses or the medical care for cancer patients. What did it mean anymore?

"Good." Gracie tried to remain diplomatic. "I assume you have some thoughts?"

"Yes, but to be honest, I am seriously questioning whether you are the person we need to take us there."

"Why would you say that?" She wasn't pleased at the quiver in her voice. His tack wasn't unexpected. Now was the time to show strength and resolve, not timidity and weakness.

"I think it would be best if I explained my reservations in writing." Gregory jerked his chin up and sniffing again.

What an arrogant bastard! Gracie wished he'd lose the uppity tic.

"So, this is something you guys have been talking about?" She folded her hands in front of her on the desk and fought the rising tone in her voice. "I thought board meetings were open to the public."

"Yes, they are. These have just been casual conversations, serendipitous meetings. But still, I don't think it would come as any surprise to you that I haven't been pleased with the direction you've taken our community resource."

"Well, I know we have our disagreements, but up to now, I had no reason to believe that you didn't think I was still fulfilling my duties satisfactorily."

It was a lie. He had done nothing for the last year but complain about how she managed things—complain and push for policies she was never going to put into place. She had expected it would come to this, a straightforward threat to take her job; she just didn't know it would be today.

"Satisfactorily, yes," he said, accepting her lie. He lowered his chin, copping a pedantic tone. "But satisfactory and exemplary are two different things. Like I said, I think it's time to take this institution to another level."

Gracie swallowed her disdain. She held his eyes. She forced her throat to relax and dropped her voice.

"Frankly, Gregory, I think that is bullshit," she said.

"No need to swear, Gracie!" Gregory pushed his ample

butt back in his chair and feigned surprise.

Gracie chuckled. Even someone as sanctimonious as Gregory couldn't be taken aback by "bullshit" these days.

"You swore plenty in your office last week," she said. "And I have no need to mince words. If you have issues with my performance here at the library, I look forward to responding to them. When are these written words of wisdom coming down to me?"

"Soon," he said. "And when you get my letter, I expect that it will not affect our little pact?"

"You mean that I won't tell anyone that you've been screwing high school girls?" Gracie gave up being diplomatic. The battle was now fully engaged, and she needed to land her punches as squarely as possible. "Is that what this is really about?"

"I don't think we need to use that kind of language." He narrowed his eyes. "But yes. I expect you will keep your word. And no, my little deal with Ísabel has nothing to do with that. Nothing to do with you, really."

"You are simply without conscience, aren't you." It wasn't a question. She was exasperated, caught between Gregory's hypocrisy and her inability to do anything about it.

"Not at all." He puffed his chest up and sniffed again. "I'm fighting the good fight here."

"While impregnating young girls."

Gregory's chest fell, and he leaned forward with his elbows on his knees, the same posture she'd seen him take while lecturing the table of men at the back of the café in the mornings.

"You see, Gracie, this is exactly what we're trying to save our children from, this kind of danger. If Ísabel had better moral guidance and fewer negative role models, she would never have come on to me in the first place."

"You have got to be kidding!" Gracie slapped her hands down on the desk. "Could you be more of a hypocrite? Would it be possible? Aren't monsters like you what we need to save our kids from?"

"Oh, come on, Gracie," he said, sitting back. "She isn't one of ours; she's not from our community. She's Mexican! And she sure as hell wasn't a virgin. Get real! She's probably hanging out behind the schoolhouse as we speak, offering to teach the boys a few things."

"I . . . I . . . I . . ." Gracie was so angry she couldn't form another sentence. Her head swam and her heart pounded so hard she could feel the veins in her stomach jump. She held onto the edge of her desk to steady herself.

Gregory rose and pulled his coat off the back of the chair, and turned back to Gracie from her office door. "And remember," he said. His voice was smarmy with sarcasm. "We wouldn't want to embarrass your little foster child by letting anyone know she got herself knocked up, now would we?"

Gracie felt like her heart had jumped into her throat, choking the blood out of her brain and turning her blind with rage. She stood up, shaking, and grabbed the first thing her hand found on the desk. A book. She threw it at Gregory, but he slipped past the window of her office, and the book landed with a thud on the floor in the library.

"Careful, Gracie." He mocked her. "You wouldn't want to get arrested for assault. You wouldn't want to leave your boyfriend alone in your house with little Ísabel, now would you?"

Gracie needed a double dose of Xanax to get to sleep that night.

✍

Gregory's letter arrived a day later.

Gracie got a notice in her post office box that a certified letter had arrived, and she immediately knew what it was. She wondered what would happen if she didn't go to the window to claim it. But what good would it do to delay the confrontation? None. Eventually, she and Gregory had to engage publicly, and it was better for the community if they got it over with.

As she waited in line to retrieve the letter, she imagined how the meeting would go. How much support would Gregory get from the other board members? Would they hide behind his leadership or speak out for themselves? Would any of her library regulars show up to support her? Gracie was glad that Jens wasn't around to witness it. He might not have gone to the meeting anyway, arguing that it wouldn't be proper for him to defend her in a public forum. But it wouldn't be about propriety, really. It would have been about his comfort level outside of a venue that he didn't control totally.

As a judge, his authority in a courtroom was unquestioned, the rules were clear, and boundaries on discussion were set by years of tradition and case law. The free-for-all of public forums was too chaotic, undisciplined for him. He twitched nervously at public hearings, grimacing at illogical strings of argument, rolling his eyes at irrelevant testimony.

Gracie knew that Richard would be different. As a respected lawyer in the community, his testimony on her behalf would carry weight, but she guessed he would argue that their relationship precluded him from speaking up. No one would believe he was unbiased, and she would have to agree.

At the post office, she handed Jamie the little slip she'd found in her mail slot. "I seem to have a delivery."

"Yes, you do!" Jamie said, as if passing along a certified letter was the most exciting thing she got to do all week. She returned with the letter, tore off the section of the sticker on the front of the envelope that required Gracie's signature, and handed it to Gracie.

"Am I getting close to the top of the list?" she asked,

watching Gracie sign the slip and hand it back. Gracie didn't have to ask what list she was talking about; Jamie had been waiting for weeks to get her hands on one of the three copies of *The Intern's Travels*.

"I'm sure you are." Gracie smiled. If only Jamie knew what was in this letter. Undoubtedly, it would condemn Gracie for buying the book. If only all of the people who were asking for the book knew what Gregory wanted to do! She had a lot more support in this town than he did, she was certain. Still, raising your voice against a religious bully—especially one so adept at public speaking—was risky and scary. Even if they knew he was intending to fire her for making the book they wanted to read available, they would likely shy away.

She was bound to lose this fight. She accepted the letter, smiled as pleasantly as she could at Jamie, and waved to a couple other familiar faces as she walked steadily out of the post office.

Gracie waited until she got home that evening to open the letter. She was in no hurry to read it. She already knew the broad outlines of Gregory's opinions, and by the time she sat down at the kitchen table with a glass of wine and slid open the envelope, she had started to script her responses to his accusations in her head.

In America, we don't accept censorship of reading materials for adults, for instance. And *the marketplace of ideas can't be robust or thrive if you limit discovery and discussion.* She imagined defending herself with arguments that would co-opt the patriotic themes he liked to espouse.

The letter was written on what appeared to be official library board letterhead that Gracie had never seen before and didn't even know existed. He must have had it printed recently. It seemed a bit over the top; did he really think his library position was important enough to require official stationary?

This letter is to serve notice to you that the board is considering some recent actions and behaviors as potential causes for dismissal was its opening salvo.

Gracie glanced quickly through the letter, looking for details about when the board would make its move. But the letter said nothing about a meeting or a public discussion. Perhaps he wanted to spring it on her at that week's meeting. If so, it wouldn't be much of a surprise.

Gracie went back to the top and read the letter carefully. Gregory had itemized the four allegations against her.

Item one delineated her refusal to draft and adopt an official policy to "protect community morality" through the purchase and distribution of "only those reading materials consistent with community standards." The letter didn't detail what the community's standards were or how they should be articulated. But in board meetings he had argued that the books carried in the town's library should promote unquestioned acceptance of American exceptionalism, unwavering support for the "free market," adherence to "Christian" values, however unspecified, full discussion of "intelligent design," and rejection of lifestyles that threatened the primacy of the nuclear family—which meant no same-sex marriages, no extramarital sex, no abortions, and no artificial means of birth control.

How out of touch he was with his own community! He had no idea what the twenty- and thirty-somethings in his own town perceived as "normal" behavior.

Item two was the expected condemnation for buying *The Intern's Travels* despite his "request to defer" to those same alleged community standards. If there were some impartial calculation of community standards with a basis in fact, Gracie thought, it would be that there were more than four dozen women and one man in Johnson Station who had put their names on the list to get the book as soon as it was available.

Item three was about her relationship with Richard: *Your cohabitation with a man you are not married to raises questions about your suitability as a shepherd of our community's children and of our community's morality.* She'd suspected he'd pull this. While it had nothing to do with how she managed the library, he would use it as a way to challenge her character and indict her for her personal behavior. The letter suggested it was proof of her failure to adhere to those community standards, again.

But item four astounded her: *You are harboring an illegal alien in your home without proper authority from the county, state, or federal government.*

First, that wasn't true. Didn't he know that Ísabel was a citizen? Ísabel was born in the states, and regardless of her parent's citizenship, she was a legal American. Apparently, he knew more about Ísabel's breast size and the warmth of her vagina than he did about her legal status, she thought, at first smirking and then checking herself. It wasn't funny.

Sure, Gracie had taken Ísabel in without expressed permission from any government agency, but as a small-government advocate, shouldn't Gregory applaud her for finding a solution to the girl's problems that didn't involve an agency of some sort or tax dollars?

But, then, he was a hypocrite. Obviously. After what he did to Ísabel, and who knew how many others, how could he hold himself up as a guarantor of the community's morality? His political philosophy wasn't nearly as well developed as his political clout; his platforms were only as solid as he needed to stand on them and wave his arms around for attention.

But how could he threaten her? He knew that Gracie was fully aware of what he had done to Ísabel. And he agreed not to lobby for someone to take Ísabel away. But he'd also calculated that their agreement said nothing about using Ísabel's residence as an excuse to fire Gracie from her job.

Then it hit her: He was calling their bluff. As long as Ísabel was too weak to stand up for herself and accuse him of rape, he was going to pursue his agenda. If doing that exacerbated the harm he'd done to the girl, it didn't matter to him. He believed she'd never tattle on him.

Had he no shame for what he had done? Gracie shook her head and threw the letter down on the counter.

"What's that?"

Gracie was startled by Ísabel's voice. She hadn't noticed the girl standing only inches behind her. Had she been reading over Gracie's shoulder? Gracie slammed the letter, face-down, on the table.

"Just a letter about the agenda for the next board meeting." Gracie tamped down the anger in her chest.

"What was that about illegal aliens?" Ísabel sat down next to Gracie. She reached for the letter.

Gracie slapped her hand over Ísabel's and grabbed the paper away.

"This is none of your business."

"Oh, I think it is." Ísabel nodded emphatically. "I think at least part of it is about me. What's going on?"

Gracie looked into Ísabel's face and their eyes held. The girl had grown up so much in the past couple of months. She'd lost the shyness, the self-deprecation, the petulance she came to the library with those first few weeks, and mostly, Gracie was glad for that. Maybe she was stronger now. Perhaps it was time to lay their cards on the table and call Gregory's bluff. Was he so sure that Ísabel wouldn't talk? Would it hurt her so much if she did press charges?

Gracie smoothed the now-wrinkled letter out on the counter in front of her and pointed to number four.

"Read this."

Ísabel glanced at the paper and returned her gaze to Gracie's face.

"I already did."

"He's using the fact that I am taking care of you as an excuse to fire me from the library," Gracie interpreted.

"That's disgusting. He's a disgusting human being." Finally, Ísabel wasn't equivocating. Gracie was encouraged.

"Well, do you think we should let him do it?" Gracie asked.

"No."

"Then what should we do?"

"Just tell the board that I'm not illegal."

"But that's only half of the problem. I have no legal guardianship over you. He could use this to pull you away and send you to some foster home."

"He said he wouldn't, remember. And anyway, Richard said he can't without a judge's order, right? And that social services person sent us that letter, right?"

"But doesn't this mean he's reneging on our deal? Don't you think maybe it's time to go to the police and tell them what he did to you?"

Isabel's face froze, her eyes lit with anger. She stood up and backed away from the table, her glare searing Gracie's face.

"What did you say?"

"He's using your silence against us! Don't you hate that?"

Isabel frowned and looked back at the letter. She pointed. "He's using it against you, not against us."

"Same thing! You're here with me only because no one has interfered. He wants you to go away."

"No, he wants to fire you. He isn't threatening to take me away. And we had a deal, Gracie! I told you I would never tell anyone else what happened, and we agreed we'd keep it that way. You said the deal would be insurance against him hurting other girls like he hurt me. You didn't say it was about you. Now you want to use that to save your job?" Her voice rose an octave and her finger shook as she jabbed at the letter. "Really? That's all I am to you? A bargaining chip you can use to save your job?"

"Hey, what's going on here?" Richard's booming voice bounced off the walls of the kitchen. Gracie jumped, startled. She twirled around and faced him. She didn't know what to say.

"Nothing," she said weakly. She hated herself for it immediately.

"It's not nothing!" Ísabel retorted. "Gracie wants to break our pact so she can save her job. I really can't believe this is happening!" She threw up her hands and headed out of the room, but Richard caught her by a bicep and pulled her back to the table.

"Let's talk," he said. "Sit down, Ísabel."

"I don't have—"

"Yes, you do!" He pointed to the chair she had just vacated. Looking resigned, Ísabel sat.

"Now, let's talk this over like adults." He took the chair across from Gracie. "I take it this is about your pact with Gregory."

"You know?" Ísabel asked. "You know it was Gregory?"

"That's what adults who are in love and committed to each other do, Ísabel," he said. "They share their most difficult decisions. They lean on each other for perspective and advice. That's what Gracie and I do. That's what you should expect from us. Now, let's not argue that point, but let's talk about what's going on."

Gracie listened, and a little smile spread over her face slowly. He really was a good guy. And now he was acting like the father he must have been for Ronnie. He wasn't trying to take over; he was mediating. That's what good parents do for each other. It humbled Gracie; she hoped she could learn to be as good to Ísabel as Richard was naturally.

"Gregory wants to argue that my *harboring* of Ísabel is one of the reasons I should be dismissed as the town's librarian," Gracie said, handing the letter to Richard. "The other three reasons I expected, but not this one."

Richard's eyes quickly scanned the letter, and looking like he got the gist of it, he handed it back to Gracie.

"But what's this about a bargaining chip?"

"She wants me to go to the police to stop him," Ísabel answered. Gracie was surprised how succinctly she had managed to summarize their argument.

"I just think he's taking advantage of her silence," Gracie said. "I think someone should call him out. He's not the good Christian he says he is. He shouldn't be allowed to run me out of town. He shouldn't be allowed to use this as a political soapbox to gain votes."

"Well, I agree with you," Richard said, "but you and Ísabel had an agreement. That's far more important than bringing Gregory down to size, isn't it?"

"Is it?" Now Gracie's voice rose an octave. She looked at Ísabel. "You think that preserving our little blackmail scheme is more important than saving the community from a jerk like Gregory?"

"Little blackmail scheme!" Ísabel got up from her chair and threw up her arms. "That's what it is to you? A little blackmail scheme? It's my *life*, Gracie. My *life* we're talking about here!"

Ísabel stomped out of the kitchen, this time successfully ducking away from Richard's grasp. She ran up the stairs and slammed the door to her room.

"Well, that was helpful." Gracie made a droll face.

"I think she's right, though," Richard said, nearly whispering.

"What do you mean? This man is making a mockery of our community! He's the biggest slime ball in town, and he's masquerading as the town's morality police. Are we so impotent in the face of evil?"

"I hear you," Richard said. "But I think your relationship with Ísabel and Ísabel's secret are worth preserving, whatever the political outcome. Or your job. Eventually, Gregory's behavior will catch up with him."

"I'm not so sure." Gracie shook her head.

"Don't you imagine he's going to get his comeuppance at

some point? Even if he doesn't, would you really risk Ísabel's emotional health to force the issue now?"

"The guy is sleeping with teenagers, Richard!" Gracie shouted. "We're not talking about a little campaign finance malfeasance. We're talking about kids' lives!"

"I get it, Gracie." He held a palm up to deflect her anger. "I know it's serious business. But maybe it's time for you to get out of the business of being the community's morality police, too. Or morality icon. Whatever it is you think you are."

That caught Gracie by surprise. Whatever she expected from Richard, she never thought he would compare her behavior with Gregory's vigilantism.

"Oh, is this now about me? Or is it about us? Is this now about the fact that I didn't want people to know about us? I thought we were talking about Gregory. But all of a sudden it's about my hang-ups?"

"I'm just suggesting that maybe it's time for you to quit holding yourself up as a paragon of perfection. That's a pretty heavy cross to bear, Gracie. Then maybe you won't feel you need to judge others."

"I'm not judging Gregory! I just want him to stop hurting girls in this town. Don't you?"

Richard didn't answer right away. He held Gracie's eyes. She held her breath and thought about what she'd just said.

"Do you really want Ísabel to have to face him in court?" he asked. "Is that what you really want?"

Angry as she was, Gracie forced herself to consider his question. It wasn't what she wanted, of course. What she wanted was for Ísabel to be happy and Gregory to go away.

"I don't know. Maybe I just want him out of my life. Out of our lives."

"I know," Richard said. "And I also know that love is powerful, and I know that you love Ísabel, and I think that will be enough to help you figure this out."

He stood up and looked down at her for a long minute.

Gracie's thoughts were too muddled to know what to say. He was right. She was right. Ísabel was right. It was going to take some serious evaluation of relative goods and evils to figure out what to do.

But why had Richard brought up her secrecy about their love life now? Was there really a connection between that and wanting to bring Gregory down?

Was it really about whose secrets were safe in this small town and whose weren't? That was really what it boiled down to, wasn't it? It wasn't about the severity of the transgression; obviously, Gregory's had been worse than hers. It was about power, and that's what irritated her the most. Gregory had more than his share, and he didn't deserve it.

Richard put his hand on her shoulder and held it there for a few seconds. "I have faith in you, my love," he said. "I know you will do the right thing."

He turned and walked up the stairs and knocked on Ísabel's door.

~21~

It wasn't until she got the letter from Gregory that Gracie remembered that John, the mayor, had said Caitlin was resigning from the board.

Fuming over her inability to bring his hypocrisy to light, Gracie decided to call Caitlin and find out what happened. She needed to have an ally in this fight, and Caitlin was her only bet. Jacob had called her to say he was postponing his return from Arizona and wouldn't be back in time for the February board meeting.

They chose a bakery-café on the outskirts of Des Moines for their rendezvous, reducing the chances that Gregory or any of his cronies would see them together that Saturday. The air was rich with the aroma of spices and sugar when Gracie walked in, and the counter where she ordered her coffee displayed the culprit: a heaping pile of freshly baked cinnamon cookies, each as big as a hand, including its fingers.

"My guess is it's pretty much impossible to get out of here without eating one of those." Gracie winked at the young man who took her order for a latté. Lattés were hard to come by in Johnson Station, and having one should have been enough of a treat, but Gracie's resistance was no match for the sight and smell of those cookies.

"Well, the good thing is they are one hundred percent calorie-free." The young man winked back at her and pulled the top cookie onto a paper plate. "But the bad thing is you'll be hungry again in a week."

While Gracie waited for both Caitlin and her latté, she worked on a crossword puzzle someone had left half-done in the *Des Moines Register* left behind at her table. "Giving up" was

the clue for seven-down. Eight letters. "Resigned?" No, it
didn't fit. "Badgered" didn't work either. But "buckling" did.
What a coincidence that it was the first clue she came across
while she waited. She hoped it didn't have some subliminal
effect on what she said to Caitlin. The brain could be pretty
stubborn.

Gracie focused on making a list of good words, words she
wanted to soak in before Caitlin arrived. "Forbearance."
"Forgiveness." "Patience." "Understanding." How about
simply "nice"?

Her drink arrived just as Caitlin rushed in the door, letting
in enough cold air to drop her latté to easy sipping
temperature.

"Hey, sorry if I'm late." Caitlin stripped off her coat and
scarf and threw them on the chair across the table. "Kids. I'll
hurry up and order something."

A minute later Caitlin came back with a matching cookie
and a cup of regular coffee and plopped down as if she'd run
a marathon before showing up for their meeting.

"Whew!" she exclaimed. "I'm really glad you suggested
this. Sometimes I don't get away from my rat race all weekend.
This is such a great idea."

"You know what I wanted to talk about, though." Gracie
sounded as apologetic as she could.

"Sure, but compared with chasing after my five-year-olds
and wrestling with six loads of laundry, it's no biggie."

Gracie gave Caitlin a minute to settle down, sip some
coffee, and take a couple of bites of her big, doughy cookie.
She was surprised at how energetic and vivacious she seemed
compared with the quiet person Gracie had come to know at
board meetings.

"Mmmmm," Caitlin moaned her appreciation. "Sugar
good!"

Gracie laughed. "You look like you run it off pretty quick,
too," she said.

"No, it's not running; it's more like schlepping. Schlepping laundry, schlepping groceries, schlepping kids. My sister has MS, and I end up taking her kids and their dirty laundry most days as well. And that's just the sixteen hours I'm not at work. At the store, it's schlepping books, schlepping files, schlepping mailbags. I mean, look at these arms!"

Caitlin held up an arm and pushed back the long sleeve of her turtleneck. Her bicep, Gracie had to admit, was impressive.

"Wow, maybe I should try weight lifting," Gracie said.

"No, how about you take the kids instead!" Caitlin laughed. It was clear, despite the complaining, that she was in love with her life.

"Thanks, but I'd hate to deprive you of your workout," Gracie said. "You might lose some muscle tone."

Gracie nibbled on her cookie, trying to decide whether to ask the obvious question: What about her husband?

What the hell. If Caitlin got angry with her, it wouldn't matter much, now that she was leaving the board. She asked, adding, "Doesn't your husband help?

"Divorced." Caitlin held up her ringless left hand. There wasn't an indentation or a white stripe that would have indicated a recent separation. Apparently, it had been a while. Gracie hadn't noticed.

"Long time?"

"Yeah, five years ago."

"Over it?"

"Except for the workload, yeah. It wasn't good. No regrets, except for the poor child support settlement I agreed on." Caitlin rolled her eyes, and then shook her head as if to dismiss the subject.

Caitlin finished off her cookie in a few more bites, slapped her hands together to knock the sugar off her fingers, and sat back.

"What did you want to talk about?"

"Why you are resigning from the library board."

"Of course. I knew that. Or I assumed. So, here's the story."

Gregory, she said, had asked her to change her position on creating the library policy and to quit fighting him in his efforts to establish a don't-read list for the library's underage patrons. She had refused, saying it went against her principles as well as the First Amendment. He had added a couple of snide comments about her divorce, and then said he would ask the mayor to replace her if she wouldn't go along.

"Do you think the mayor would actually do that?" Caitlin asked.

"I don't know," Gracie said. "I ran into him a month or so ago, and he seemed different. He seemed like he had taken a page out of Gregory's prayer book."

"Wow. That town is changing!" Caitlin said. "My mom said when she was a kid, there was a socialist mayor in Johnson Station. But that was back in the sixties."

"I take it you didn't agree to change your position?"

"No, I didn't."

"Did you think about talking to the mayor about it?"

Abruptly, Caitlin's face drooped, and she looked tired. She looked down at her hands and started folding her paper napkin into smaller and smaller squares.

"No, I guess I was intimidated a bit." Caitlin sighed. "And, I'm sorry, but I already have enough battles to fight. I didn't want the public embarrassment of being kicked off the board, and having my dirty laundry, so to speak aired, so I resigned."

"But you could have stuck it out and let people know you couldn't be bullied." The word "buckling" hovered over her thoughts, and she fought to keep it at bay. "And a divorce isn't dirty laundry in today's world. My God, half of the population of the country gets divorced!"

"Yes, I know." Caitlin looked chagrined. "Look, I have

two kids. I'm a single mom. I have laundry. I have a job that takes sixty hours a week. This week the refrigerator quit making ice and the idle on the car started racing, burning up about ten gallons of gas per mile. I had to figure out how to get a repairman to come to the house when I could be there, and how to get the kids to daycare and myself to work while the car was in the shop. Sometimes I just want to get through the week without fighting all of this stuff and having to fix things."

Gracie let the sound of Caitlin's whine settle a second before reacting.

"Hey, I'm sorry," she said. "I am sorry. I wasn't accusing you of being a slacker or not standing by your principles. I'm sorry. I just wish this one man wasn't getting to the point he's running our town. But I don't blame you. He's a handful for anyone, even me. And he's all I really have to worry about."

"Well, there's something else," Caitlin said, almost under her breath. "It's something I need to tell you. It's part of the context here, part of why I was so willing to resign."

Gracie said nothing. She looked Caitlin in the eye and nodded.

"Do you remember Sara?"

Gracie thought for a moment, and then nodded. "Oh, of course I do. I hope she found those books helpful. It can't be easy trying to help a young man navigate his sexuality in the midst of so much prejudice. Especially these days!"

"Yeah, well." Caitlin stopped and glanced around the shop, as if to see who was within earshot. She lowered her voice. "She doesn't have a son."

Immediately, Gracie knew. It all came together: Sara's visits to Johnson Station. The "dirty laundry" Caitlin was referring to. One five-year divorce and one very recent one. The cover story Sara had employed: a son who needed help coming to terms with a sexual identity. The novels that were well beyond appropriate for a teenager. Why hadn't she seen it before?

"I will tell you the story," Caitlin offered. Gracie nodded.

Caitlin had first met Sara in the bookstore in Des Moines two years before. The way Caitlin described it, the encounter reminded Gracie of Sara's first visit to the library; she'd been just as reluctant to tell Caitlin what she was looking for. But eventually, she let Caitlin help her find books on divorce and abused women. Eventually, Sara's marriage ended, and with it, most of her disposable income. She wasn't able to buy books anymore.

As the two of them grew closer and started to fall in love, Sara started to spend weekends with Caitlin, and now they were adjusting to who they were: two lesbians. But it was harder than that: two lesbians in a very conservative small town.

"I feel so stupid," Gracie said. "I should have known. I could have been more sensitive. To you and to Sara. I'm sorry."

Caitlin nodded and took a deep breath. "Wow, it's good to have that off my chest."

"But why didn't you just bring home some books for her? Why send her to the library?"

"Because she needed to discover her own answers, find her own way. That's what libraries are for. That's what you're there for. But I don't need to tell you that. You know that better than I do."

"Thanks." Gracie thought that might be one of the nicest compliments she'd ever received.

"I think you are the only one in Johnson Station who knows about Sara and me, and I need to ask you to keep it that way. And I didn't want to give Gregory any incentive to pry into my life. That's also why I quit. If he could chastise me for my divorce, imagine what he'd do with this?"

"I admire your strength," Gracie said.

"Well, I appreciate your strength, Gracie" Caitlin reached

over and squeezed Gracie's forearm so tightly it hurt a bit. "I promise you I'm not abandoning you. I promise I'll find a way to help win this fight. It just can't be with me on the board."

Gracie couldn't imagine what Caitlin could do, but she nodded her gratitude.

"There are a lot of people behind you, you know," Caitlin continued. "It's the new silent majority. But people have gotten to the point they don't want to fight these ideologues. They just keep coming. It's like pushing a rock up hill, you know. Like Sisyphus."

"Yes, but at least Sisyphus knew what his role in life was," Gracie said.

"Yes, and thank you, Albert Camus." Caitlin laughed and Gracie laughed along.

But her heart was heavy. She was just getting to know Caitlin, and now she was losing her.

ॐ

Gracie was starting to feel like defeat was inevitable. She was either going to have to implement and enforce Gregory's new policies at the library, or she was going to lose her job. Before she gave up, she decided to pay a visit to the mayor. Maybe there was a third way.

Gracie remembered when John first came to Johnson Station as a salesman at the Ford dealership. At the time, he had Jens do some work for him—something to do with John's parents' estate. He talked big when he arrived, telling everyone that his plan was to own the dealership in a few years. However, after the farm economy collapsed in the mid-eighties, the town began to shrink, and the dealership went bankrupt—long before John had saved enough money to buy it from his boss. He sold cars in Des Moines after that, and with no wife or kids to support and the chance to own a dealership gone, he had no need to work. He retired in his early fifties and ran for mayor in Johnson Station.

John had held onto his post for twenty years, largely because no one else really wanted the job. He ran unopposed for all but his first four-year term. A little more rotund, a little more humble, and now a lot more conservative than he was when he first moved to town from Ohio, he still had another year before he was up for re-election, and Gracie knew of no reason he should have been worried about any competition for his mostly ceremonial position. Unless, of course, he challenged Gregory's growing hegemony.

His powers were limited; he broke ties in town council votes, appointed planning and zoning commissioners, and named library board members. Otherwise, he mainly showed up at charity events and ribbon cuttings, always in the same blue blazer, gray pants, and dark-gray fedora. It was the only hat Gracie had ever seen anyone wear in Johnson Station other than baseball caps with seed-corn and Major League Baseball logos.

Although Gracie hadn't seen him since the night she and Richard ran into him at the Olive Garden, she knew he had to be around. He was not a snowbird, and she had heard him bemoan the fact that the shrinking town couldn't support as many bars or restaurants as it once did, and he hated having to leave for a night—or day—out.

She called him under the pretense of having some names to suggest for the empty library board seat vacated by Caitlin. He sounded jocular on the phone and happy to hear from her. He was glad to meet with her in his seldom-used office in the town hall on Tuesday.

"What else do I have to do?" he asked by way of saying "yes" to her request to meet.

At his office door midmorning, he shook her hand vigorously, as if he'd been storing up handshakes for some time. "No one ever comes to see me much anymore," he admitted.

"Well, it is winter," Gracie offered, as she took the chair across from his desk. "You would probably see more of your constituents if you went to Arizona."

"Well, yes. And even if they were here, they have figured out where the power is in town these days, and it isn't in this office," he said obliquely. "No one needs to see me much anymore."

Gracie was surprised at his willingness to share his political impotency with her, and she couldn't resist encouraging him to continue. "What do you mean?"

The mayor leaned back in his old wooden desk chair and rubbed his bald head, as if he were trying to decide how much he wanted to say.

"Gracie," he finally answered, rocking forward and putting his elbows on his desk. "You and I have known each other for a long time, and we've both seen time fly by and dreams dashed. So, I don't mind being honest with you."

"About what?"

"Don't get me wrong," he said. "I believe that Gregory has the community's best interests at heart, and with all of the businessmen in town behind him, I don't feel I can make a move without consulting him first."

"But this is supposed to be a democracy," she said. "Even at the municipal level, we have elected officials and bureaucrats and courts—you know the three branches of government."

"Yes, and Gregory can buy them all."

"I wish you hadn't said that."

"I wish I didn't believe it. Gracie." He looked beaten down by his admission. "Never underestimate the degree to which Johnson Station is now Gregory Thungaard's town."

"Can I quote you on that?" Gracie was only half joking.

"I will deny I ever said it."

"Sad day in America."

"Yes." John nodded.

They sat in silence, and Gracie suddenly wanted to get out of there. She reached into her purse and pulled out a sheet of paper with two names on it—Terry, the minister; and Jackie, her friend and a former English teacher.

"Here." She handed the paper to John. "I think both these individuals are well qualified to stand up for the interests of Johnson Station's reading public. I would like you to consider them for the open library board spot."

"I think that's already been decided." The mayor barely looked at the paper. "I'm not sure who it is yet, but I can't appoint anyone that Gregory doesn't nominate."

"Seriously?"

The mayor threw up his hands. "Yup. You're lucky his son isn't old enough to be appointed to the board. And the town council. And to the town manager's job."

"That's just wrong!" Gracie nearly shouted. "One man can't usurp the entire democratic process and name himself emperor!"

"I'm afraid he can, if he can afford to."

Now Gracie wondered what else Gregory had gotten his fingers into. What other controls did he have his grubby hands on? And how exactly had he bought such power?

"Can I ask you something?"

"I don't know. What about?"

"The food bank. Did you cast a tie-breaking vote?"

"Yes. Gregory didn't think we needed it anymore."

"But what did you think?"

The mayor ignored her question. "He said the illegals had been sent home, and they were the only ones using it."

"You know that's not true," Gracie said. "There are plenty of people, perhaps even some the deported left behind, who need that help."

"Gregory thinks we don't necessarily need to keep them in the community," the mayor said.

"But your population is declining," Gracie countered.

"Don't you need more people, not fewer?"

"Not those kind." He knitted his eyebrows and nodded at her as if it would help her understand. "Perhaps if we don't coddle them, they'll go somewhere else."

"And they'll be someone else's problem?"

"Maybe."

"Real Christian of you. And him. And what does your man Gregory think about all of the empty buildings downtown here?" she asked. "If he wants to better this town, perhaps he's got an idea of how to turn things around. Two more businesses closed last week."

"What's happening to our economy isn't Gregory's fault. It's those trade deals and illegal immigrants. The fat cats in Washington don't care about us out here in Iowa."

"Did Gregory tell you that too? Does he provide you with a script these days?"

John pretended he hadn't heard that. "Downtown isn't Gregory's problem."

"But it certainly is yours," Gracie countered quickly. "I know I must sound like a broken record to you, harping on this all of the time, but what are you going to do about it? If Gregory is such a valuable resource to you, perhaps he has some ideas. Or maybe you have some."

The mayor said nothing. He squinted as if he was trying to figure a way out of the conversation. Then suddenly his entire attitude changed, as if he realized he had allowed the discussion to go wrong. His face turned to stone, and he sat up in his chair.

"I'm sorry you and Gregory don't get along," he said. "But, you know, it isn't all bad. We could use a little moral integrity around here, a kind of discipline and guidance that might save us from meth labs and teenage pregnancies and our pandemic of divorces and adultery. I think Gregory is onto something. Perhaps this could help us clean up our community and rebuild it on our Christian traditions."

Gracie realized she had lost him. In an instant, he had gone back to being Gregory's mayor. Arguing about the validity of "Christian traditions" in government wasn't going to get them any closer to agreeing. And leaning on Christian values wasn't going to do anything about those boarded up buildings on Main Street.

"How much time are you spending with Gregory these days?" she asked.

"Quite a bit." It sounded like an exaggeration and a boast. "I was asked to be on his campaign committee. Not bad for an old car salesman, huh?"

"Well, everyone has his price." Gracie stood up.

The mayor's face went blank.

"Nice talking with you, Gracie," he said stiffly. "I hope you'll keep my confidence. I shouldn't have said most of what I said today. I hope we're good enough friends you'll keep it between us."

She waited for him to look up and meet her eyes, but after a few uncomfortable seconds, she decided to let him off the hook. She turned and left without saying good-bye.

Gracie couldn't believe her luck; no sooner had she left work at the library that afternoon than she ran into the would-be emperor himself at the little grocery store down the street.

He was standing in the middle of the canned-vegetable aisle, holding onto a grocery tote. Next to him, a tall, immaculately coifed blonde about his age studied the label on a can of tomato juice, reading glasses perched on the end of her nose and attached to a leather strap that looped behind her neck. Her camel coat was open, revealing a nicely tailored gray suit, its jacket buttoned at the waist, showing off the kind of figure Gracie had envied for herself twenty years ago and totally dismissed as possible today.

Gracie had never met Gregory's wife, but she had always imagined her to be a mousy little thing stuck back in the farmhouse, barefoot and in the kitchen, taking whatever abuse her dictator-husband dished out. This woman couldn't be his wife. Gracie assumed he was having another affair, this time with a grown-up.

"Oh, Gracie." Gregory's voice was much sweeter than the one he usually used when he addressed her. "How pleasant to see you. Do you know Barbra? Barbra, this is Gracie, the librarian I've told you about."

Taken off guard, Gracie defaulted to her best behavior. "How do you do?" She held out her hand. "Is that Barbra as in Streisand, or Barbara as in Bush?"

"How clever of you not to jump to conclusions!" the woman answered, reaching out with a gloved hand to shake. Her grip was firm and businesslike. "It's like Streisand."

"Barbra is a top money manager for high-net-worth individuals in the investment arm of Principal in Des Moines," Gregory said, sounding very proud of that fact.

Gracie was confused. "So you manage Gregory's money?"

The woman chuckled softly. "No, my dear," she said. "I'm his wife. He won't let me *near* his money."

Being addressed as "my dear" was embarrassing enough. To have mistaken the woman for his money manager rather than a wife was even worse. Why would his money manager be shopping for groceries with him?

In fact, Barbra seemed to be thinking the same thing. "So, I've heard so much about you." She emphasized the word *you*. She turned to Gregory with a questioning frown. "Is this the woman . . . ?"

Gregory nodded nearly imperceptibly, and Barbra stopped and turned back toward Gracie.

"I hope Gregory isn't beating up on you too much."

Gracie considered how to respond. Barbra looked more

successful than Gregory, and she came across as smarter, too. How did she feel about their debate over censorship? Worried that a discussion about it would devolve into an argument, Gracie simply smiled and looked back and forth, studying their faces, trying to discern the true nature of their relationship.

She was rewarded. Barbra dug into her coat pocket and took out a Kleenex. She reached over, straightened Gregory's tie, and tried to discretely hand him the tissue while looking at aa spot on Gregory's chin.

"You have a little barbecue on your face," she whispered, but Gracie heard it. "You might want to wipe it off."

Gregory pushed her hand away just like Janice used to do when Gracie tried to clean her face in public. He looked away, avoiding both women's eyes.

So, this was where his money and his ambition came from. How did a woman as powerful and successful as Barbra settle for this weak link in the first place?

"We must get running, dear." Barbra stuffed the Kleenex back in her pocket and grabbed Gregory's elbow. A weariness had crept into her expression; was she tiring of the role as the grown-up in the family? "We both have meetings tonight. So nice to meet you, Gracie."

Gracie stood, mesmerized, and watched them push down the aisle. *You don't deserve her, Gregory, you smug bastard.* Barbra clearly could have done better.

Gracie stood for a moment, trying to remember what she was looking for when she chose this grocery aisle. Instead, she saw two images from the day floating in her mind's eye: the mayor, distraught and beaten down, slumping in his big official chair; and Gregory's wife, full of competence and poise.

What if, she wondered, Gregory suddenly had to choose between them—between his political ambitions or his wife? Better yet, what if his political career failed, and as a consequence, so did his financially advantageous and respectable marriage? What if in trying to save one or the other, he ends up losing them both?

She couldn't help but think that if he did, Barbra would be better off.

~

Ísabel and Gracie had barely spoken since she received Gregory's letter and Ísabel had read it over her shoulder. Gracie owed the girl the apology, not the other way around, but she hadn't found time to sit down and do it right.

Ísabel had started going straight home from school rather than stopping at the library. She had a computer in her room in Gracie's house now, and Gracie didn't doubt that it was a lot easier for her to do her homework there. So she didn't take it as a sign that Ísabel was avoiding her. However, Gracie knew she needed to cultivate a reconciliation before Ísabel's resentment hardened into Janice-like antipathy.

Oddly, it was Janice who warned her not to wait too long.

"Mom, that's the thing that always got me about you," Janice said in one of their now-weekly phone conversations. Since Christmas, she and Janice had reached a kind of truce, and their rapport was starting to warm a bit. Perhaps Janice's jealousy made her want to try harder. Or perhaps Gracie had started to adjust her approach as she learned from Ísabel.

Whatever the provenance, finally Gracie and Janice were talking without throwing accusations back and forth, as they had for years. And while it wasn't easy, Gracie was relieved it was happening. It had never seemed right to be so estranged from her only blood relative left in the world.

"What?" Gracie asked Janice on the phone. "What did I do?"

"You were so good at managing all of the physical stuff about being my mom, but you had trouble letting grudges go. You'd hold things against me for months."

"No, I didn't—" Gracie started. Then she stopped. She was learning to take her daughter's criticism, even if her first instinct was denial. "I'm sorry, go on."

"I finally quit trying to get your love back," Janice said. "I just decided your affections were too conditional. I don't know what happened between you and Ísabel, but maybe you should let this go. Whatever reason you have for being mad at her, let it go. Go say you're sorry. And don't say 'I'm sorry, *but* . . .'"

Gracie agreed, grudgingly. "Things have been busy around here, and I've been using that as an excuse. But you're right. I need to talk to her sooner, not later."

"And you have some trouble saying you're sorry," Janice added. Gracie thought that was unnecessary, but she let it slide.

"How'd you get so smart?" she asked instead.

"Therapy," Janice said. So, Richard was right. "Years and years of therapy."

That evening when Gracie got home from the grocery store with makings for lasagna, she called up the stairs to Ísabel.

"Are you done with your homework?"

"Why? What do you want?" Ísabel yelled back through her closed door. Ísabel could be as stubborn as she was, Gracie thought, smiling to herself. They were quite the pair.

"I was wondering if you could help make supper. Richard is coming over, but not in time to help me."

As soon as Ísabel opened her door and appeared at the top of the staircase, Gracie turned back to the kitchen. She pulled a stockpot out of the cupboard and filled it with water, listening to Ísabel's steps down the stairs.

"What do you want me to do?" Ísabel stood behind her. Gracie was relieved to hear the girl's neutral tone. She didn't sound particularly mad.

"Could you brown the sausage and hamburger? We're

making lasagna."

Gracie waited until Ísabel was settled over a sauté pan stirring the meat with a spatula to start her apology.

"I'm sorry, Ísabel," she said.

"About what?"

"About suggesting we break your agreement with Gregory."

Ísabel said nothing, leaving Gracie to fill in her silence.

"I was thinking about myself and not about you. That's not always wrong, but in this instance it was. I'm sorry, and I'll never push you to change your mind about it again."

"Okay," Ísabel said so quietly that Gracie barely heard it. Gracie sighed deeply, letting go of much more tension than she knew she was holding. If that was all it took to get beyond her big mistake, she was lucky. The girl could have held a grudge for a very long time.

Gracie started chopping herbs on a cutting board by the sink, and Ísabel looked over and watched.

"You're really good at that," she complimented Gracie. "I like the way you hardly move the knife but you chop it all so fine."

"Practice, Ísabel." Gracie didn't look up. She didn't need to cut off a finger just when the girl had praised her ability with a knife. "That's all it is. Do you want to try?"

"Nah, I'm happy doing this. Would you like me to make the salad, though, once the meat is done?"

"That'd be great. I bought some Romaine and some tomatoes. Cucumbers, too." Gracie pointed to the refrigerator with her knife.

They worked silently for the next few minutes. Gracie finished chopping the herbs and added them to Ísabel's meat mixture. She stirred in a large can of diced tomatoes, and then started to work on the cheese mixture, while Ísabel tore tiny pieces of lettuce into the salad spinner.

Ísabel broke their silence. "Are you going to lose your

job? Is Gregory going to fire you?"

"Probably," Gracie answered softly. "But I think that was going to happen anyway. And you know what? I think it's about time I left anyway. I've been thinking about retiring, maybe traveling to South America."

She let that notion hang in the air for a moment.

"And Richard and I were thinking maybe you'd like to come along. You know, take the summer and be our Spanish translator. Maybe he and I can pick up some of the language with your help. And then when your mom gets back, she and I can get to know each other a little."

She looked over at Ísabel, who was smiling broadly. She nodded vigorously, tears welling in her eyes.

"I can't wait to tell my mom!" she said. "Can I go call her now?"

"Sure. But hurry back. I still need help constructing the lasagna."

Maybe she was reading too much into their relationship, but Gracie was getting a feel for Ísabel in a way she had never found with Janice. If everyone had a second chance to learn this mothering thing, maybe they'd all get good at it. She chuckled.

"What's funny?" Ísabel asked, suspiciously, turning back at the doorway.

"I am just thinking how much I love being here for you, Ísabel." Gracie looked up into the girl's eyes with tears in her own. "You have no idea what a gift you are for me."

~22~

Marcia didn't have to wait as long as she expected to find out about the internship. Apparently her qualifications had been such a great fit with what the microfinance group needed that they called her up and offered her the position as soon as they received her application on Friday.

When she received the call at work, she told Gracie later, she got up from her desk, walked into her boss's office, and resigned on the spot. She didn't give two weeks' notice, but she did offer to help anyone who took over her loan portfolio over the phone if they had questions. That wasn't necessary, her boss had said.

"I'm relieved," she told Gracie. She had packed up the small box of personal items in her desk, taken them out to her car, and then hurried over to the library to tell Gracie the good news. "I really need a clean break. After that idiot mistake I made with Carl, I just wanted to put the entire business behind me and move on. But I didn't know if a woman my age could get hired anywhere."

"I guess this calls for a celebration," Gracie said. "I wish I could throw you a party, but the board meeting is Tuesday, and I don't think I have time."

"Well, let's just have a private toast, then," Marcia said. "Do you have any coffee?"

Marcia stayed for an hour, excitedly relaying her plans to pack, drive her old Cadillac across the Rockies and Cascades to Seattle, find an apartment near her new job, and then wow the agency with her enthusiasm and expertise. She might leave as early as the coming weekend, she said, although she allowed that it was likely it would take her longer to get ready.

Gracie felt herself withdrawing from the conversation, lapsing into a kind of abstract distance, even as she nodded and encouraged her friend to continue. Was it a defensive reaction to loss? Was she proactively mentally and emotionally separating herself from Marcia to protect herself from the loneliness she would feel once her best friend was gone? But maybe she was too jealous to be civil. Or too preoccupied with the upcoming board meeting to focus on Marcia's big news.

Marcia left at noon, giving Gracie a long, generous hug before tripping out the door with the light step of a newly minted graduate off to start the job of her collegiate dreams. Gracie glanced at her watch and decided to take her lunch hour out of the office. She called Terry to see if she could bring him a sandwich and spend her lunch hour in his office in the back of the church.

"Turkey on rye," she announced fifteen minutes later, handing him a butcher-paper-wrapped sandwich fresh from Blixt's Café. "I hope that's good. I forgot to ask you what you wanted."

"It's great." He accepted her offering and motioned for her to sit with him at the small conference table in the corner of his office. "But not as great as seeing you. You've been busy, I gather."

Gracie wondered how much she should share with him. Certainly not Ísabel's abortion, and since she was sworn to secrecy, not her pregnancy nor Gregory's role in it. She needed to limit her musings to the problems she was having at the library and her concerns about the political trends in Johnson Station, and leave her personal problems out of it.

"How is Ísabel?"

"Thriving," Gracie said, leaving it at that.

"And Richard?"

"Very good. He really enjoys Ísabel's company. They've been on a classic movie binge the past month."

"Are you two going to get married, do you think?"

Gracie smiled. Of course he would ask that. He was probably concerned for her soul, she thought.

"No, I don't think so," she admitted. "I imagine you think that is pretty sinful, but it's just not who I am right now."

"No, Gracie." Terry offered her a bottled water out of the apartment refrigerator he kept in his office and sitting down. "To me, sin is not breaking mankind's rules and regulations. Far worse is not knowing who you are and who you want to be. I applaud you for knowing you don't need to get married again."

The minister opened his sandwich and got up again to retrieve a jar of Grey Poupon from his refrigerator. "Since it's not about a wedding, what was it you wanted to talk about today?"

"I'm not sure," Gracie said. "I just found out my best friend is leaving town, and suddenly, I felt lonely, like I needed to talk to someone. I've told you before, you're my go-to guy."

"Well, I'm pleased to be reminded of that."

Gracie took a bite of her sandwich. It bought her a little time while she tried to figure out how broach her subject.

Finally, she jumped in. "Something is on my mind," she said. "Something I'm worried about."

"What is that?"

"The direction our town is headed," she said. "I know that sounds a little grandiose, like I'm a community guardian or something."

"In a way, you are." He tipped his head slightly in the way he often did that seemed to solicit further explication. "Even Gregory recognizes that."

"Well, thanks, but I'm not sure I want the role."

"Anyway . . ."

"It's funny, but I guess what's concerning me is this push to adopt a so-called Christian morality that seems to be anything but Christian to me. Not that I know anything about being religious, of course. In fact, that's why I wanted to talk to you."

"Of course."

"I mean, how can we be a community that considers itself so Christian that we have to limit the books kids can read, and yet not Christian enough to keep the food bank open? How can we be Christian enough to kill sex education in school, but not Christian enough to accept those who suffer the consequences of unwanted pregnancies? Or not Christian enough to take in a young woman who is abandoned by her parents?"

"These are very good questions," Terry said. "I suppose they have come up because of the political ambitions of a certain someone."

"Yes, it is political ambition that I think is at the bottom of this. And what concerns me is it seems that some people really don't care about Christianity except as a brand on which they can build their political campaigns."

"You are probably right about that," Terry said. "So, what did you think you need to do about this?"

"Well, I think my job is to take care of the people I love, and at the same time, stick to my guns about what I think are fundamental rights that I'm charged with protecting. Specifically, the right to read anything we want to read. And to help people find it."

"That sounds like a good strategy," Terry said. He focused on his sandwich as if he was looking for some spiritual sign in the dark and light swirls of the rye bread. "I think you should do exactly that. And I don't think you should worry about those who are pursuing their political ambitions."

"But what if it destroys this town? What if we end up in a kind of totalitarian community where only certain opinions and behaviors are tolerated? Wouldn't that be something I should care about?"

Terry nodded as if he agreed. Then he disagreed in his own diplomatic way. "Your ambition is also pretty expansive, then, isn't it?"

"Well, I can't stick my head in the sand and pretend I don't see what's going on."

"But you've never suggested that was your plan," Terry said. "Your plan is to protect the First Amendment rights of Johnson Station's residents. That is not sticking your head in the sand."

"But is it enough?"

"Probably not, but, Gracie, you are only one person," he said. "The community may have to go through this process, but I'm certain that these things go in cycles. Eventually, we will see our way to the other side of this."

"But doesn't it bother you that the hypocrites among us get by with their hypocrisy? That no one calls them out?"

Terry took the last bite of his sandwich and folded up the butcher paper while he chewed. He swallowed, took a big swig of water, and smiled at Gracie.

"In the end, Gracie," he said, "everyone from the king to the pauper must make an accounting to God. I'm confident your accounting will be satisfactory and even laudatory. I'm not so sure about the other guy."

"It helps if you believe in God," she said. "It gives you a life after death to look forward to, and some kind of righteous judgment."

"Believing in God and believing in life after death are two different things," the minister said. "You never hear me talking about an afterlife as a reward for good behavior. Good acts, loving acts are reward enough in themselves."

Gracie tried to think back to all the sermons she'd heard him deliver on Sunday mornings. He was right. He never promised a heavenly reward in return for Christian benevolence. The "accounting" he talked about wasn't the same as a reward.

"Hey." He interrupted her thoughts. "But I'm wondering. You have a board meeting next week that I hear is pretty important when it comes to that First Amendment issue. Have you recruited some support?"

"No." Gracie sighed. "I started to at one point, but lately, I've not had any time. It's amazing how much a teenager can soak up your energies."

"Well, good luck to you, then," he said. "I've got a meeting with a new parishioner in a few minutes. But call me if you want to get together again, Gracie."

&

The next Tuesday, Gracie turned the library over to her assistant to set up the table for the board meeting and walked home for supper. Richard had promised to have meatloaf and mashed potatoes—the ultimate in comfort food—ready for her so she could eat and get back to the library within the two-hour window she'd have between her workday and the big board meeting.

Still, she had trouble working up an appetite. Her stomach seemed to be absorbing more than its share of the nerves that jangled through her body as she anticipated the nasty conclave.

Walking back downtown for the meeting, she rued the fact that she'd never found the time to build a cadre of supporters like she had planned way back in December, when it was clear Gregory was going to push his agenda. With her regular job duties, Marcia's issues, Ísabel's pregnancy, and Richard's companionship, she'd had enough on her hands. And even if she had pulled together some kind of posse to save her job, she expected it would have been futile in the long run, just as she had told Ísabel.

Oddly, though, she had a feeling that losing her personal battle with Gregory didn't signal the end of the war. This meeting would be difficult, she may end up losing her job, but it may have been worth it to fight, anyway. Her personal crusade to protect the library from a censorious conservative not only demonstrated Gregory's disinterest in the town's real problems, it also exposed the community leaders as petty, insular, and beholden to his interests. The mayor was up for re-election in a few months, and unless the downtown businessmen came up with some magic to revitalize this dying town, she thought anyone who wanted to run for his position had a good chance of winning.

It had finally snowed again, and Gracie trudged through six inches of wet snow in her big boots and a down coat, steeling herself for what was coming. How she wished the next three hours were already over. She consoled herself by recalling all the times she had returned from vacation, wondering where the time had gone, thinking how quickly it passed. This too would be over soon.

As she turned onto Main Street, she wondered what was happening downtown. Cars, minivans, and pickup trucks lined the curbs, and it didn't look like there was a free spot for blocks. Usually she knew every event taking place in town; how could she have missed this?

"Oh, that's it!" she said aloud as she walked through the heavy library door. While she hadn't had time to recruit supporters for her position on library policy, it appeared that Gregory had—dozens of them. Right by the front door, Tony was holding court, lecturing a small circle of fellow businessmen: the balding mortician, the redheaded insurance agency owner, the tall construction contractor, and the nerdy computer repairman. She couldn't catch the drift of Tony's monologue, but she bet it wouldn't improve how she felt about the coming meeting.

Lowering her head, Gracie pushed through the crowd to her office, unlocked her door and ducked inside. Even with the door closed, the din of the accumulated crowd was enough that she barely heard the knock on her window.

She looked up. Smiling through the glass at her were Ísabel and Richard.

Thank God. She hadn't expected them to follow her to the library, but now she'd have at least two friends in the crowd. Still, she wouldn't expect either of them to stand up and say anything in her defense.

Gracie waved them in, and they closed the door quickly behind them.

"Hey, could you make copies of this agenda, Ísabel?" She handed the girl a two-page agenda that, as usual, would start the meeting with the most mundane items: selecting a bid to refurbish the ancient air conditioner, a list of small capital improvements she wanted to recommend for the building, and approval of a draft operating budget for the physical plant for the next year. She had also written a toned-down—she hoped innocuously phrased—proposal for the Spanish-English children's reading hour that Ísabel had agreed to help run.

She didn't think the bore of it all would dissuade any of Gregory's pals from sticking around for the debate over policy or her continued employment, but it would at least quiet them down for a few minutes.

"My God, this is intimidating." Gracie shook her head at Richard. "I don't think we've ever had more than one spectator at a board meeting in the twenty-five years I've been librarian. There must be forty people out there."

"Well, they're not all here to support Gregory, are they?" Richard peered out the window at the milling crowd.

"What else?" Gracie asked, pulling together the materials she'd prepared for the meeting earlier in the day.

"Well, I see Terry out there, and I don't think he'd be here at Gregory's request, would he?"

Gracie looked up and walked over to the window. "No," she said. "I don't think Terry is a fan of Gregory." She caught her minister's eye, and he smiled and waved at her. She recognized the two women he was chatting with: Marcia and Jackie. Marcia must have postponed her trip to Seattle. And there was a heavy woman next to them. Even from the back she knew it was Belinda.

"I had no idea those guys were coming," Gracie said. "Okay, now I have five—maybe six—friends. I'm not sure which way Belinda is leaning these days."

Gregory stuck his face in the window and knocked at her door. He opened it enough to stick his head through.

"Are we ready?" he asked. "We should probably get started. It's a little after seven."

"Where are all of these people going to sit?" Gracie asked. "If you were going to invite so many friends, shouldn't you have let me know? We could have set out some chairs."

He looked offended. "I only invited two people," he said, "and Tony invited a half dozen of his friends. I don't know where these other folks came from. Not my fault."

"Well, there are about two dozen chairs back in the storage area," she said to Richard. "Why don't you find Karen and get some guys to help her set them out? At least some of the older folks can sit."

Gracie gathered up her stack of files and loose papers and Richard held the door for her. She slipped through the crowd to the board table Karen had set up in its usual location towards the back of the open area of the big room. She was relieved to see Caitlin already there. Apparently her replacement was not yet in place. She was likely to get at least one vote of support.

Gracie sat down at the end of the table as usual. Gregory took the center seat facing the room, and the other board members slowly pushed through the crowd and sat flanking him. Gracie read over her notes on the budget matters while the audience shuffled out of the way so that Richard and two other men could set out the folding chairs.

The seats quickly filled, and as she organized the files in front of her, Gracie refrained from looking over the crowd. She really didn't want to know how many enemies she had that she didn't even know about or how many friends Tony could call on, friends willing to brave the cold and dark for a Tuesday night meeting in the middle of the winter to support Gregory's agenda.

Finally, the crowd settled down, and Gracie looked up. All the chairs were full and about a dozen and a half people remained standing behind them. She nodded at Gregory to start.

"All right, we'll call this meeting to order."

~23~

Gracie pulled the agenda copies Ísabel had made off the top of her pile of papers and handed them to Caitlin on her left. The board members passed them down, and Gregory studied his copy. Gracie then passed copies of the air-conditioning bids to Caitlin, and once again, the pages were passed down the line.

"Thanks, Gracie," Gregory said in his finest oratorical voice. He was already playing to the crowd, and he hadn't even entertained them with the air-conditioning bids yet. "But I think we'll probably be able to turn this agenda upside down tonight. I don't think all these people are here to hear us debate which plumbing and heating guy we're going to choose."

The crowd murmured its agreement.

"As chairman, I'm going to unilaterally elect to start the meeting with item number five," Gregory continued. "It's a discussion of the policy regarding book purchases and book access that we asked you to prepare back at the meeting in November, Gracie. Do you have copies of your policy for us to look at?"

He knew the answer. The board packet she had sent out didn't contain any such policy, and in the note she had sent along with the packet, she had explained why.

"As you know," Gracie started. She paused. Her voice was shaky, and that made her angry. She was letting Gregory and his crowd intimidate her, and an intimidated, mousy old lady was not the person she wanted to see when she looked in the mirror that evening. She took a deep breath and started over, pushing as much air out of her lungs as she could to match Gregory's strong delivery.

"As I told you in December, I agree with the American Library Association's position on this matter. May I read an excerpt of that policy for our audience, as I believe they may not have had a chance to see it before?"

Gracie spread out the pile of files in front of her, and found the one she'd prepared for the policy discussion. She turned toward the audience, without making eye contact with anyone.

"Any of you who would like a copy of this Library Bill of Rights issued by the library association, you can find it on their website, or ask me for a copy later, and I'll get you one."

Gracie looked down at the copy she'd printed out earlier that day and started reading.

The American Library Association affirms that all libraries are forums for information and ideas, and that the following basic policies should guide their services.

One. Books and other library resources should be provided for the interest, information, and enlightenment of all people of the community.—

"Hold on, Gracie!" Gregory interrupted her. "I think everyone here is capable of reading this on their own. But it's irrelevant. Let's stick to the management issue at hand. Did you or did you not follow the board's directive to prepare a policy that would direct you, as librarian, to select books for this community's library that are consistent with this community's standards of morality?"

He read the last sentence off the sheet in front of him. Obviously, he had expected this.

"I'm trying to explain why I didn't prepare such a policy," Gracie said. "I believe it's inappropriate—"

"What's inappropriate is for you to decide which of this board's directives you should follow and which you shouldn't," Gregory retorted, much more loudly than necessary, given the silence that had fallen over the room. He sniffed and jerked his head back in the arrogant tic he'd developed over the past year.

He continued. "But because I did not see any such policy in the packet you prepared for this meeting, I have taken the liberty of penning one myself." He pulled the reading glasses off his face and addressed the audience. "I would be happy to provide copies of it to any citizen of Johnson Station who would like to help us protect the morality and Christian values of our community."

"Resident." Gracie interjected.

"What?" Gregory turned to scowl at her. "What did you say?"

"People are *residents* of a community," she said. "You can only be a *citizen* of a country. Citizen of the United States. Resident of Johnson Station."

Gregory glared at her with disdain. The room was silent except for a solitary snicker in the back of the standing crowd. Gracie glanced over in its direction and saw Jackie covering her mouth as if trying to keep more noise from escaping.

Gregory also searched the seats for the snickering culprit before replacing his reading glasses and clearing his throat.

"The Johnson Station Library is committed to promoting a community standard that reflects and encourages a wholesome environment for children and families. The library encourages all its citizens to become aware of this standard and to promote it for the good of the entire community, particularly for its future—our children," he read.

Gregory looked up over his reading glasses and scanned the crowd. It was a pause for effect, Gracie guessed. He wanted to be sure the audience knew how important this was. He continued.

Johnson Station's community standards are best defined by what we will not accept: material that promotes homosexuality, nudity, bisexuality, transsexual and other deviant sexual behaviors; communism, socialism, and other destructive political philosophies that threaten our democracy; atheism and cults that promote Satanism and other religions that do not accept the word of Jesus Christ; drugs and a drug culture; and any other deviant behaviors that are recognizable on their face.

Books and other materials that contain or promote such unacceptable themes will not be purchased by the Johnson Station Library and the librarian shall remove any such items from its shelves. Further, the library will facilitate physical separation of materials deemed appropriate for adults only, restricting access by underage patrons.

Gregory paused, pulling off his glasses and scanning the crowd as if expecting applause for his well-crafted prose. Hearing none, he frowned, remounted his readers and continued.

Actions to fulfill this policy will commence immediately and be completed within one year of its adoption by a resolution of the board of directors of the Johnson Station Library.

Gregory pulled his glasses off again and glanced at the board members on either side of him. On cue, Tony raised his hand.

"I move that we adopt a resolution that directs the Johnson Station librarian to begin implementation of such a policy as proposed by our chairman," he announced.

"All in favor?" Gregory asked.

Tony, Gregory, Paul, and Lorena all answered "aye." Somewhere along the line, Gregory must have convinced Lorena to change her position.

"Opposed?"

"Nay," Caitlin said loudly.

"The ayes have it," Gregory said. "Now let's move on to

the next item. We will—"

"Excuse me!"

Gracie and the board members looked up to see Terry standing in the back, raising his hand.

"Mr. Chairman, isn't there going to be some public discussion of this so-called policy?" Terry asked.

"Oh, Reverend!" Gregory smiled full-toothed at Terry. "Nice to see you here. I'm so sorry, but this is not a public hearing. It is a board meeting. We generally do not take public comments at the board meeting."

"But on a matter in which you assert some kind of consensus as to what our quote-unquote community standards are, it seems that you would want to have some feedback from the community," Terry argued.

"Thank you for your suggestion," Gregory said. His frown clearly indicated that he wasn't grateful for it at all. "But this board has been appointed to represent the community, so as for all representative governmental bodies, we are charged with representing you all by proxy."

"Well, if you intend to argue you are a governmental body then I would argue that any discussion of appropriate and inappropriate religious materials is totally out of the question. There is a general doctrine of a separation of church and state in this country, is there not?"

Gregory sat back. He looked confused. Perhaps he had expected Terry to support him, particularly on matters pertaining to religious materials. But while Gracie knew Terry well enough to expect him to argue that the state should stay out of the business of religion, apparently Gregory did not.

"Once again, this is not a public hearing, Reverend," Gregory said.

"Why not?" Now Jackie had raised her hand.

"That's not how these things work." Gregory sounded as if he was losing his patience.

A collective groan rose from the crowd, and for the first

time, Gracie took a good look to see who was among those seated and standing before them. She spotted Caroline, the reader of child-rearing manuals; Liz, the anorexic cookbook reader; Armand, the avid critic of historical fiction; and Betty, the Blixt's Café waitress. She didn't even read; what was she doing there?

Jackie and Marcia were sitting a couple rows from the front, and she caught them smiling at her. She recognized another dozen or so occasional library patrons and a number of Terry's regular parishioners. Suddenly she realized she had more supporters in this crowd than Gregory did. But were they too cowed by his accumulated political heft to do anything other than show up at the meeting and groan?

How did they all end up coming? Then it hit her. Terry didn't have a meeting with a parishioner on Friday afternoon; he had hurried her out of the office so he could collect the posse of supporters she hadn't had time to stir up herself.

Gracie tried to catch Terry's eye to give him a nod of thanks, but he wasn't looking at her.

"Now, without further interruption," Gregory stuck his glasses back on his nose, "I'd like to discuss our next item, and that involves the employment of the town's librarian."

Another murmur rose up from the crowd, and Gregory peered over his glasses and shook his head. He returned to a sheet he had lifted out of one of the folders in front of him.

"I would like to make a motion to terminate the employment of Gracie Jensen as Johnson Station Lib—" He got no further before a collective roar from the crowd drowned him out.

"This is a disgrace!" she heard someone exclaim.

"You have no right!" yelled another.

"Impeach!"

The chorus grew louder, and those who had been seated were nearly all on their feet.

"You can't do this!"

"This is wrong!"

It wasn't exactly an angry mob, Gracie thought, as much as a disorganized, multi-tonal chorus. She looked from face to face.

Yes, there were Gregory's sycophants, right there in the front row. Seated, they wrenched themselves around and motioned for the crowd to sit down. Everyone ignored them.

"I don't think we can continue with this meeting if you don't all settle down now!" Gregory shouted, standing up and spreading his arms.

The unruly audience threw out a few more invectives before slowly quieting down, and as their noisy protest declined to a disgruntled buzz, Gregory started reading his motion again.

"Dismissal is grounded in the following complaints. Number one: Gracie Jensen has refused to draft and adopt an official policy to protect community morality through the purchase and distribution of only those reading materials consistent with community standards despite being directed to do so by the governing body of the Johnson Station Library. Two: Gracie Jensen recently purchased three copies of *The Intern's Travels* despite this board's request to defer its purchase until the formation of such a policy to protect our community standards."

At that, Gracie heard several groans—possibly from those who had borrowed the very book in question.

"Three: Gracie has conducted her personal life in such a manner as to indicate she is not cognizant of nor respectful of this community's standards of behavior."

Gracie felt the heat rise in her face and dropped her eyes to her lap. But in a matter of mere seconds, her embarrassment was washed aside by anger. She looked up at Gregory, who avoided her eyes.

The chutzpah of his hypocrisy was too much. He was the one whose personal behavior was disrespectful of community standards. What community condoned rape of teenage girls? But what could Gracie say without messing things up with Ísabel?

"What does that have to do with anything?" she heard someone shout from the seats. She thought it sounded like Marcia.

"This is none of your business!" shouted someone whose voice Gracie didn't recognize.

"What are these alleged sins you refer to?" asked Terry, stepping forward in the crowd.

Gracie looked out to watch Terry, but her attention was drawn to Barbra. Impeccable, proper wife of Gregory, Barbra was sitting directly in front of Terry, holding her head high, a beatific, professional smile stuck on her perfectly made-up face.

She had ten times the poise of her husband. Without her, Gregory was nothing. Barbra didn't need Gregory or his political career to retain her status or lifestyle. But without her support, he'd still be a retired farmer just like the handful of other retired farmers in the audience. Of course, there was nothing wrong with being a farmer or ex-farmer, but Gracie doubted it was what he considered his highest and best calling. County supervisor would be a little better. State senator or governor even better than that.

Gracie caught Barbra's eye and flashed a big, happy smile at her. She saw Barbra's brow crease in surprise. Gracie imagined her confusion: She must have been wondering how Gracie could be happy.

"Well, I guess I should let her in on a little secret," Gracie whispered to no one.

The audience's murmurs quieted down, and Gracie turned back to Gregory.

"Is this really the forum where you want to have a debate over our relative sins?" she asked him calmly, raising her voice enough to guarantee no one in the room would miss a word.

Gregory frowned, and Gracie imagined the fear and doubt suddenly racing through his mind: His "sins" could mean only one thing. Would she really say something about Ísabel in front of all of these people? And with Ísabel herself in the room?

"Do you want to open that can of worms in front of this audience?" Gracie continued, holding Gregory's eyes. He looked away, nervously.

"Don't try to change the subject, Gracie," he said. "This meeting is about who the librarian that represents our community should be."

"No," Gracie retorted. "You've just questioned my morality and behavior, which have nothing to do with the library. You opened this subject. Now, I suggest we explore it fully, both directions."

Gregory's face turned red and he clenched his fists on the table. "You promised—" he whispered harshly, and then stopped. She hadn't expected him to make a mistake this quickly.

"What? What did I promise?" Gracie feigned ignorance, raising her eyebrows. It was becoming obvious that he really didn't have the right temperament to be a politician—especially one under fire. He had just done exactly the opposite of what he should have done: he admitted she had something on him. He would have to get better at controlling his emotions if he was ever going to rise above library chairman or the school board. "I promised I wouldn't go the police. And I won't."

"You and I agreed—" He stopped again. That wasn't any better, he seemed to realize. 'You are treading on dangerous legal waters here, lady. That other is a matter between you and I."

"You mean 'you and me,'" Gracie said. Sometimes it was fun being a pedant. "If you plan to run for governor, you might work on your grammar."

"My grammar isn't the subject here either."

"Well, I agree. Let's back up a moment," Gracie said. She was surprised; she was enjoying this exchange. Maybe she had a future as a politician. Finally, she felt like she had some control over the proceeding, and if Gregory didn't like it, it was own fault. "What you and I agreed to do was protect the privacy of a victim of your behavior. And I intend to do that. But now that we've broached the subject of our relative immorality, do you want to rethink our agreement?"

"What are you talking about?" Tony interrupted, looking back and forth between her and Gregory. "What does this have to do with the library?"

"Exactly!" Gracie answered, nodding and smiling happily. "I would suggest we return our discussion to matters that affect the management and efficacy of our community's library, not the sins of the library board's chairman or its librarian."

She looked at Barbra in the audience and winked at her. "Don't you think that's a good idea?"

Barbra stared straight ahead, her smile now replaced by a poker face she had probably honed in hundreds of negotiations in boardrooms. Gracie imagined the conversation Barbra and Gregory would have on the drive home later that night.

Gregory looked like he didn't know what to do next. He cleared his throat and shuffled his papers. Gracie thought she could see his hands shaking.

"Let's get back to business here, can we?" he snarled. His jaw was clenched as tightly as his fists. "Gracie, the grievances we have against you will be detailed in a confidential report that will not be released to the public in the interest of protecting your privacy."

At that, half of the crowd rose to its feet again, some shouting protests, some talking amongst themselves loudly, and Gregory sat back, clearly unsure about how to regain control over the room. He pulled off his glasses again, sniffed, jerked his head back, and despite the noise, continued.

"I move that we dismiss Gracie and hire a new librarian. Do I hear a second?" he yelled.

"I second it!" Tony answered.

"All in favor?"

Gracie couldn't hear who voted aye and who voted nay, but she knew immediately it wouldn't matter. Gregory would write in his minutes that the motion had passed. She was through.

"Meeting adjourned!" Gregory yelled through the roar of the crowd.

The commotion had made continuing impossible, and the air conditioner bids would have to wait for another day. As Gracie stood up and gathered her papers, a dozen of her friends and library patrons rushed forward to console her and pledge to do whatever they could to undo Gregory's action. Not surprisingly, a few wanted to know what Gregory had done that was so secretive.

"I've agreed not to tattle," she told the curious. The damage to his squeaky-clean reputation had been done, and she didn't need to say more.

As the crowd slowly dispersed over the next half hour, Gracie wondered just how much Gregory would suffer from what she had said. Probably a little, although it was going to take some time before the community figured out how to take back some of the power he'd already accumulated over them. Even if they got it back, she was ready to leave the library; even if her termination were to be reversed, she knew she didn't want the job anymore.

Gracie scanned the departing townsfolk for Richard and Ísabel. She saw Terry standing at the back of the room, caught his eye, smiled, and nodded. "Thanks," she mouthed.

"You're welcome," he mouthed back. He waved and left with the last of his parishioners.

Still sitting in the middle of the otherwise empty rows of chairs, Barbra looked smaller than she had when Gracie first caught sight of her that evening. Her poker face had sunk and her lips were moving as she stared at her purse on her lap. Gracie imagined that she was practicing what she was going to say to her husband that night. She felt a little sorry for the woman; however misdirected her ambitions were, she probably didn't deserve Gregory's betrayal.

By then, most of those left in the library were Gregory's sycophants, who crowded around him in front of the board table, talking in low tones. As she picked up her files, Gracie ignored them. She didn't care what they were talking about. Whatever it was, it had nothing to do with her anymore.

She started to walk back to her office when Ísabel strolled up to the front of the room. Head high and steely eyed, she stepped right into the middle of Gregory's friends and reached out to hand him a book. She was only five feet tall, but somehow she towered over the men around her.

"Here," she said to Gregory in a strong, steady voice. "I thought you might want this back. You left it in my room that night in Des Moines, and I figured you might want to return it. It belongs to the library, you know."

The businessmen surrounding Ísabel stepped back from the girl as if she were carrying an explosive device. Gracie leaned in to see what Ísabel was proffering.

She recognized it immediately. It was the library's missing copy of *Fifty Shades of Grey*.

❧

The *New York Times* didn't catch wind of Gracie's firing and didn't comment on the grave injustice of it all. Even the local *Johnson Station Newsweekly* didn't mention it. It was too controversial a matter for the editor, and didn't fit into one of the paper's regular columns: "Visitors", "School Lunch

Menus", "Fifty Years Ago in Johnson Station", and "Letter from Our Congressman".

The publisher's income was dependent on Gregory's campaign advertising, so it didn't surprise Gracie that he ignored what had happened, and that was fine with her. She had her moment in the spotlight, and she had seen how many friends she had. She was proud of what she had done, standing up to Gregory, rediscovering some of the courage that had allowed her to jump into those trading pits in Chicago decades before. She hoped it had jump-started a movement to reverse Gregory's virtual take-over of the town.

She was even more proud of what she had accomplished over twenty-five years: building a library that people cared enough about to show up and fight for. Maybe that indicated they'd finally stand up for their town as well.

~24~

Gracie walked to the library slowly.

She had left her house early, intending to concentrate on every square slab of sidewalk, every crack in the concrete, every manicured green lawn, every weed-free flower bed, every neat shutter and chimney on her three-block walk, in order to burn them into her memory. But after only a few steps, she realized the effort was unnecessary. After twenty-six years, every sight, every smell, every incline, decline, and curb cut of her three-block walk was already permanently stored in her brain.

Most of the town's residents, she realized, were comforted by that. Nothing new would come along to frighten them; nothing would happen to challenge their happy assumption that Johnson Station would look pretty much the same as long as they lived and probably long after they died.

Every so often, someone in one of the neat houses she had passed every day would die, the adult children would sell the place, the newcomers would apply a new coat of paint, repave the driveway, and change the color of the petunias in the flower beds. Or, if the house was too old to attract buyers, it would fade and sag and eventually be torn down. But that would take fifty years. Meanwhile, nothing would change enough to turn a head in surprise.

Gracie crossed Main Street, stood outside the library, and waited for the new librarian. She had never met the woman Gregory had hired in her place. She hadn't even been shown the resume or told why this woman was supposedly the best choice to replace her.

She glanced at her watch; she was fifteen minutes early. It was a pleasant day to wait, though. The warm, late May breeze was a harbinger of a hotter-than-usual summer, and Gracie smirked at the realization that she wouldn't be there to suffer through it.

It had been a long three months since the board fired her. At the mayor's request, she'd continued to show up to make morning coffee, re-shelve and help her patrons find books, dust the shelves, and pay the bills until someone was hired to replace her. She was told that the new hire would be chosen for his or her willingness to "understand and commit" to the new policy authored by Gregory and adopted at the February meeting, the last to which she was invited. Meanwhile, Gracie ordered no new books and removed none from the shelves.

As expected, Caitlin had resigned from the board, and the mayor had replaced her with a woman Gracie didn't know—handpicked by Gregory, of course, who worked on the county Republican Party committee.

"Did you hear what Barbra did? She cut him off!" Jackie had burst into the library in April to announce. "Now he's scrambling for donations. He might have to drop his campaign! You did it, Gracie! You did it!"

Without any further explanation, Gracie knew exactly what Jackie was talking about. They had no way of knowing what had happened behind Gregory and Barbra's closed door that night after the library meeting, but everyone in town surmised that it had to have been ugly. Shortly after that, Gregory had rented the old apartment Isabel and her parents had vacated above the dry cleaners, and had turned it into both his sleeping quarters and his campaign headquarters.

"I'm quite sure it wasn't me." Gracie quickly deflected the credit for Gregory's problems. "Do you think they're getting a divorce?" She wasn't sure she wanted to be responsible for breaking up the marriage, either; she had only wanted to knock him off his self-constructed pedestal.

"I don't know," Jackie said, "but she's definitely pulled his campaign funding. I can only imagine how embarrassing this must be to her."

"Well, she should thank me for one thing."

"What's that?"

"That his philandering was exposed long before she had to stand next to him at some press conference five or ten years from now, smiling stiffly while he apologizes to the rest of the state for messing around with young women."

Shortly after that, Gregory surprised her by calling her at the library and asking to meet with her privately.

"Why?" she asked. "What could you possibly have to say to me?"

"I'd like to propose a truce."

"What would a truce do for me?" She noisily clicked the keys on her computer keyboard to communicate disinterest in the conversation. "I'm not interested in any truce. I'm done at the library as soon as you find a new librarian."

"I was thinking that maybe there might be some kind of compromise."

"Compromise?" Gracie let her voice carry her incredulity.

"Can we meet?"

"No."

"Okay. Then, let me offer this now. I'm willing to allow you to stay in the library, and in return, you would support my candidacy for county supervisor."

Gracie smiled. She knew where this was coming from. At the coffee klatch and after church services, she'd heard more and more discussions that made her optimistic about the possibility for change in Johnson Station—a local revolution, perhaps. Her firing had been a catalyst of sorts, bringing together a group of residents who talked Armand into running against John for mayor. From the sounds of things, Armand had the support of the teachers and administrators in the school district, with the exception of the principal. A good number of her library patrons had pledged their support to Armand as well—they called themselves Armand's Army.

The de-funding of the food bank had been another catalyst. John had cast the tie-breaking vote to cut off the city's contribution and people were holding him responsible for it. Terry had pulled together enough donations to keep the food bank's shelves full and in place for another year, and so far, the town's efforts to fill the industrial park hadn't brought it any competition for the space.

All of this cast a dark cloud over Gregory's political ambitions. If he lost support of his hometown, it would be harder for him to build the momentum he needed for his climb up the political ladder and for his eventual run for governor.

He might have been aware of the change in the town's pulse, but it seemed that the town's entrenched politicians, Main Street businessmen, and insurance and real estate agents weren't. In every store front and insurance agency window, they posted signs for John for mayor and Gregory for county commissioner. Were they both arrogant *and* deaf?

Gracie was biased, but she couldn't help but believe that one of the things that held this town together so far—in many ways made it better off than some other towns in the state— had been the library. Why didn't those businessmen see that?

She worried about what would happen to the library under the new librarian, but she wasn't worried about her "legacy." That was too grand; legacies were for presidents of universities, presidents of the United States, wealthy philanthropists. She knew her role in the community as a voice of progress and moderation would be filled by Armand, Terry, and a cadre of women, including Liz, Caroline, and Jackie now. Marcia, too, if she ever came back.

And while Gregory still pretended to be nothing but optimistic about his own political future, he had to be worried, too. He'd seen how much support she had in February.

His phone call was proof of that.

"I'm not interested in your political career," Gracie said. "And I'm not interested in keeping this job. It has taken me some time to realize that I'm not the only one in this town who can stand up for free speech. Now that the revolution is underway, others will."

"Revolution. What revolution?"

Gracie ignored his question; if he truly didn't know, he'd find out soon enough. "I'm going to travel with Richard, however immoral you may think that is, and if I have my way, neither I nor Isabel will ever run into you again."

"I asked what revolution? Do you think you've started a revolution?"

"Well, maybe that's a bit grandiose, Greg." It was the first time she'd ever called him by a nickname, and she felt powerful doing it. "But, I think things are going to change around here, and you just might find yourself out of step soon."

"You are being stubborn, Gracie." Gregory clearly didn't understand what she was saying. Or maybe he had chosen not to hear it. "You have to realize that this is politics, it's not personal—"

"You!" Gracie spat into the receiver. "You are the one who made this personal! You publicly attacked my reputation and my morals. You impregnated a young girl and then tried to use her embarrassment against me. If you don't think it's personal, then you have ..."

Suddenly, words failed her. Gracie stopped. She didn't want to talk with Gregory about anything, not even to berate him. She wanted him out of her life, and she had the power to do make that happen. Maybe she was overestimating how much Johnson Station might change, but she had the power to hang up on him.

And so she did.

ᐁ

None of this, Gracie realized with satisfaction as she
waited for the new librarian to show up, had required her to
betray Ísabel and her secret to anyone else. If anyone guessed
that Gregory's misbehavior had anything to do with Ísabel, the
young woman had volunteered that herself by publicly
returning *Fifty Shades of Grey* to him that night. After that
meeting, Gracie rarely heard anyone venture a guess as to what
Gregory's sin was that she had referred to, or who Gregory's
victim was. Her coffee klatch asked if it was Ísabel, but when
she refused to say, even they dropped it. Small-town gossip
could be devastating, for sure, but in this case, small-town
decency had risen to the occasion, and no one pursued the
matter, at least to her face.

Gracie hated that Gregory had gotten by with what she
still thought of as rape of an underage girl, and she would
never forgive him for it, but she ended up preserving Ísabel's
love and loyalty in return for her discretion, and that was a
pretty good bargain.

Worse than that, she hated the fact that she had failed to
find a way to save the library from his meddling. A library
restricted the way Gregory intended couldn't serve its
community. She wondered if the town was going to survive
now. How central were healthy libraries to communities?
Were they as important as schools, or diversity, or new blood?

The only silver lining for Gracie was this: Now that her
battle with Gregory was over, she'd been forced to face the
fact that she had been stuck in a rut. It helped her see what a
priceless gift Ísabel had been as well. She'd been waiting for
something come along and shake up her life a little, and Ísabel
had shown up just in time.

Ísabel had made the most of the last four months of the
school year. She joined the school golf team, largely to please
Gracie, but the coach, Armand, reported to Gracie that she

was picking it up quickly. Even better, she had made new friends on the team, and they had become regular visitors in Gracie's home. Ísabel was introducing them to film classics and a new reading list.

"Hi!"

Startled back to the present, Gracie turned around to face Caitlin's friend Sara. She hadn't seen her for months.

"Sara!" Gracie exclaimed. "What are you doing here?"

"Well, I'm the new librarian." Sara smiled and held out her arms to pantomime "I'm here!"

"It's you?" Gracie put her hand up on the brick wall to steady herself. "You are the Sara he hired? How ... What ... What the hell? Does Gregory know?"

"Know what?" Sara smiled a broad conspiratorial smile. "Know that I'm a single, former school library volunteer? That I am willing to move to town to be close to this job? That my father was once the chairman of the Republican Party in the county?"

Gracie laughed out loud.

"Yeah, he knows all that," Sara said. "What else is there?" She acted out a big obvious wink. "So, here I am!"

"But what will you do when he starts pushing you around? Asking you to wipe out entire shelves of books?"

"I will box them up, put them in my office, wait for him to win his county supervisor seat, and put them back. He'll be totally unaware. By then, he'll have much bigger fish to fry. I will be surprised if he doesn't give up his seat on the board. Johnson Station will be too small for him."

Gracie thought Sara had figured out his ego quite quickly. Perhaps Caitlin had helped with the character study.

Gracie remembered her conversation in the coffee shop with Caitlin last winter. Caitlin had promised she'd find a way to help the library, even if she wasn't on the board anymore. And she had. She had helped Sara get through her interviews and get this job.

Sara looked happy, as if running the Johnson Station Library would amount to embarking on the greatest adventure of her life. She smiled broadly and pushed her long graying curls away from her face. The wind blew them back.

"And for the second time in my short tenure in Johnson Station, I thank you so much for being here!" Sara said with an enthusiasm that made Gracie smile.

"Absolutely!" Gracie handed Sara her key. "Let's go in and get started."

Sara fumbled with the key, finally setting her purse down on the sidewalk in order to unlock the big front door. Gracie thought about how sad it was that no hardware store owner was around anymore to offer to fix that recalcitrant lock.

"I appreciate you showing me around," Sara said, bracing her tiny fame against the big door to hold it open and let Gracie pass through first. "You didn't have to do this."

Gracie knew what Sara meant. She wasn't obliged to do anything to help the new librarian get settled. In fact, Gracie's friends had argued that she should just wash her hands of the mess and let her replacement sink or swim. If Sara didn't know what she was doing, it wasn't Gracie's problem.

"It's Gregory's problem and the fault of his pansy-assed board," Marcia had said.

However, the library had been the center of Gracie's life after Jens had died and Janice graduated from college. She loved it. She loved the old cranky furnace, the inadequate air conditioner, the too-heavy front door. She loved those dusty stacks and the old card catalog—even the neat little bathrooms. She enjoyed locating Caroline's next child-rearing fantasy fix, watching Liz drool over a new cookbook she'd never use, and Armand discover another historical novel he could pull apart. She relished the serendipity of someone asking for a hot new nonfiction tome she'd just put on order.

She loved the fact that she'd helped both Sara and Ísabel find their way in a confusing, conflicted world.

Gracie stood for a moment in the doorway and breathed in the dusty old-book smell.

"Are you going to miss this?" Sara asked tentatively. "You've been here a long time."

"Yes, I am going to miss it. Some of it," Gracie said. "But some things, no. The politics, no. Some of my people, yes. Some people, no. In balance, I'd have to say I'm glad that I'm leaving."

Who would have thought that getting fired was so liberating?

Now, protecting the town's library, this precious asset, would be Sara's job, not Gracie's. The one role that had fulfilled Gracie and imprisoned her at the same time for the past two and a half decades was no longer going to define the person Gracie saw in the mirror. Now she was an adventurer. An intrepid, curious wanderer. A person who experienced life, not from an armchair, not from a book, but up close and in person—and with two people she loved.

Tomorrow she and Richard would take Ísabel to South America for the summer. And after that, who knew?

She showed Sara where she kept her purse during the day and the hook inside her office where she kept the key so that she never lost it.

"Sara," she said, stopping the new librarian as they headed back out into the main room. "I have one favor to ask of you."

"What's that?"

"Would you consider developing an after-school program aimed at keeping our young girls from getting pregnant until they intend to? I mean teaching them something beyond abstinence. I don't think the schools are doing that anymore."

Sara looked puzzled. She had no way to know why this meant so much to Gracie, and Gracie didn't intend to tell her. She gave Sara a moment to consider it.

"Certainly." Sara finally nodded. "I think that sounds like a good use of our resources. I'll work on it whenever Gregory isn't looking."

The two women smiled at each other conspiratorially.

"So, now let's start with the nasty old air conditioner." Gracie pointed at the thermostat by the front door. "And then I can show you how to make coffee."

THE END

ABOUT THE AUTHOR

Marj Charlier lives in Palm Springs, California, with her husband, Ben Miller, a free-lance journalist. She worked as a business reporter for twenty years, including eleven at *The Wall Street Journal*. She worked in corporate finance for another twenty years before retiring to write novels. This is her seventh novel.

ACKNOWLEDGMENTS

I grew up in a small town in central Iowa, one that has been luckier than many others its size due to its proximity to a big university. While the setting of Johnson Station was in many ways inspired by Story City and therefore may lead some to think I'm writing about it, none of the tales or characters in Gracie's story were based on anything I recall happening or anyone one I knew there. This is totally a work of fiction.

That said, I owe most of what I know about small towns and their sad demise from my experiences there as a child, my visits as an adult, and my work as a reporter at *The Wall Street Journal*, where I covered rural America and agriculture.

I owe much of the happiness of my life to my safe and stable upbringing in small-town Iowa, and many of my best memories are of my childhood adventures with my best friend (and Iowa editor), Diane Mathre (now Larson), her brother, Larry, and my late brother, Bruce.

I owe any success this novel might have to several people who helped it come together: First to Rose Baldwin, whose willingness to tell me the truth about the early drafts was a godsend. This wouldn't be the same book without her calm, sharp critique. To Diane; my husband, Ben Miller; my beta readers, Kristin Kirby and Lynne Spreen; and my copyeditor, Rhonda Erb, thanks for helping this come together. Thanks to Mark and Bob at the Brown Street Inn in Iowa City, who never forget to find non-gluten bread for me and put up with my complaints about the Iowa humidity. And many thanks to my friends at the Iowa Writers Workshop's Summer Writing Festival for their advice.

And finally, I owe many thanks to my librarian role models: the late Frances Bartlett, Story City's long-time librarian; Aunt Wilma Scott, the librarian in tiny Gilman, Iowa; and Tom Lutgen, librarian in Rancho Mirage, California, whose faith in me and support for my work I will never deserve and can never repay.

DISCUSSION QUESTIONS FOR BOOK CLUBS

1) What do you think gave Gracie the courage and the desire to stand up to the library board chairman, Gregory? Could she have done this at the beginning of her career? Does this say anything about the benefits of age?

2) Why do you think it took Gracie so long to decide she didn't care what people thought of her personal life? What do you think it's like to live in a small town like Johnson Station?

3) Is Ísabel a typical teenager? In what ways does being a first-generation American define who she is and how she acts? What do you think about the way she felt toward her father's home town in Mexico?

4) The novel suggests various reasons for the decline in small rural communities. Do you think these are real? Can you think of others?

5) Although we never hear Gracie voice an opinion on abortion, she helps Ísabel get one. How did that affect your opinion of her? How does it help us understand her ethics and her character?

6) What feminist themes do you sense in reading this book? Since they aren't overt, does this strengthen or weaken their impact?

7) How important do you think libraries—especially small town libraries—are in these days of e-books and other digital media? In what ways do you think they've lost importance? Do you agree with Gracie that the future of the town and the survival of the library are connected? In what ways?

8) Does Johnson Station remind you of any place you've lived or visited? In what ways does it seem familiar and in what ways is it different?

9) What do you think it would take to turn around the fate of Johnson Station? Will electing new leaders make a difference? Do you think there is a real chance of saving the town?

10) What do you think Gracie's friends mean by a "revolution"? Do you think such a revolution is possible in rural communities?

THE SECOND
JOHNSON STATION NOVEL COMING SOON:

Jackie's Campaign

~1~

The Johnson Station City Hall had occupied the first floor of an impressive early-twentieth-century building that took up a half-block of the business district on Main Street, since the 1950s. The building also once housed the town's "Opera Hall"—a pretentious label for a stage that never presented anything more refined than a vaudeville act.

Seven hundred miles from the nearest earthquake fault, and sitting on top of some fifty feet of black Iowa loam, its red-brick exterior hadn't developed a single serious crack in more than a hundred years. Its dark wood floors sagged and creaked, but structural engineers had assured the town they were safe, even if a pen dropped on the floor was likely to roll downhill twenty feet before coming to a stop on a countervailing slope.

Ducking through the big double doors off Main Street, Jackie slipped into the cool, dark hall leading to the town offices. Any time she was in there, she had a hankering to work there just for the ambiance of the old building. In the winter, the blocky radiators along the walls provided both reliable hot spots and an oddly comforting cacophony of clanging and hissing. In the summer, the heat and humidity seeped in from outdoors and drew the aroma of varnish out from the woodwork, reminding her of the hallways of the town's ancient Romanesque elementary school where she had taught for nearly thirty years.

Jackie never found out when a town hall job was open before it was too late to apply. It wasn't like she needed the money. She had retired five years before with a nice pension from the school system, and Nils was the plant manager at the window factory at the edge of town, one of the highest paying jobs in Johnson Station. It afforded them a comfortable life in this rural town. Still, Jackie wished she had something more productive to do than run errands for her lazy sons, babysit for her granddaughter, and serve as a domestic servant for her husband, Nils.

She stopped at the long service counter and poked the little chrome bell to announce her presence.

"Be right there!" She heard Sophie call from one of the interior offices.

"I'll just leave this here, Sophie," Jackie called back. "It's just a building permit application. We're getting new siding on the house."

"Okay, Jackie!" the disembodied voice of the town clerk's administrative assistant answered. Johnson Station was small enough that most adults in town knew each other by voice. The joke around town was that no one used turn signals because everyone already knew where they were going.

Jackie left her forms and the application fee anchored on the counter by the chrome bell, retreated down the hall, and pushed out the big doors into the late summer afternoon. The sun temporarily blinded her as she stepped down onto the sidewalk, and her shoulder bumped into someone. She shielded her eyes with her hands, and looked down into the face of John, the town's mayor. He was a half-foot shorter than she was, and lucky for him, he was quite a bit stouter, too. He had been able to stay on his feet when she sideswiped him.

"I am so sorry!" she exclaimed, jumping backwards and barely keeping her own balance. "It's so bright out today!"

"Sure is," John said. "Another beautiful day in paradise! What business did you have with us here at the city today, Jackie?"

Jackie cringed. The last thing she wanted was an extended conversation with John. She still resented him for backing last winter's campaign by the town's ambitious politician, Gregory Thungaard, to fire her best friend, Gracie, as the town's librarian. In spite of wide support from Johnson Station residents for Gracie, Gregory had prevailed. Now Jackie's friend was taking advantage of her forced retirement by traveling abroad, and Jackie missed her.

"Just a building permit. New siding," Jackie answered tersely. The mayor knew how she felt about him. Did he really think that engaging in friendly chit-chat on the sidewalk would win her vote for his reelection in November? He hadn't been particularly friendly to most of the town's residents, back when all he needed was Gregory's financial and political support to win seemingly endless successive terms of the town's top office. But after dozens of people showed up to protest Gracie's dismissal at a town meeting last winter, John had suddenly become the nicest guy in Johnson Station. Everyone had noticed it.

"I've been meaning to come over to your house one of these evenings!" the mayor called after Jackie as she hurried down the sidewalk. She turned around abruptly.

"Why?" She let her face show how distasteful she found the idea of having him there.

"I was going to see if Nils would work on my campaign," he said. "You know I have always supported anything the factory has wanted from the city."

"That's because it makes up about a third of your tax base," Jackie said, walking back a few steps so she wouldn't have to shout. "And at least ten percent of your constituents work there, now that the chicken plant is closed."

"Yes, that's true. But you can't accuse me of focusing only on political expediency."

"Yes—" Jackie stopped herself. Did she really want to get in an argument with the mayor in the middle of Main Street with the sun beating down on them and the humidity climbing? Was this a good time to tell him what she really thought of him? She'd only seen him a couple of times since the night Gracie was fired, and both times she'd avoided any conversation with him. If you can't say anything nice, she'd been taught, keep your mouth shut.

Now she was pissed. The mayor knew she was close friends with Gracie. Or did he think since Gracie was now traveling the world, Jackie didn't care about her anymore?

"Yes," she finally continued. She straightened her shoulders and lifted her chin to exaggerate her height advantage. "Yes, I can accuse you of political expediency, and I do. You let Gregory fire Gracie because he was funneling campaign money to you. You knew Gracie was a town treasure, but you sold out, John. You sold Gracie out."

"Gracie was fighting a losing battle, Jackie," John said, rubbing his bald head, his usual gesture whenever anyone challenged him, as if he was thinking so hard his head hurt. "The community's moral standards have been declining for years, and I think we all owe Gregory a big thanks for getting us back on track."

Jackie felt her heart rate pick up and considered walking away before she said too much. But she hated to back down from a fight. "I don't know what community you are talking about," she said, anger tightening her throat and thinning her voice. "The community I have belonged to for the past thirty years has been a fine, respectable place to live. I don't think you should be denigrating the very residents who have elected you to office, how many times?"

"Four," John said, taking the opportunity to puff out his chest with pride, which caused his pants to fall down below his bulging middle. He hiked them up proudly as if the gesture demonstrated manliness. "My guess is the citizens of Johnson Station will vote their support for me again this fall. You aren't thinking of backing the other side, are you?"

The other side was Armand, a retired high school history teacher and John's only competition in the November mayoral race.

"Well, I am thinking that," Jackie retorted. "I worked with Armand for years."

"What does that Armand think he knows about running a city? He's never run anything more complicated than a high school history class in his life."

"Teaching high school is a bit harder than you think. It certainly requires more skill than sitting around taking money and orders from the town bully." Jackie couldn't help herself. Some things had to be said.

"Well, I guess I should talk to your husband," John spat back. "Maybe he can talk some sense into you."

"That is just the kind of backward thing I expect from one of Gregory's sycophants!"

Jackie was shaking. She hated getting angry; she wore it so poorly. She pulled her purse up to her chest and hugged it with both arms to resist taking a punch at the mayor's round nose. She wanted to walk away but needed John to retreat first, or it would look like she was backing down.

The two held their positions on the sidewalk for a long minute, saying nothing more. John was apparently as stubborn as she was. How long could they stand there, fuming, facing each other?

"Mayor?" Sophie saved them both by sticking her head out the big front door of town hall. "You've got a phone call. Do you want me to take another message? This guy has called three times in the last hour?"

"No, I'll be right there," John said, not taking his eyes off Jackie. "I'm sorry Mrs. Nilsson, but we'll have to cut our little tête-a-tête short. I look forward to continuing this fruitful exchange another time."

Jackie was glad for the interruption that let them both off the hook, even if she didn't care for his sarcasm. Free at last, she took a deep breath to calm down and shot across the street to walk on the shady side. In two more weeks, it would be time for the weather to break, and Iowa's hot, humid summer would turn—probably overnight, if the usual pattern held—into cool, crisp autumn, her favorite time of the year. But now, the oppressive temperatures only added to the steam she had worked up in facing off with John.

WATCH FOR *JACKIE'S CAMPAIGN*
ON AMAZON.COM AND FOR
NEWS OF THE JOHNSON STATION SERIES
AT HTTP://WWW.MARJCHARLIER.COM